Elle eased the s[...]
H&K .45 and pu[...]
the door. It was unlocked.

She raised the gun and swung into position just inside the door. The soft blue-white glow of a computer monitor filled the bedroom. Data streamed across the screen.

And the illumination fell across a figure lying in the middle of the floor. She knew exactly what the black dot in the centre of the body's forehead was.

Silently, a shadow separated itself from the darkness. She pulled the gun up and fired. A man cursed in surprise.

In the next handful of seconds, her feet were swept from under her as a weight fell on top of her, knocking out her breath. "Stop," a deep voice said as she crashed a forearm into his nose and eye. "I didn't kill him."

She went still. "Then let me up."

Cautiously, the man lifted his head and looked at her.

She gasped. "You!"

Available in November 2006 from Silhouette Sensation

Awaken to Danger
by Catherine Mann
(Wingmen Warriors)

Living on the Edge
by Susan Mallery

Breaking All the Rules
by Susan Vaughan

Look-Alike
by Meredith Fletcher
(Bombshell)

Blue Jeans and a Badge
by Nina Bruhns

Ms Longshot
by Sylvie Kurtz
(Bombshell)

Look-Alike

MEREDITH FLETCHER

First published in Great Britain 2006
Silhouette Books, Eton House, 18-24 Paradise Road,
Richmond, Surrey TW9 1SR

© Harlequin Books S.A. 2006

Special thanks and acknowledgement are given to Meredith Fletcher
for her contribution to the ATHENA FORCE mini-series.

ISBN-13: 978 0 373 51404 5
ISBN-10: 0 373 51404 2

18-1106

Printed and bound in Spain
by Litografia Rosés S.A., Barcelona

MEREDITH FLETCHER

doesn't really call any place home. She blames her wanderlust on her navy father, who moved the family several times around the United States and other countries. The one constant she had was her books. The battered trunk of favourite novels followed her around the world when she was growing up and shared dorm space with her in college. These days, the trunk is stored, but sometimes comes with Meredith to visit houses high in the Colorado mountains, cottages in Maine, where she likes to visit lighthouses and work with fishing crews, and rental flats where she takes moments of "early retirement" for months at a stretch. Interested readers can reach her at MFletcher1216@aol.com.

To Drs Donna and Brian Johnson, staunch
supporters of Athena Force and of my
writing. And to my editor, Natashya Wilson,
who loves romance adventure as much as I do
and helped me straighten all the wrinkles.

Prologue

Outside Suwan, Berzhaan
The Middle East

"Please! I beg you! Don't kill me! I made a mistake! Just a mistake!"

Seated in the back of the luxury limousine, Vasilios Quinn listened to the man beg for his life. It was music to his ears. A return to days he hadn't seen in many years.

Soundproof windows kept the man's panicked cries from reaching the dark night outside the limousine. Less than five miles from Suwan, the capital city of Berzhaan, they were in desert highlands filled with hard stone ravines and shifting sandstorms.

It was the perfect place for an execution.

"I swear to you! It will never happen again! I will not allow myself to be so tempted!" Tears ran down the man's quivering jowls. He was in his thirties yet covered in mounds of baby fat. He hadn't known the hard life so many of his countrymen had suffered.

Berzhaan was part of the Middle East and had faced a precarious existence all its life. The current government, headed by Prime Minister Omar Razidae, suffered from internal strife. The United States was believed to support Berzhaan's Kemeni guerrillas, who wanted control of the country. As a result, the native terrorist network—the Q'Rajn—attacked the government and the Kemenis alike to drive out the U.S., as well as American sympathizers. Death did a daily business in Berzhaan.

Quinn's business was with the Q'Rajn. The man on the limousine floor had acted as go-between to the terrorists.

"I trusted you, Malik," Quinn said.

Malik sobbed. "I swear, you can still trust me!"

"Unfortunately," Quinn said, "trust is like virginity. Once given, it can't be given again. You have to be careful whom you extend it to. I have been very careful. You—" he pointed the silenced Glock .45 at Malik's nose "—are my first mistake in over twenty years."

"I can fix it! I swear!" Malik clasped his hands in front of him. Held on his elbows and knees as he was, dressed in a robe and trembling, he was a poster child for subjugation.

Quinn had been at a soiree when his security team had called him to let him know they had Malik in custody. When he finished here, he intended to return to that soiree. His gray hair was carefully coiffed, and though he was a big man, his tuxedo fit him perfectly.

"You brought someone to our meeting," Quinn said. "You knew I didn't operate that way."

"She won't talk!" Malik said. "She's just a girl! Young! She doesn't know anything! I give you my word!"

Quinn almost laughed. The two bodyguards holding Malik grinned and shook their heads. Of course, they had already killed the girl and dumped her body.

Quinn's cell phone rang. He wasn't pleased at being interrupted. "Yes."

"The breach in security may be more severe than we had believed."

Quinn cursed and leaned back in the limousine. He'd thought dealing with Malik would be the end of it. "I thought you had a handle on this."

"I still do." The voice at the other end of the connection was calm and assured. The caller's name was Arnaud Beck. He was a mercenary leader with international contacts, and Quinn had never met a more efficient killing machine. "Our competitors are working more quickly than we had imagined."

The competitors were an intelligence team that Quinn hadn't yet identified. His intelligence people had tracked them back to a nebulous agency that had ties to a Web site, www.AA.gov. The site appeared to be the home page of an all-girls school, but its advanced firewalls and security countermeasures had stymied every attempt Quinn's people had made to crack it. Even the information brokers Quinn had access to had as much rumor as fact about the organization behind AA.gov. Maybe it was a cover for interagency information, or maybe—as a few reports indicated—it was an enforcement arm that stopped short of assassinations.

The most curious facet about AA.gov was the connection to the school just outside of the Glendale/Phoenix, Arizona, area in the United States. From circumspect investigation, Quinn had learned that the Athena Academy for the Advancement of Women had many ties to the United States government. Many of the school's select graduates went on to important positions within federal and state agencies.

"They've already placed an agent in the field," Beck went on. "I've sent you a file."

Turning, Quinn pulled the back of the seat down beside him, revealing the computer. A small dish at the back of the limousine connected him to a satellite array.

He opened the e-mail feature and decrypted the message, then linked to the Web site where Beck had posted his progress. One long minute later, a digital image flickered onto the LCD screen.

The woman was young, perhaps midtwenties, and beautiful. Her white-blond hair fell to her shoulders. Ice blue eyes. In the picture, she looked like a tourist, dressed in light summerwear. For some reason that he didn't understand, she looked hauntingly familiar.

"Who is she?" Quinn asked.

"She's in Amsterdam now," Beck replied, evasive. "She made contact with a man who sells me information on a regular basis. She asked him about Tuenis Meijer. Once she had Meijer's address, she went there. But, of course, Meijer hasn't returned yet or I would have him."

"How do you know she was asking about Meijer?"

"The man who sold her the information called me and gave me her picture."

"What have you done about her involvement?"

"I've got two men on her now. She's currently at the railway station awaiting an arrival."

"Not departing?" That would be too good, Quinn thought. Too easy. And too much to hope for.

"She hasn't bought a ticket. I tracked her arrival into Amsterdam through computer records. Her passport says she's Crystal Downing. From Newark, New Jersey."

"She's not?"

"Her name is Samantha St. John. She's an Athena Academy graduate. She fits the profile for the AA.gov background we have access to. I got her picture and name from a school yearbook."

Cursing, Quinn closed the computer and stored it behind the seat again.

He struggled to remain calm. For over twenty years, his secret had been safe. At least, relatively safe. There was one woman who knew more about him than she should, a woman who some said was only a myth, a black widow who seduced and killed her mate and any man she found useless once she was done with them. For the last twenty-plus years, she had been blackmailing him.

That blackmailer was believed to have one of the most sophisticated information networks in the world, with secrets that could cripple or topple major corporations and nations. Despite years of searching, Quinn had not been able to find his blackmailer or discern her identity. Now, if he moved quickly, he had a chance to find that woman and kill her. Perhaps, if he moved quickly enough, he might even hope to learn the secrets she knew. They were worth a lot of money. But he needed Meijer.

"My path may cross the competition's," Beck said.

"If she gets in your way, kill her."

There was no hesitation. "Yes, sir."

"And let me know as soon as it's dealt with." Quinn hung up the phone and put it back in his jacket.

"Sahib," Malik whispered tremulously from the car. "Please?"

Ruthlessly, Quinn knotted his fist in the man's hair and yanked him from the limousine. Ten feet from the car,

Quinn put the silencer to Malik's head and squeezed the trigger. The body dropped onto the shifting sand.

Quinn breathed in the cool, dry desert air, held it a moment, then let it out. *Everything is controllable,* he told himself. *With enough money, enough blood, enough determination, everything is controllable.*

He would spend all to protect himself.

Chapter 1

Amsterdam, The Netherlands

Once you get to Amsterdam, Sam, your life will be in danger. You can't trust anyone.

Remembering Allison Gracelyn's last warning before she'd boarded the plane in Phoenix, Samantha St. John stood waiting in the lobby of Central Station, Amsterdam's main railway station, and forced the tension and doubt away. *You were warned about the danger,* she chided herself. *You didn't tell your lover about it, but you told your sister.*

Guilt stung her, but she didn't give in to it. Riley McLane was her lover and had been a big part of her life for almost nineteen months now. But she wasn't used to sharing everything in her life. There were parts she wasn't ready to share—didn't know *how* to share. Being alone was natural; being part of a couple wasn't.

Riley was a CIA agent, as she was, but with a lot more fieldwork experience than she'd had. Normally she acted as support, specializing in languages and computers. Riley was definitely hands-on for retrievals and terminations.

Riley had a tendency to be overprotective and a control freak, which could be endearing, Sam had found. But for her current mission, she needed backup with no questions asked. Since she and her sister had been planning to get together for a while, Sam had elected to ask Elle to come with her.

Sam's sister was an intelligence agent as well. Elle worked for the Russian government's SVR, which was that country's equivalent of the CIA. Although they'd known each other less than a year and a half, Sam knew Elle wouldn't ask a lot of questions if Sam asked her not to. That was one of the things Sam truly appreciated about her sister.

And if things truly got dangerous on the assignment, it would be easier to disappear with Elle, who had been to Amsterdam several times before, than with Riley, who had only a passing acquaintance with the country. Sam told herself that was the real reason for her decision, but she knew she didn't want to put Riley in harm's way if she couldn't tell him why she was doing it.

And she couldn't tell him, because she didn't know. Only Allison and Alexandra Forsythe's request, and the Athena Academy bond between them, had moved her into action.

Dozens of other people waited for the train as well. Night lurked dark and mysterious outside the station windows, and the red glow of the red-light district in the distance held the promise of forbidden ecstasy. Music in several languages boomed from personal entertainment systems. Children and teenagers played video games while parents consulted travel brochures. Monitors broadcast information and news from around the world. The hustle and bustle of the station became an ocean of sight and sound that pressed against her senses.

Sam wore dark blue notch-tab capri pants and a white scoop neck sweater. She'd left her shoulder-length, white-blond hair loose, and dark sunglasses hid her ice-blue eyes even though it was dark outside. According to the tourist pamphlets, the area was rife with pickpockets and purse-snatchers. At five feet three inches tall and slender, she knew she'd be a target for predators. As a safeguard, she carried her ID, passport and cash in a pocket. She felt naked without a weapon.

And she was nervous.

You have every right to be nervous, she told herself. *You're meeting your sister in person for the fourth time in your whole life.*

For all of her childhood that she could remember, Sam had been an orphan raised in foster homes. She'd learned to be quiet and self-contained. She wasn't used to family. Most of the foster homes she'd been in preferred not to see their charges. She'd learned to spend incredible amounts of time surfing the Internet.

Ultimately, it had been her interest in computers that had saved her, though her salvation had taken a strange route. When she'd been nine years old, she'd hacked into a sensitive government site, not really knowing what she was getting into, just plugging away at a barrier that had stymied her young mind. Her success had triggered an armed invasion by federal forces.

But a judge's decision and government intervention had brought her to the attention of the Athena Academy for the Advancement of Women. The seventh-through-twelfth-grade school was a special academy set up for the smartest, most promising young women to learn and explore their every potential.

While there, Sam had come to know the only family she'd ever felt part of. The Cassandras. Her orientation group had all been assigned at random, but their senior student leader, Lorraine "Rainy" Miller, had united them into a group of best friends. Even graduation hadn't ended that relationship.

Rainy's recent murder and the fallout from their investigation and eventual exposure of the killers had only drawn the Cassandras closer. Sam hadn't needed anything outside that world.

Until she'd found out about Elle Petrenko.

Last year, Sam had been detained by the CIA and accused of being responsible for a double-cross in Berzhaan that had triggered a lot of adverse publicity for the United States. No one expected Sam to have an evil twin.

But Elle Petrenko *was* her twin, separated from Sam when they were barely toddlers when their parents, who had been Russian double agents for the British intelligence agency MI-6, were murdered. The events around those deaths and how Sam eventually was abandoned in America still hadn't been explained.

Thankfully, Elle hadn't been an evil twin. She'd merely been a Russian agent performing her own mission in Berzhaan. Neither Sam nor Elle had known the other existed, but once they'd met, each of them had felt as if a missing piece had been restored to them. Though their lives were worlds apart and filled with covert responsibilities, they made an effort to stay in touch by phone and e-mail and meet when they could.

So, for the fourth meeting, Sam thought glumly, *it's all,*

"Come to see me in Amsterdam and try not to die." *What kind of sister am I?* She sighed, because she truly didn't know the answer to that question at present.

She had mixed emotions. On one hand, she wanted to see Elle and they'd already made arrangements to be together this week, which had been hard to plan to begin with. Giving up the time wasn't something Sam was willing to do. But neither was turning away from a request Allison and Alex had tendered, knowing full well Sam was planning on seeing Elle.

On the other hand, Sam knew how valuable Elle would be in Amsterdam, a place Sam had never been. Being a good agent was all about having resources in place in the field. *So what are you?* she asked herself. *A sister, an agent or a rat?*

"Hi."

Startled, Sam turned to look at the speaker. He'd come up behind her quietly.

The man was tall, at least six foot three, with broad shoulders and lean hips. His shaved head gave him a look of menace, and a reddish soul patch made a point on his lower lip. Gray-green hazel eyes, like those of a big jungle cat, surveyed her impassively and held deep melancholy. The black biker leathers and heavy-metal concert T-shirt didn't give much away. He could have been a dockworker or a Goth.

"Are you American?" The man spoke English flawlessly.

Because she felt contrary and because she didn't want to let anyone know her business, Sam answered in French. "I don't speak English. Do you speak French?" Languages and computers were her specialty at the CIA.

He switched to German, which she also understood. "No French. I speak German."

Sam decided to cut the guy a break. He might even know more languages. She spoke in German. "Your German is very good."

"I'm told my English is really good, too," he said.

"I wouldn't know," Sam replied.

The man shrugged. "I'm amazed."

Sam arched an eyebrow.

"You're so gifted linguistically."

"What makes you think that?"

Again the shrug, just a slight lift of the broad, leather-covered shoulders. "You speak French. You speak German." He reached out slowly, without threat, and touched the pamphlet in her hand. "And you *read* English. Quite an accomplishment."

Glancing down, Sam saw that she was indeed holding an English language pamphlet. "Busted." She smiled, but she was wary at the same time. The man was very observant.

"I came over because you look like a tourist. This is a dangerous place for tourists."

"You just volunteer to wait with strangers in the train station?"

He gave a slight nod. "It's a hobby."

"Maybe," Sam said sweetly, "you should seek counseling."

Perhaps he had a comeback for that, but Sam didn't find out. At that moment the warning Klaxons went off, filling the station with noise and vibration. The crowd moved around her, getting ready for the train's arrival.

In that moment, Sam got a clue as to what the man's real interest was. Two men dressed in casual streetwear moved toward the platform. They had short, military-style haircuts and wore light jackets. An air of danger clung to both of them.

The big man, dressed in black, moved with them, shifting so that they stayed in his view.

The two men kept their distance.

Sam looked at the man in black. *Are you hunting them? Or avoiding them?* The situation intrigued her.

The train stopped with a grinding screech of brakes. Seconds later, the doors opened and the passengers began to debark in a press of moving bodies.

Sam stood on tiptoe to peer through the crowd.

Elle Petrenko stepped out from a middle car. She was carrying a baby and chatting amiably with a woman only a little older than her, who was carrying another toddler.

A baby? Sam was shocked. Elle hadn't said anything about a baby. But then, there was a lot Sam didn't know about her twin. Elle seemed outgoing and friendly, always willing to share her life, but Sam didn't do that because of her upbringing. Naturally she assumed others held back things they didn't want known as well. *But a baby?*

Three meetings in person over the last eighteen months, combined with several phone calls that were, no doubt, monitored by their respective intelligence agencies, and off-the-grid e-mails—none of it could complete a relationship that had a twenty-three-year gap.

Elle wore caramel-colored twill pants and a black, short-sleeved turtleneck that flattered her slender figure. Boots and a carry-on tote completed the ensemble. Unlike Sam, Elle wore her hair up.

After a brief conversation, Elle handed the baby to the young woman, who waved goodbye and managed to head out under a full head of steam with both kids. Sam released a breath, but a bit of wistfulness tugged at her heart. She was beginning to understand what it felt like to be a sister, but what would it be like to be an aunt? Just the sight of

Elle holding that baby had started a whole kaleidoscope of possibilities tumbling through Sam's head. She'd never really thought about family before. Now she was seeing generations of it ahead of her.

Glancing across the waiting area, Elle spotted Sam and walked over.

"Hello, sis," Elle said, sounding totally American instead of Russian.

"Hi," Sam replied.

Elle glanced up at the man beside Sam. "Who's your friend?"

"You're twins," the big man observed.

Elle smiled but didn't take her ice-blue eyes off the man in black. "He's cute, but has he always been this slow?"

The man frowned at her.

"I don't know," Sam admitted. "I just found him."

Looking a trifle uncomfortable, the man crossed his arms over his broad chest.

"He's big," Elle said, grinning slightly. Her blue eyes sparkled. "Can we afford to feed him?"

"He's not staying," Sam said. "Do you have bags?"

Elle patted the carry-on. "Just this one. I knew you said we'd be on the go tonight, so I made arrangements to have my bags delivered to my room."

"Good." Sam was already feeling antsy to be moving. She looked up at the big man. "Well, good luck finding another tourist to guard."

He nodded.

Elle fixed him with the full force of her ice-blue eyes. "Do you have a name?"

"Joachim," he said, then looked a little irritated.

Sam thought maybe it was because he'd answered before he could stop himself. Elle had that effect on men.

Even though they were twins, Elle was able to do more with her looks and her personality than Sam was. *She's just more willing to take risks than I am,* Sam thought for what must have been the thousandth time.

"I'm Elle." She offered her hand.

Joachim took Elle's hand and held it for a moment, then seemed reluctant to let go.

"Are you going to be in Amsterdam long?" Elle asked.

"A few days."

"Maybe I'll see you around."

Sam didn't think that was a good idea. Joachim was rousing her warning senses. Maybe it was the quiet way he moved, or the fact that he'd avoided the two suspicious-looking men who now seemed to have disappeared, or maybe even the fact that Elle was acting twitterpated over him, but Sam wanted him gone.

"Perhaps," Joachim replied. He offered a small wave. "Have a safe trip." Then he was in motion, walking away from them.

Elle watched him go.

Despite her misgivings, and feeling a little guilty because Riley was back home missing her, Sam also watched the big man walk away. The tight leather pants hugged his firm butt in ways that Sam could appreciate even though she was spoken for.

"Wow," Elle said.

"Wow?" Sam grumbled.

"Definitely wow," Elle replied. "He's one of *those* guys."

"What guys?"

"Those guys you hate to see go but you love to watch leave."

Sam grimaced. During the last year of getting to know Elle, she'd found her sister was much more outspoken than she was. "Personally, I thought he was creepy. He appeared behind me, out of nowhere. He told me he thought I was a tourist and shouldn't be alone."

"Doesn't sound creepy to me. Sounds like a nice guy." Elle glanced at her meaningfully. "You've already got a nice guy. Maybe that's why you're invulnerable to Joachim's mutant abilities."

"Mutant abilities?"

"It's from a children's cartoon show," Elle explained. *"The X-Men."*

"In your country?"

"In yours." Elle gave her a perplexed look. "You know, it surprises me sometimes how little you know about being a kid."

I didn't get to spend a lot of time being a kid, Sam thought.

"What *mutant abilities* does he have?" Sam asked.

"Irresistible charm and devastating looks. Definitely. Oh, and brooding menace."

"I must be invulnerable."

"You," Elle countered, "have Riley."

The crowd flowed steadily out of the building as the train powered up to depart again. Joachim and the two other men were nowhere in sight.

"What's on the agenda?" Elle asked. "You said part of this little get-together was going to be a working vacation."

"I've got to find someone."

"We already found someone. You let him go."

"Look," Sam said, more shortly than she intended because she was tired and tense from meeting with Elle and dealing with Allison and Alex's unexplained request, "if you hurry, you might be able to catch up to him."

A calm look filled Elle's face. She touched Sam's arm. "Hey, just joking, Sam. I've been really looking forward to seeing you again. It's been three months. I'm kind of jet-lagged from the trip. To make this happen, I've had to be up and running for the last thirty-seven hours. I'm not at my best."

"I'm sorry," Sam said. *My sisterly skills could definitely use some improvement,* she thought. During their time together, Elle was always the more relaxed one, more able to accept everything that happened. As a foster child, Sam had always fought to maintain security and familiarity. She didn't like it when things changed.

"No biggie," Elle said. "Buy me a mocha latte along the way and you'll find I can be all about forgiveness."

Sam smiled and shook her head. "Do you realize that sometimes you sound more American than I do?"

"I," Elle replied, "take that as a compliment. I've worked hard to sound that way." Leaning in, she whispered conspiratorially in a thick Russian accent that she had once assured Sam came from *The Rocky and Bullwinkle Show*. Sam had gotten on the Internet to learn who those cartoon characters were. "Eet vas all included een my secret spy training, comrade."

"Terrific," Sam said. "Are you ready?"

"Yes. Why haven't you already found the guy that you were sent here to find?"

Sam led the way out of the terminal. "It's possible that I've been looking in the wrong places."

"Where did you look?"

"At his house."

"Hmm. That's a good place to start. He wasn't home?"

"No."

"What about his place of work?"

"He's a criminal," Sam said. "He doesn't keep regular

hours or an office. He lives on a houseboat, so even his res-idence moves around a lot."

"Makes it more difficult, but not impossible."

Sam nodded. "This guy has pissed off a lot of the wrong people from what I've been able to find out. Someone may have killed him."

"So instead of a person," Elle said, "you could be looking for a boat anchor or fish chum."

"Exactly," Sam said. "I have to tell you, this could be dangerous."

"You don't have to tell me," Elle replied with a smile. "I'm a secret agent. I figured it out all on my own. C'mon. If I'm going to have to stay on my toes, we need to find me that mocha latte."

Chapter 2

Standing in the shadows in front of Central Station, Joachim Reiter watched the two young women leave the building. They headed toward the red-light district and that didn't please him. Although the sex shops and brothels were tourist attractions, they were also places were people got into trouble and sometimes got killed.

And those two women—or maybe only the one he'd first met at the train station—were in trouble. Otherwise Arnaud Beck's men wouldn't have led Joachim to them.

The last hour had been quite the circus, Joachim reflected. Tension and nervousness rattled through him. He didn't want to be there, so far from home and his family. Being out of the country right now threatened everything. If any of his subterfuges were found out, he was dead. More important, so was his family.

He exhaled and avoided the fear clamoring inside his

mind. *One step at a time, Joachim. You won't make any mistakes. Just get this done and get back home.*

But things had already gotten more complicated than he'd guessed. He'd been sent to Amsterdam to find a man named Tuenis Meijer and had tripped across Beck's men while gathering information about his target. Thinking that Beck's men might lead him to Meijer, Joachim had followed them, staying out of sight. They'd never known he was there until he let them see him in the railway station.

Then they had locked on to the young blond woman at the station. Joachim still didn't know who she was or what threat or possibility of gain she represented to a man like Arnaud Beck, but he'd known he couldn't let them kidnap her or kill her.

Although *he* had, in the past, kidnapped and killed other men, Joachim couldn't stand idly by while something happened to the woman. He wasn't that kind of man. And he didn't want to be the kind of man Günter Stahlmann paid him to be.

He was working on a way out. If trying to get there didn't get him or his family killed in the process. Still, he played that deadly game by his rules and he'd made Günter respect them. Rule number one was that Joachim would never harm an innocent.

That was why he had broken his cover and revealed himself to Beck's men. Although they'd had their quarry in their sights, his presence there had upped the stakes. For them all, he ruefully admitted. No one was supposed to know he was there, either.

That decision was going to bring him trouble. He took trouble one step at a time, though. He'd learned that from years spent living between the crush of evil and the law. None of it had been easy. Even the way out he was now reaching for couldn't promise he would live out his life instead of getting a bullet through his head or a knife across his throat for his betrayal.

But the women had gone one way and Beck's men, now wise to his presence, had gone another. It was a stalemate that he could live with at the moment. What happened to them later was out of his hands. If something did happen, he hoped he would never know.

One of his cell phones chirped for attention. He pulled the device from inside his jacket, but his eyes stayed on the two blond women walking toward Oude Zijde.

A freighter passing in the north canal on the other side of the station sounded its horn, the tone mournful on the night air, like some lonely beast.

"Yes," Joachim said into the phone. He spoke Russian now. Like his German and English, his voice carried no dialect.

"I have an address for you," the young woman's voice on the other end announced. "Your target lives on a house-boat called *Satyr Dreams* down on Achterburgwal. It's near the intersection of Rusland Street."

"I can find it." Joachim paused, wondering how much he should reveal. But then, there was always the possibility that the woman was tracking his progress. "Beck's men are here."

Some of the confidence vanished from the young woman's tone. "Are you certain?"

"One of them is known to me. He's a criminal named Felix Horst. He specializes in armory and wetwork." Wetwork was a euphemism for murder and assassination. Joachim knew people who did such things, but he would never be one of them.

"You knew that it was likely you would cross paths with Beck. I told you that."

"You did. But if Beck, or at least one of his lieutenants, is here, it affects what we are able to do in the future. If you have any influence with him…"

"Beck is not part of this organization. I told you that, too."

She had, but Joachim hadn't necessarily believed her. The fact that she knew Beck, and knew what kind of man he was, made her information on him suspect. Most people outside the criminal syndicate and law enforcement didn't know about Beck. That she did told him he needed to be careful.

"Concentrate on your mission, Joachim," she chided him. "Call me when you reach his houseboat."

The phone clicked in Joachim's ear. He closed the cell phone and replaced it in his pocket. Slowly, he turned and surveyed the street. *Is she watching?* He wasn't certain.

Paranoia was a constant state of his profession. The feeling was one of the things that kept him alive all these years. His world was filled with gunrunners and black marketers, dope dealers and blackmailers, thieves and murderers. The sad thing was, he felt more at home in that world than any other.

Sometimes, when he let his own doubts and limitations plague him, he lost hope that he would ever be out of the sewer he was in. All his life that he could remember had been about violence, about crime that boiled down to sex and money. Even if he got out of it, got away from Günter and men like him, Joachim wondered how he was supposed to live like a normal man.

He would never be normal.

At the canal he flagged down a water taxi and gave his target's address, wishing he knew more about why he was there.

And why a man as dangerous as Arnaud Beck was, too.

* * *

As Sam walked toward the area, Amsterdam's red-light district pulsed neon against the encroaching night. It was just after 10:00 p.m. locally and the nine-to-five crowds had given the city over to the nightlife. The clubs and bars were full, and music stained the air, but traffic was sparse.

The city was shaped like a horseshoe, built on the old streets that had accommodated horse-and-buggy traffic. The canals had always offered transport, and the majority of destinations were within walking distance. Small parties and big groups walked through the streets and window-shopped.

She and Elle walked alone.

The Voorburgwal Canal lay to their right and the Achterburgwal Canal to their left. Buildings were crammed together in the space between. Trees and boats lined the canals and bicyclists weaved between the pedestrians.

The red-light district created a ruby bubble of illumination in Oude Zijde, the old side of the city. Although she hadn't been there yet, Sam knew sex shops and brothels filled the area. What she was probably going to see intrigued her, but at the same time she was put off by reports of sexual slavery. Willing adults putting on a sex show in a window was one thing, but she had to wonder if some were forced to perform.

"When was the last time you were in Amsterdam?" Sam asked, curious about her sister's life.

"Five months ago. Perhaps six."

"You never mentioned it."

"I was working."

"Ah." Although they'd shared a lot about their lives, Sam knew they kept secrets from each other. Given the nature of their professions, they had to.

However, the unclassified bits and pieces gave them

much to discuss. Like who to bribe in Rio de Janeiro to get weapons and transportation, or who to lean on in Paris to get information about the black market network. Several of the people they'd met on missions had been the subject of more than a few laughs over beer and pizza.

Sam couldn't help wondering if the mission they were presently on would be something they'd laugh about later. The fact that she hadn't found her quarry yet spoke volumes about how difficult it might become.

Neither Allison nor Alex had given many clues. They'd simply come to Sam and asked her to find the man. Sam knew that Allison had been digging around in some of the secret files they'd found during their investigation of Rainy's murder. The files' importance had taken on a new dimension when Alex had connected them to the death of Allison's own mother, Athena Academy founder Marion Gracelyn. She'd felt certain that the mystery assignment came out of those, but she had no clue what it pertained to.

Now, in the middle of Amsterdam, misgivings rattled against her confidence. She didn't doubt that she could find Meijer, but the danger quotient was doubtlessly going to go up.

And I invited my sister to do this, Sam thought. *Way to go.*

"Who are you after?" Elle asked.

"Tuenis Meijer. He's a—"

"Computer cracker," Elle said.

She used the correct term for the man's chosen illegal profession. *Hacker* was a term used by the public as a result of movies and misinformation. True masters of the craft referred to themselves as *crackers* because they cracked the code that protected information. "Right," Sam said.

"Sorry," Elle said. "Didn't mean to spoil your briefing.

It's just that I've dealt with guys who have done business with Tuenis in the past."

"It's okay," Sam said. "I knew you were familiar with Amsterdam. That's one of the reasons I asked you to meet me here instead of canceling out. Your knowing Meijer is a plus."

"He's truly slime."

"That's what I gathered."

Elle stopped and gazed south. "He keeps a houseboat on the Achterburgwal near Rusland Street."

"I know," Sam said. "I've already been by there. He wasn't home."

"Do you have a destination in mind?" Elle asked.

"I thought we would cruise the strip. Find out where the action is." Sam walked along the Voorburgwal. Neon shimmered like stripes of runny rainbows in the dark water of the canal. A passing motorboat created a pulse of vibrant noise. Waves slapped against the houseboats moored at the canal's edge. "Tuenis has a predilection for sex clubs."

"Yes, he does." Elle smiled. "This should be interesting, since you haven't been here before." She turned and headed into the nearest alley. "You won't find the ones Tuenis will be interested in out on the street. He's a truly bad boy. At least, he thinks he is. We'll need to hit the alleys. That's where you find the more aggressive clubs."

In just a matter of steps, Sam felt like she'd been transported into another world. Narrow, long and winding, the alley slipped between tall buildings filled with large picture windows on the lower floors. Red lights ringed windows in which provocatively dressed, semiclad and nude women lounged, danced or moved in open invitation to voyeurism.

It was like nothing Sam had ever seen before. But she couldn't help smiling, thinking about what Riley would say if she showed up in his bedroom dressed—or *undressed*—

in one of those outfits. In fact, she was pretty sure he wouldn't be able to say anything until he managed to pull his jaw up from the ground.

The woman in the booth smiled back at Sam and blew her a kiss.

"Sam?" Elle called.

"Yeah?"

"Problem?"

Sam turned to her sister. "Before we leave Amsterdam, we have to go shopping."

Elle shook her head. "Poor Riley. He's not going to know what hit him."

"That's exactly the point," Sam said. "You don't catch him off guard often."

Elle glanced at the women in the windows. "That will do it. I know just the place. After we find Meijer." Turning, still grinning, she continued down the alley.

Keeping his face forward, Joachim performed a walk-by near *Satyr Dreams*. Darkness filled the houseboat's deck. His senses tingled with alertness the way they had since he was a boy and had first learned to break and enter back in Leipzig. Back then, stealing had been a way of survival. Forced entry was merely one of the skills he employed in his current vocation.

The houseboat was spacious but looked old. The fabricated metal exterior held pockmarks from hail and other abuse. Rocking on the waves from passing vessels, *Satyr Dreams* slapped against the side of the canal with quiet, hollow thuds.

He felt confident he could get inside.

At twelve he had started breaking into the homes of affluent people on the outer edges of the old neighborhood.

That had been the year his father had been killed while trying to commit an armored car robbery. The Berlin Wall had fallen only a few years previously and West Germany was still working out the details of absorbing East Germany. The difference between the two countries' economies had been like night and day. For a time, West German business had taken advantage of the East German labor pool, paying them only slightly more than they had already been getting paid. It wasn't a good introduction to Western ways.

But crime had been good. Joachim's father hadn't been a bad man, just one who liked living easy and grew attracted to the danger of taking what he wanted. But he'd always been kind and gentle and soft-spoken. Until his father's death, Joachim and his mother and sister hadn't known his father had been a criminal.

Joachim's mother had worked, but she hadn't been able to make enough to keep a roof over their heads and feed them after her husband's death. Joachim had tried to find a job, but no one wanted to hire a twelve-year-old boy and pay him enough to make up the difference his mother fell short on every month. In the end, he'd become a thief.

At first, Joachim had taken only food and small things he could trade for more food. Later, he had worked with a few partners and started stealing from corporate warehouses, targeting electronics and vehicles, moving into higher risk theft for a chance at a higher paycheck.

One night, one of his friends had been shot while they'd stolen a car. The boy had bled to death in the seat beside Joachim. The man Joachim had sold the stolen Mercedes to had docked the price for the blood on the seats. Joachim had been forced to dump his friend's body in an alley as if it were common trash. He hadn't been able to speak to his friend's mother ever again.

Joachim knew the world wasn't fair, and he'd quickly gotten harder to match it.

Since the age of fifteen, Joachim had been involved in organized crime. His mother had turned a blind eye to the money he'd brought into the house, and his sister had never known what he did. By the time he'd gotten old enough to get a legitimate job, he was too entangled to get out.

The people he did business with wouldn't let him step out of their circle without paying a heavy price. They feared snitches.

Joachim had started as a numbers runner for Günter Stahlmann. At eighteen, Joachim had proven he could survive on the streets, and Günter promoted him to enforcer. For the next five years, Joachim had collected from habitual criminals who owed Günter money for sports bets and had tracked down those who had stolen from Günter. Joachim had been shot and stabbed on several occasions.

The last two years, though, he had graduated to a position of specialty assignments. The current assignment to Amsterdam came under that heading. Lately, Günter had managed a working arrangement with the mysterious woman who was currently calling the shots on the mission to capture Tuenis Meijer. Joachim didn't know the nature of that arrangement, but he was paying careful attention.

Getting sent after Meijer couldn't have happened at a worse time. Joachim was close to getting away from Günter for good. During the last year, pursuant to the agreement he'd made with the German police, Joachim had been steadily betraying his employer, easing out of the shackles of crime that had bound him for all these years.

It hadn't been an easy trick to accomplish. His life was currently several layers of lies deep.

But he desperately wanted out. Enough so to risk everything he had in the attempt.

Joachim stepped into the dark shadows that draped the houseboat. With a lithe coil of muscles, he leaped onto the rear deck. He tried the door, because he'd learned while collecting for Günter that doors weren't always locked.

This one was.

It was also armed with an alarm.

Kneeling, Joachim pulled on a pair of thin surgical gloves and took out an electronic lock-pick kit from his pocket. Working quickly, he held a small pen-flash in his mouth for light and then cut into the alarm wiring. He bypassed the secondary alarm, then popped the plastic cover on the main alarm and connected the lock-pick's alligator clips to the circuitry leading to the operating system. A quick tap on the electronic lock-pick device sent the digital readout scurrying to chase out the alarm code.

Less than a minute later, the readout flashed the eight-digit code. He pressed the activation button and the lock opened with a quiet *snik*.

Pocketing the electronic lock-pick, Joachim opened the door and went inside.

The boathouse smelled like the inside of a gym locker. Joachim breathed through his mouth. Evidently Tuenis Meijer spent his ill-gotten gains on sex and drugs but not on maids. He pulled the shades and played his pen-flash around.

It looked like a dirty clothes bomb had gone off inside the living area. Pizza boxes and fast-food containers littered every flat surface. The only thing that looked clean was the computer desk.

Joachim left the computer alone for the moment. During

his time as a collector, he'd learned that people who used computers as their preferred weapons often left them boo-by-trapped. He wasn't proficient in computer usage. Günter had other people for that.

His cell phone rang.

Taking it out, he opened it and said, "Yes."

"Hey, kiddo," Günter said in his deep voice. He was a large, broad man with a nose that had been broken many times and a thick shock of black hair only now going to gray. He liked American movies, particularly the crime dramas known as noir.

"Hey," Joachim said. Neither of them used names. It was a practice of many years because they both knew their phone lines could be tapped at any time.

"How's it going?" Günter asked.

"I'm still looking for our package."

Günter sighed, and the sound was filled with all the sadness old Germany could muster. "I'm counting on you to pull this out, kiddo."

"I will." Quelling the unease that talking to Günter created, Joachim made a quick circuit of the galley. The clutter continued there. *How can Meijer live like this?*

Intrigued by the closet, Joachim tried to open the door. It was locked. He set the pen-flash on the galley table so the beam played over the door and he could free his hands. Reaching into his jacket pocket, he took out two lock-picks, shouldered the cell to his ear and knelt to work on the lock.

"I just want to warn you to stay on your toes," Günter said.

"I am. I always do."

"Don't trust anybody over there."

"I never do." The lock clicked open.

"And you'll let me know the instant you find the package?"

"Of course." Joachim put the lock-picks away and

pulled the closet door open. Once the lock was released, the door opened quickly, forced into frantic motion by the weight on the other side. Stepping back, Joachim reached for a long knife in the cutlery block on the galley table. The cell phone tumbled from his shoulder to the floor.

A man sprawled at Joachim's feet, barely illuminated by the pen-flash's wide beam.

Joachim brought the knife up smoothly, the blade positioned along his forearm so it wouldn't easily be knocked from his grasp. The technique didn't allow him to immediately stab an opponent, but he could slash an opponent's face, hands, arms or stomach. Once an enemy started to bleed, it was only a matter of time till he succumbed.

The man at Joachim's feet didn't move.

Picking up his pen-flash, Joachim surveyed the man. A neat round bullet hole between the man's eyes showed blue-black. A tiny streamer of blood zigzagged down his face.

"Hey, kiddo," Günter called from the phone. "Hey."

Senses flaring wildly, sensitive now to the rocking motion the houseboat made on the water, Joachim waited in the darkness. He fully expected to hear police sirens and helicopter rotors overhead.

"Hey," Günter called out a little more strongly. "Can you hear me now?"

Moving slowly, making himself breathe and not bolt off the houseboat, Joachim scooped up the phone. "Yes."

"What happened?"

Joachim shined the pen-flash down on the man's face. His head rocked slowly back and forth with the houseboat's motion.

"We have a problem," Joachim said, struggling to keep himself calm. But he knew the problem was his. With everything so delicately balanced in his life, with all the lies he'd told, he felt certain that something had fallen through the cracks. He didn't doubt for a moment that he'd just been set up. He could already feel the jaws of the trap springing closed on him.

Chapter 3

Elle's mind buzzed as she rounded the corner of the alley and stepped onto the sidewalk. She automatically swept the street, looking for suspicious pedestrians, parked vehicles and passing cars. Nothing pinged the personal warning system she'd developed since becoming an intelligence agent.

Sam remained behind her, alert and ready. Remembering how they'd met in Berzhaan, how Sam had beaten her in an unarmed fight, Elle knew her twin could take care of herself. But the situation Elle was leading them into was doubtlessly going to turn ugly fast. She had a history with the man they were going to see.

"The place we're going," Elle said, "is going to be dangerous."

"All right." Sam never missed a beat or showed any sign of hesitation.

"The men we're going to see are killers," Elle continued. "Jan, the man we want to talk to, will have at least two bodyguards. The store he runs is a cover for his other business. He traffics in drugs and weapons, but he has a lot of contacts and knows a lot of things. Tuenis Meijer is someone he'll know."

"Good."

"He may also try to kill me on sight."

"Why?"

"A couple years ago, I cost him a major portion of his business and almost got him killed. I also put him in the hospital because I nearly burned his face off."

"That would do it," Sam said lightly.

Elle glanced at her sister. Sam looked a little tense. Then Elle focused on the street in front of her. She was feeling nervous herself. Jan wasn't a good man to meet under any circumstance. The history they had made it worse.

For just a moment, Elle wondered why Sam wanted Meijer and what her twin wasn't telling her. Elle didn't like walking into operations without knowing everything that was going on. If it had been anyone else, she wouldn't have been involved. But this was her sister. Family meant everything to Elle. Her parents, the people who had raised her and loved her, had taught her that.

She just hoped there would be no regrets and both of them would live through the experience.

They passed a small group of street hookers complaining in English, German and French about the slow business of the night, the weather and assorted personal problems. Pedestrian traffic flowed around them, barely slowed by even the most aggressive sales tactics.

The front of the shop that was the sisters' destination held a large picture window garishly outfitted with provocatively attired mannequins sporting black leather, masks, whips, chains and furry handcuffs. Two of the kneeling mannequins had red ball gags in their mouths. Monitors played movies featuring paddling, restraints and degradation. Neon tubing advertised Sex Videos, Sex Aids and Fantasy Sex.

Elle went through the door without hesitation. The bell overhead rang to announce her arrival. Five people were inside. Jan stood behind the counter while his two body-guards sat at a small table beside a rack of DVDs with covers that left nothing to the imagination. A young couple peered at a swing contraption made of leather and wood that Jan was showing them.

Jan was a thick-bodied man with a bored air. His dark hair was neatly clipped and gold chains hung around his neck. He wore a New York Yankees baseball jersey. As he looked up to greet them, recognition flared in his gray eyes.

"Hella," Jan called in English, scrambling to reach under the counter. "Kill her." Then he did a double take, seeing Sam behind Elle. "Kill them both."

The scarlet neon from the tubing played over the burn scars on Hella's face. He moved smoothly, showing years of practice. He was at least fifty, his hair white with age, smooth shaven like someone's kindly grandfather. The coat slid away from the cut-down double-barrel 12-gauge shotgun hanging from a whipit sling on his right arm.

Elle ignored the bodyguards, trusting Sam to handle them. With the men spread out inside the sex shop, the danger was spread across two fronts.

Sam stepped toward Hella, got in close and blocked the man's attempt to bring the weapon to bear on Elle, who was closing the distance on Jan. The shotgun erupted in a deaf-ening blast. Neon light shimmered on the picture window as the concussive wave hammered the plate glass. The swarm of double ought buckshot cut a mannequin in half, blowing the top part off the bottom in a popcorn spray of hardened plastic.

The couple at the counter dove to the ground and covered their heads. The woman screamed hoarsely and didn't stop.

Elle felt bad for them. They'd appeared a little embarrassed just to be in the sex shop, and the negative experience they were going through was partly her fault. But they'd provided the distraction she'd needed that allowed her to get close to Jan. Now the trick was to keep them safe. She didn't want innocent blood on her hands. Even as she moved, she kept track of her sister, hating the fact that she was distracted. It wasn't professional.

Sam put a hand on the top of the shotgun to push it down to the floor just as Hella discharged the second blast. Pellets tore holes in the linoleum and shredded leather outfits and rattled chains.

With the shotgun empty, Sam released the weapon, slid back, then delivered a snap-kick to the front of Hella's knee, another to his crotch and—when the man bent over—a roundhouse kick to the face that drove him sideways.

By that time, Jan was bringing up the weapon he kept beneath the counter. Elle placed her hands on the countertop and vaulted over almost effortlessly. Balanced like a gymnast, she drove both feet into the center of Jan's chest.

A painful explosion ripped from Jan's lips as he stumbled back and slammed against the wall behind him. Shelves filled with sex toys tumbled down around him, but he fought his way back up, cursing vehemently. Elle landed on her feet and threw herself at Jan again, reaching for the weapon. She caught sight of Sam using Hella to block his partner's efforts to get at her.

The second man had cleared his pistol and brought it up but couldn't get a clear shot because Sam kept his partner between them. Moving quickly, Sam stepped around Hella and caught the man's gunwrist with one hand while with the other she rammed the Y between her thumb and forefinger into the man's throat. He *hurked* and dropped to his knees.

Shifting, Sam scooped up the fallen pistol. It was a Heckler & Koch .45, heavy and solid. Oil gleamed on the black metal barrel. She slid into a modified Weaver stance, left foot in front of the right, left palm cupped under her right palm.

Hella groped for the shotgun with one hand. He held two fresh shells from his jacket pocket in his other hand.

Voice calm, as if she were in situations like this all the time, Sam spoke in English, modeling Jan. "Touch the weapon and I *will* kill you."

Evidently Hella believed her. His hand withdrew from the shotgun.

Elle stopped admiring Sam's technique and fought Jan for the pistol. Although the man was larger than her, she maintained leverage over the weapon. If he got free, she knew Jan would kill her and Sam without a second's hesitation. Unexpectedly, she broke the hold she had on the pistol and sunk in on Jan. She moved like an automaton, delivering devastating elbow and knee strikes in bruising syncopation. The style was *Krav Maga*, the close-in fighting katas often used by Israeli Mossad and special forces.

Jan stumbled back. For a moment, he dropped to the floor, then fought his way to his feet. The pistol bounced away. He reached for a wooden dowel on the wall behind him, part of the erotic swing kit he'd been showing the couple.

Elle reached into her pocket and pulled out a flick knife. Expertly, she flipped the weapon twice, baring the blade and locking the handle grips together, then drove the sharp point through Jan's hand and impaled it on the wall. She didn't even think about the pain she caused her opponent.

Her father had taught her to distance herself from such things. Pain was a tool she'd learned to use just as she'd learned to use weapons and martial arts. Many agents were too squeamish to use such tactics. In the beginning, Elle had felt a strong reluctance to employing measures like this, but time often meant lives. Her father had told her that.

On one mission, Elle had been with a senior agent who hadn't used methods like this to get an answer quickly. The woman they had tried to save, a mother of two who'd been taken as a kidnap victim for ransom, had suffocated in a shallow grave before they reached her. It was a lesson Elle had never forgotten.

With a man like Jan, Elle never hesitated to go to extremes early. It saved time.

With a cry of pain, Jan stood as if transfixed. He swore in English and Dutch and French.

Not even breathing hard, Elle kept her hand on the knife handle. She distanced herself from her own emotions, going numb inside as her father had taught her. "Hurts, doesn't it?" she asked.

Jan cursed at her.

Elle wiggled the blade and the man groaned, sagged against the wall, then pleaded with her to stop.

Elle spoke in English. "The last time you saw me, you swore that you would kill me."

Face trembling in agony, Jan stared at her.

Still holding the knife, Elle said, "Now I'll make you a promise. If you try to kill me again, I'll kill you. It won't matter what information I want from you. There are other places to get it."

Blood ran along Jan's arm and dripped to the floor. He blinked his eyes rapidly. "My hand," he whispered.

"Not yet. For the moment, I like your hand where it is." Elle closed her fingers around the knife handle.

"What do you want?" Jan whispered.

"A man named Tuenis Meijer."

"Dmitri's," Jan gasped. "Try Dmitri's. There's a girl there that Meijer thinks he's in love with."

Silently, Elle pulled the knife from the wall. The man cradled his injured hand to his stomach and sank down on his haunches. He gave Elle a harsh look.

Squatting, Elle wiped the blade clean on Jan's pant leg. He didn't move to avoid her. "Don't think about following me. Don't think about warning Meijer I'm coming. Do you understand?"

Jan's reluctance to be bullied into an answer lasted only a moment. "Yes. Yes, I understand."

"Good," Elle said. She stood and walked away. Her eyes met Sam's briefly. "Are you ready?"

Sam had to try twice to speak. "Yes."

She's never seen anyone do something like that, Elle realized, recognizing the trauma in her twin's eyes. Then she remembered that Sam was relatively new to the field. Not only that, she'd been primarily relegated to translating documents and hacking computer systems. She was good at fighting, but violence was still somewhat new to her. She hadn't seen the things that Elle had.

Not knowing what to do or say to ease her twin's discomfort, hoping that she hadn't crossed a chasm that would permanently hurt their relationship, Elle led the way out of the shop and Sam followed.

The hunt was still on. Elle gave herself over to that.

"What is the matter?" Günter demanded at the other end of the phone connection.

Joachim stared down into the dead man's face and struggled to remain rational and calm. Panic gnawed at him with small, rat's teeth. "I found a body."

"Is it the man you were sent for?"

Kneeling, Joachim shone the pen-flash down and went through the dead man's pockets with his free hand. "No," he answered. "Someone else."

The dead man was easily ten years older than Tuenis Meijer but was just as shaggy and unkempt.

Joachim didn't like surprises. They tended to upset his ability to handle a situation. Everything in him screamed to get off the houseboat.

Playing the pen-flash around, he examined the floor. Neither the weapon that had killed the man nor a spent casing was in sight. Further examination of the closet where the man had been concealed revealed that he'd met his end there. Blood and brain matter clung to the closet walls and pooled on the floor.

"I've got to call our contact," Joachim said.

"Yes. Let me know how that goes."

"I will."

"And be careful, Joachim," Günter said. "You are very important to me. I would not see you injured."

A pang ripped through Joachim at the coming betrayal. Despite his murderous approach to his business and the long line of bodies that had led up to his current standing, Günter seemed to truly care about Joachim.

For months, Joachim had agonized over his decision to align himself against Günter. The crime czar had family and he was good to them, even though his daughters and sons didn't appreciate the things he had done for them. Günter's wife, ex-wives and mistresses only used him for what they could get. Günter hadn't had good experiences related to family or friends. He didn't trust many people.

But he trusted Joachim.

At fifteen, Joachim had been caught looting the home of a man who fenced stolen goods. That night, Günter had been with the man. The fence had wanted to shoot Joachim and call the *Stasi*. The East German police agency, with all the proper payments in place, would have condoned the decision because Joachim had been a thief and Leipzig had been filled with young thieves.

Only, Günter had liked the way Joachim had stood his ground and asked that his mother and sister be spared the details of his death. They didn't know he was a thief. They'd believed he worked at odd jobs.

Günter had kept the fence from killing Joachim that night. The next night, he gave Joachim his first numbers-running assignment.

"I will be careful," Joachim promised. He hung up the phone and reached for the third cell that he carried. His nerves jangled and the urge to run almost overcame him. He pressed numbers with his thumb and held the phone to his ear.

"Trouble?" a quiet, calm voice answered at the other end. Pitor Schultz was close to forty, a quiet man with dangerous eyes. Most people wouldn't assume he was a threat until it was too late. For almost twenty years, he'd been an agent for the *Bundesnachrichtendienst*. The BND was Germany's Foreign Intelligence Agency but they also operated inside the country when they had to.

"I'm going to send you a picture," Joachim said. "If possible, I need the man in it identified."

"All right. Send it." Schultz hung up.

The BND agent's ability to cut to the chase and ask only those questions that were pertinent was one of the things that made Joachim feel more secure about dealing with him. That and the fact that Schultz had been clever enough to catch him and compromise his freedom.

Joachim held the pen-flash on the man's face and used the cell phone's camera function to capture his image. A few buttons later, the image was on its way to Schultz.

Crossing to one of the houseboat's windows, Joachim slid the heavy blinds out slightly and slowly, to peer outside. Passersby continued on their way without a glance in his direction. If a team was watching, Joachim couldn't spot them.

He called Schultz's number again.

"Yes?" the BND agent answered.

"You have the picture?"

"I do. I don't know him. Is he connected to your present endeavor in any way?"

"Not that I'm aware of." Restlessness filled Joachim. He wanted desperately to be out of the houseboat. It was a floating trap.

"Be careful," Schultz advised.

Joachim ended the call and slipped the phone back in his pocket.

The dead man rolled slightly as the boat shifted. Since rigor hadn't set in, Joachim knew the man hadn't been dead long.

He took out the phone that connected him with the woman and punched the Send button. Schultz had tried tracking the number at one point, but it was carefully managed at the other end. A series of ever-changing cutouts made it seem as though the end connection was in several places in the United States, South America, the Caribbean, Russia and Asia.

"Do you have the target?" the woman asked.

"No. There's been a problem."

"There are not supposed to be any problems." Her voice took on icy suspicion.

"This problem was here before I arrived," Joachim replied. Anger stirred within him. "I found a dead man on the boat."

A brief pause stretched between them. "Who?" she asked.

"I don't know."

"What about your target?"

"Not here. The target could have been taken when this...other problem came up."

"One thing at a time. Is the computer still there?"

Joachim glanced at the computer. "Yes."

"Is it operational?"

"Give me a moment." Crossing the room, Joachim pulled the computer tower out, slid the cover off and checked for antipersonnel mines. Finding nothing, he left the cover off and switched the machine on. Despite his search, he still grew tense as the computer powered up.

"Well?" the woman asked.

"It's operational."

"Good. Now here's what you're to do..."

Following the woman's direction, Joachim settled in at the computer, opened up the high-speed Internet connection available through the houseboat's satellite dish array and allowed her access to the computer from a remote site. She— or whoever worked for her at the other end of the connection—took control of the cursor and the computer's functions.

"While this runs," the woman said, "I need you to stay there and monitor the computer."

"I'm not comfortable with that," Joachim replied. "I'm exposed here."

"You don't have a choice," she said coldly.

"I do." Joachim stood.

"Leave before I say you can and I'll make sure your mother, sister and niece don't live to see the dawn."

The threat hammered Joachim squarely between the eyes. The woman knew about his family. He was certain Günter had not told her. Whatever else Günter was, he wouldn't expose his family or anyone else's to danger. It only proved that the woman's knowledge of Joachim went deep.

"All right," Joachim said. He seethed inside. He'd moved his sister and mother to Munich so his and Günter's enemies wouldn't hurt them. "I'll stay here until you're finished." *Then, if you ever cross my path again, I'll kill you.*

Chapter 4

Dmitri's Private Entertainment stood in the middle of one of the long alleys in the old side under an office building. The alley rode up a hill and the sex club was near the top. Recessed back under a tall building, a short flight of stairs led up to the establishment. The offices above were strictly low rent, but the sex club offered the promise of more exciting fare.

Dark red neon lights that blazed like coals spelled out Dmitri's. Information about club hours was painted on the dark glass in English and Dutch. No cameras were allowed. It wasn't a place she'd willingly have gone by herself. She didn't feel comfortable with the prospect now.

But Elle showed no hesitation.

The club lobby was ornate, furnished with Old World splendor. Antique chairs and tables sat on either side of the room under soft nude photographs of women with tigers, in the show and lounging on high-performance cars. Fresh-cut flowers filled the vases on the tables. The whole package looked expensive and exotic. The two security guards in black suits added *dangerous* to the mix.

Elle fished money out of her pants pocket and paid the cover charge to the young woman at the desk inside the club's lobby. "I'm looking for someone," Elle said, catching the woman's hand and curling the change up into her palm. The offer was evident.

The young woman considered the bills rolled up into her hand. "Perhaps," she said, obviously desirous of the cash she was holding.

"A guest," Elle said. "Not anyone who works here."

Regretful reluctance filled the woman's eyes. "Our clientele is most important, miss. I cannot abuse the trust that they—"

"Tuenis Meijer," Elle went on.

Both security guards stood.

Sam turned slightly to address them. Her hand dropped to the bag containing the .45, but she hoped she wouldn't have to use it to threaten them.

The hostess considered for a moment, then rolled her hand up to more tightly clutch the money. She waved the two security guards back into their chairs. "Some guests are more welcome than others." She glanced at the LCD computer monitor built into the top of the desk. "In room nine. He's awaiting Fatima."

"Where's room nine and who is Fatima?" Elle asked.

"Go through those doors." The young woman pointed an elegantly nailed finger at the entrance to her left. "That gets you into the main room, where clients meet the girls. Stay to the left and go up the stairs. Room nine is marked at the landing. Fatima is one of the club employees. Tuenis Meijer has a special…interest in her.

She's not the first. I suspect she won't be the last. He's…impressionable."

"Thank you." Elle started for the ornate double doors. They didn't open.

The hostess looked at her. "If anyone inside is harmed, you won't make it back out of there."

"Understood," Elle said.

With a nod, the hostess tapped a sequence on the keyboard in front of her. The double doors unlocked with an electronic hum.

Raucous rock music from inside the room slammed into Sam as she followed Elle into the room. Furnished in more of the Old World furniture, primarily sofas and deep chairs, the sitting room looked large enough accommodate forty people. At present, most of the twenty-three there were scantily clad young women posing their wares for prospective clients. Some of those clients, Sam was surprised to see, were women.

With calm confidence, Elle led the way.

Sam followed with more trepidation. The club was a closed arena. The walls held no windows. She knew there had to be other ways out, but she didn't know them. Elle didn't appear daunted. *Has she been here before?* Sam wondered. There was so much she didn't know about her sister.

The door to room nine was unlocked. Elle turned the knob and walked in.

Tuenis Meijer lay in the tangled scarlet silk bedclothes. Sam recognized the man from the digital images Alex and Allison had sent.

The computer expert was better groomed than he had been in most of the images. Shaggy hair shadowed his narrow, pinched face and he looked younger than his late thirties. Slightly built and maybe an inch or two taller than

Sam, he didn't look threatening. Especially while he was naked and had an expectant smile on his homely face.

The smile wilted as he surveyed his two visitors.

"You're not Fatima." Tuenis reached down to pull the sheet up to his neck.

"No," Elle agreed. She took his clothes from the folding butler and tossed them to him. "Get dressed."

"What?"

"Dress," Elle said. "Now. Or I'm going to hurt you."

With a single jerk, Elle tore the sheet from the computer expert's naked body. He yelped in embarrassment and dove for his clothes.

Sam's silence bothered Elle. At the train station, her sister had seemed glad to see her, even though the present assignment had hung over both of them. Now, Sam seemed a million miles away. It was more than a little unsettling.

From Dmitri's, Elle led the way to Achterburgwal Canal and flagged down a water taxi. The pilot didn't ask about Tuenis Meijer, who had sat between them with his hands taped behind him. In Amsterdam, Elle knew from past experience, only the ordinary seemed to attract attention after dark.

They left the water taxi only a short distance from Rusland Street where the houseboat was moored. According to Sam's information and Tuenis's very believable honesty, he lived there alone.

"What's bothering you?" Elle asked. She spoke in Russian because it wasn't a language Tuenis was reputed to know.

For a moment, Sam continued on in silence. "Tonight didn't go as I'd planned."

"You have the man you came to get."

"This should have been simple."

"It was," Elle argued. How could her sister not think to-night's activities were anything *but* simple?

"We got into a gunfight in a sex shop."

"How would you have gone about getting our guest, then?" Elle asked.

After a few steps, Sam admitted, "I don't know."

"You said time was of the essence."

Reluctantly, Sam nodded. "It is. But I know a simple retrieval op shouldn't be as high profile as this one has been." She paused. "Obviously you have your own way of working, Elle, but it's not my way. It's not what I feel was warranted in this situation."

Elle stopped and stopped Tuenis as well. She held on to the man's elbow possessively. Tuenis shrank away, as if afraid he was about to be ripped apart.

"You've never been to Amsterdam before," Elle accused. "You don't know how things are done here."

Sam said nothing.

Her sister's silence infuriated Elle. How could she stand there so calmly and make no response? "Couldn't your agency have sent someone more experienced in this area?"

"I was asked to pick up Tuenis by Alexandra Forsythe and Allison Gracelyn," Sam said.

Elle matched the names from stories she'd shared with Sam. "They're both from Athena Academy."

"Yes." Sam sipped a breath.

Trusting people was hard for Sam. Elle understood that. Though Sam had grown up in the more affluent American world, her life had been lacking in so many ways that Elle's hadn't been. Knowing that allowed Elle to be patient.

"Something came up in an investigation they were conducting," Sam said. "Several files involving blackmail schemes were all grouped together under a folder headed Spider."

A surge of excitement rattled through Elle. The SVR had its own Spider files involving blackmail and payoffs as well as political corruption.

"Allison managed to track some of the Web activity back to a domain hosted and operated by Tuenis," Sam went on. "I'm supposed to bring him in."

"Without CIA backing?" Elle shook her head. "How are you supposed to do that?"

"Allison is working on that," Sam replied. "If we hadn't basically abducted Tuenis, I was hoping to talk him into accompanying me."

"Or getting into his hard drive and Web space," Elle finished.

"There's something else, too," Sam said.

"What?" Elle wasn't happy now. She was certain her mood matched her sister's.

"One of the files that Alex and Allison pulled had to do with our parents."

A wave of uncertainty and fear filled Elle. Their parents, their lives and their deaths, remained mysteries to her though she had looked at their files. Despite her attempts at acceptance and her adoptive father's apologetic reassurances that she wouldn't ever know what had happened to them, she still longed to know. "What about our parents?"

"All the files were encrypted and coded," Sam explained. "It takes time. Allison is working on breaking the encryption and code. She thought perhaps she would have it broken by the time I got back. As soon as she knows, she'll tell me." She caught herself and rephrased her answer. "Us."

Turning, Elle gazed at the houseboat only a short distance away. "You also want access to Tuenis's records aboard the houseboat, then, right?"

"Or to acquire access to them from his machine long enough to copy them," Sam agreed.

At that moment, the iPAQ in Elle's jacket went off. She took the PDA from her jacket and consulted the flashing screen.

"It's a silent alarm," Tuenis said. "I have it tied to the boat's computer wifi. Someone has broken into the boat."

Elle made the decision. She pushed the iPAQ into Sam's hands. "Let me borrow the pistol you commandeered."

Without hesitation, Sam handed the weapon to her. "Be careful," Sam added.

But Elle was already in motion, striding toward the houseboat.

Chapter 5

Pulling Tuenis into motion, Sam walked to a position beside a forty-foot yacht moored at the side of the canal. She immediately attracted the attention of the boat's security officer, but he remained at the railing twenty feet away.

For a moment, Sam saw Elle slinking through the shadows along the canal, then her sister was gone—vanished into the darkness provided by the boats tied to cleats. Party music—industrial, techno and old-fashioned rock and roll—thundered from the nearby boats and from clubs that dotted the area. Amsterdam was proving louder by night than by day.

"Who are you people?" Tuenis asked.

"Quiet," Sam snapped. The thought of Elle encountering whoever was on the boat by herself didn't rest easy. Maybe Elle had more experience with the city, but she wasn't invincible.

"Are you guys criminals or government?" Tuenis asked.

Sam silenced the man with a sharp glance. "Another word," she promised, "and I'll tie you to an anchor and heave you into the canal."

Tuenis nodded weakly.

Sam took her cell phone from her pocket. Chipped for international use, the phone also had a GPS locator. The global positioning satellite system accessed at least twelve of the twenty-four satellites in fixed orbit around Earth at any time.

She punched in Riley McLane's number and waited.

Riley answered on the second ring. "Miss me?" he asked, and she could hear the mocking grin in his voice.

"Yes."

"Look, I've been thinking," Riley said, "I shouldn't have gotten angry the way I did. I know that—"

"I need help," Sam interrupted.

Riley paused.

"At least, I may need help."

"What do you need me to do?" he asked.

That was one of the things Sam loved about Riley. He was more talkative and chatty than she was, and more willing to reveal his feelings—maybe even more certain about how he felt—but he knew when to listen.

"Can you access a satellite view of my position?"

"Yes. Give me a minute."

Tensely, Sam waited in the shadows.

Elle crept close to *Satyr Dreams*, then put a hand on the houseboat. As a water taxi sped by, she ducked to avoid the splash of light that ran along the vessel's gunwales.

Getting the rhythm of the houseboat, she leaned her body weight on the side and pulled herself over as it rocked on the wave. Lithely, she rolled to her feet and flattened beside the stern door. A quick glance at the security system told her it had been bypassed.

Holding the H&K .45 in her left hand, Elle eased the safety off and put her hand on the door to test it.

It was unlocked.

Readying herself, Elle raised the gun and swung into position just inside the door.

The soft blue-white glow of a computer monitor filled the bedroom. Data streamed across the screen.

And the illumination fell across the dead man lying in the middle of the floor. She knew exactly what the black dot in the center of the man's forehead was.

Silently, a shadow separated itself from the darkness. Only motion gave her attacker away. She pulled the gun up and fired. The pistol kicked back against her palm as the weapon's silenced "cough" wheezed into the houseboat cabin.

Inside the room, a man cursed in surprise.

CIA Headquarters, Langley, Virginia

Standing in the ops mission control room, Riley McLane stared at the images on the wall screens. He was a little over six feet tall and dressed in a brown turtleneck and tan slacks. Although he was currently riding a desk job, he wore his pistol in shoulder leather. His wavy black hair hung just above his eyebrows. His cheeks were smooth, freshly shaven.

Amsterdam. What the hell are you doing in Amsterdam, Sam? The question chafed at him.

The mission control room was quiet except for the hum of the computers and electronic equipment. Occasionally whispered conversations over the headset reached his ears.

"C'mon, Tolliver," Riley coaxed. "This connect isn't going to take all night, is it?"

"No." Tolliver was young and intense. He kept his hair trimmed to baby-chick down that was golden yellow. Round-lensed glasses reflected the wallscreen. His fingers flew knowingly across the keyboard, then he hit a final sequence and leaned back. "We're in."

The view on the center four screens changed, opening up on a night view of a canal in a busy metropolitan area. Sam's phone GPS showed up as a pulsing orange dot.

"Can you get closer to Special Agent St. John?" Riley struggled to keep the tension out of his voice.

"I'm on it." Tolliver worked the keyboard again and brought up a closer image. "You are going to get permission for the use of this spy satellite, aren't you, Special Agent McLane?"

"You bet." Riley would, of course. But it wouldn't be permission he was seeking. Rather, it would be forgiveness. In the spy trade, he'd learned that it was often more productive to everyone involved to ask for forgiveness rather than permission. Permission usually never came, and forgiveness was generally around the corner and most of the time no later than the next presidential election.

Sam stood in the shadows of a tree along the canal. Riley could tell from his lover's posture that she was worried. He wished he could put his hand on the wallscreen and touch her.

"Start capturing images, Tolliver," Riley said. Although he was more inclined to fieldwork, Riley was also being groomed as a handler. He didn't want to come in from the violent world that he loved, and felt that he could do the most good in the trenches, but he knew that sooner or later he would be forced to do it.

Tonight, however, he was thankful he was in a position

to help Sam. He clicked over to Sam's phone connection. "I'm here."

Tolliver worked quickly, downloading image after image and saving it off to a file.

"I'm here with Elle," Sam said. "She's in a houseboat about two hundred feet southeast of my position. Farther along the canal."

Covering the mouthpiece with a hand, Riley said, "Back out. There's a houseboat on the canal. A second agent is aboard."

"What agent?" Tolliver clicked the keys and the view backed out. The houseboat came into focus.

"It's a need-to-know, Tolliver. Just acquire the images."

"Yes, sir."

Riley didn't want to have to explain how Sam happened to be in Amsterdam with her twin sister, who happened to be an excellent Russian spy. He had no clue himself.

"What am I looking for, Sam?" Riley asked.

"Someone broke into the houseboat," Sam answered. "Elle went to find out who."

"Is the person or persons still there?"

"I don't know."

Riley heard the irritation and frustration in Sam's voice. As carefully guarded as she was with her emotions, he doubted many people would have noticed. "What are you working?"

"Private business."

"For the school?" Riley knew from recent experience that Athena Academy graduates had a tendency to operate quietly in the background to deal with their own issues.

"There's no time to talk about it now."

Shelving his irritation, Riley studied the screen, finding Elle standing beside the houseboat's stern door just as the woman moved out of the shadows. An instant later, a quick illumination flared into being, then just as quickly disappeared.

"That was a gunshot," Tolliver said.

"I know." Tension swirled inside Riley. He knew the flash indicated a weapon had been fired. He'd spent years out in the field. "Does Elle have a weapon, Sam?"

Joachim didn't get a good look at the woman as she came through the door. He'd gone after her immediately, hoping to catch her by surprise. Instead, she'd caught him almost flat-footed by firing so quickly. There had been no hesitation. Whoever she was, she intended to kill him.

He twisted as he saw her hands shift. The bullet grazed his chest, sliced through his shirt and pulled at his jacket as it ripped through. Another inch or two and he'd have been a dead man. He wrapped both hands around the woman's and forced the pistol from his direction.

She fired again, and the muzzle flash ripped through the cottony darkness. The bullet slapped low into the wall behind him, letting him know she was a pro because she was firing at the center of his mass rather than panicking for a head shot.

In the next handful of seconds, Joachim found out he had a hellcat on his hands. Her elbows and knees lifted, crashing into his body rapidly, going for his crotch and his face—softer tissue areas. He maintained his lock on her hands, then swept her feet from under her and fell on top of her, knocking the breath from her with his weight. He was more than a foot taller than her and had her by at least a hundred pounds. She shouldn't have given him much trouble. But she did.

He made the mistake of lifting his head to look at her

and identify her. She responded by crashing a forearm into his nose and left eye. Blinding pain screamed through his head and he lay on top of her again, somehow managing to knock the pistol away.

"Stop," he said. "I don't want to have to hurt you."

"Like you didn't hurt the guy on the floor?" She continued struggling, but—for the moment, at least—he had her arms pinned.

"I didn't kill him."

She went still. "Then let me up."

Cautiously, Joachim lifted his head and looked at her. With the blue monitor glow washing over her, he saw that she was one of the blond women he'd met earlier at Central Station. Not only that, she was the one he'd been so intrigued by. Almost instantly, he grew aware of how her body lay pressed under his. Before he knew it, his body responded and he was pressing with more than he'd intended.

He didn't know what surprised him more: that the woman was the one from Central Station, that his body could react so quickly under the circumstances...or that she arched her back and headbutted him in the face.

Bright pain ignited inside Joachim's skull. If his nose wasn't broken, he was going to be further surprised. Blood dripped into his vision from a cut over his left eye.

He cursed.

"You," she accused. Those beautiful ice-blue eyes widened in shock.

Shifting, straddling her uncomfortably now with his excitement hard against her belly, Joachim held her wrists and sat up. He looked down at her. "What are you doing here?"

"You were following us."

"How could I be following you if I got here in time to kill that man before you did?" he asked.

Another thought occurred to Joachim. "Where's your sister?"

She glared at him.

Joachim growled a curse. "Don't play games. That could get your sister killed. There are worse people out tonight than me."

Sam waited anxiously after the muzzle flash. Riley's question kept wriggling through her mind. *Does Elle have a weapon?*

Then the second muzzle flash blazed to life inside the houseboat.

"What's going on?" Tuenis asked.

For a moment, Sam considered releasing the man and going to her sister's aid. With luck, they could find Tuenis again. Then Riley spoke into her ear over the phone.

"Sam, you've got trouble." His voice was deadly calm. "Three men—no, *four* men are closing on the houseboat. You've got to get out of there."

Instinctively, Sam pulled Tuenis back into the shadows with her. She scanned the street with her peripheral vision, not trying to *see* the men, just opening her vision up to spot approach patterns.

Two of the men came into view at once. Both men were unknown to her, but both moved liked predators closing in for the kill. A moment later, she spotted the third and fourth. All of them converged on the houseboat.

"Who are they?" Sam asked.

"I thought you could tell me," Riley replied.

"No." Desperate, Sam glanced around and spotted a small seventeen-foot speedboat moored behind the yacht. The canal was the fastest way out of the area. She pushed Tuenis into motion. "Move," she ordered.

At her direction, Tuenis clambered into the speedboat. Their movement had attracted the attention of the four men, temporarily freezing them in place. By that time, Sam had cast off the lines to the mooring cleats. She jumped to the wheel and reached below, jerking out wires to hotwire the boat. It felt like years before the engine fired, and she shoved the throttle forward and cut the wheel sharply. The speedboat powered out into the canal, bumping against the yacht ahead of it and drawing a string of curses. A water taxi sped by, missing her by inches. She kept the throttle buried and headed for the houseboat.

No more muzzle flashes came from within. Sam wondered who was left alive and prayed she hadn't lost the sister she'd so recently found.

Chapter 6

With the computer glow playing across his face, Elle recognized the man from the train station. Stay centered, she told herself. You can't help Sam if you're dead.

"Your sister may be in danger," Joachim repeated.

Blood from the cut on his forehead tracked down his handsome features to his nose and chin, then dripped off. Beneath the cut his eye was already starting to swell. Elle noticed that other parts of him had swelled, too, though she doubted that had anything to do with the headbutt.

Two phones, each with a distinct ring tone, went off in Joachim's jacket. He ignored them.

"Popular tonight, aren't you?" Elle asked.

"What are you doing here?" he asked.

A third phone buzzed. This time Elle realized it was hers. She wore it at her waist.

After a brief hesitation, Joachim shifted Elle's wrists

into one massive hand and with the other reached for her phone. He flipped it open and said, "I've got your sister."

Riley Connor listened to the phone ring in his ear. He scanned the wallscreen. Tolliver had tagged the four identified predators with red triangles over their heads. Blue triangles marked Sam and the houseboat. An orange triangle stayed over the head of the unidentified man with Sam.

One of the men pulled a long, tubular device from under his jacket.

"Magnify," Riley commanded, listening to the phone ring in his ear again. Sam was on hold on another line, but he could clearly see her in the speedboat she'd liberated.

Tolliver threw a rectangle over the man and blew up the image onscreen. The details fuzzed out a little, but Riley was able to identify the tube.

"Is that a rifle?" Tolliver asked.

Fear screamed through Riley's system. He barely walled it off. "No. That's a LAW. A light, antitank weapon. A disposable rocket launcher."

The phone rang again and was picked up on the other end. Riley had called Elle's number, knowing that she would either answer or not. After the shots fired in the houseboat, it was a safe bet that her presence was known.

Instead of Elle's calm voice, so like Sam's except more worry free, a thick male voice with the hint of a German accent barked, "I've got your sister."

"This is Special Agent Riley McLane of the United States Central Intelligence Agency," Riley announced, cutting the man off. "There are four men outside the houseboat closing in on your position. One of them has just taken aim at you with a rocket launcher. I don't think they intend to take either of you alive."

* * *

Rocket launcher. The words she'd overheard burned into Elle's mind. She forced herself to relax, to focus. She'd been under fire dozens of times in urban places and military zones. She could rely on her training.

Atop her, Joachim shifted, striving to see through the covered window. Bucking her hips, Elle shoved him off and threw herself in pursuit of the pistol. Her hand closed around the gun butt. At the same time, Joachim's hand closed around her ankle. Turning and twisting, she powered through his grip—hoped that he didn't sprain her ankle or her knee—and came up in a sitting position.

She aimed the pistol at the center of his face.

Joachim froze. His lips moved in a silent curse as he grimly accepted his fate.

"I know that was Riley McLane," she said. "If he told you there's someone out there with a rocket launcher, there is."

Joachim nodded. "What do you propose?"

"That we get the hell out of here."

Taking his hand from her ankle, Joachim pushed himself to his feet. He drew the curtain aside just a fraction and peered out.

Immediately a hail of bullets crashed through the window and the houseboat's wall. Glass, wood and insulation sailed into the air. The bullets continued on to the other wall, tearing through again. At least two or three smashed into the computer monitor.

Elle jumped to her feet and into a run. She moved smoothly in the zone she had created for herself.

Joachim followed her.

Anticipating that the gunners might assume their prey was coming out the stern door, Elle aimed for the forward door.

She ran through the galley, shoved her way through the cluttered mess of the bedroom and had her hand on the doorknob as another volley of shots tore through the wall behind her.

She tried the door. "Locked," she told Joachim.

"Stand aside." He ran at the door and hit it with his shoulder.

Propelled by Joachim's size and strength, the door ripped from its hinges and slapped onto the houseboat deck. Elle stumbled out, caught by surprise for just an instant. Joachim steadied her with a hand under one elbow, then dragged her toward the prow.

"Jump!" he roared.

Reaching the side, Elle shoved her hands forward while maintaining the death grip on the H&K .45 and leaped over the side. A fiery comet's tail from the LAW rocket reflected on the canal surface just before she hit.

In disbelief and horror, Sam watched debris from the houseboat sail up into the night then come raining back down.

The phone clicked in her ear. "Sam."

"Riley," Sam choked out, powering down the boat.

"She made it," Riley said. "She jumped from the bow of the houseboat before the rocket hit. I've got her onscreen. She's safe. So is the guy with her."

"What guy?" Sam peered ahead, but although the flames from the burning houseboat illuminated the nearby area, the light seemed to make the darkness beyond their reach even darker.

"Look out," Riley called. "Portside."

Glancing to her left, Sam saw another powerful speedboat coming at her from the other end of the canal, facing her. A man with an assault rifle stood to the boat pilot's left.

Ducking down, Sam slammed the throttle forward

again. The propeller ripped into the canal water and the speedboat shivered like a wet dog as it leaped into motion and hydroplaned up to the surface.

The man with the assault rifle fired immediately. Some of the rounds took off a corner of the Plexiglas window and others trip-hammered the length of the speedboat. Pieces of coaming leaped into the air.

Staying low, Sam aimed the speedboat at the other vessel. She couldn't veer away. If she did, she'd leave herself at the mercy of the gunman.

Instead, the man piloting the other craft pulled out of her way. Sam steered after him. Her speedboat juked and quivered, then slammed against the other boat. Shudders passed through the other speedboat as it rode higher out of the water. For a moment Sam thought it might even flip. Then the enemy speedboat dropped back down into the water.

The gunman tumbled from the boat into the canal.

She followed Achterburgwal south, listening to Tuenis bleat in terror behind her. When she looked back over her shoulder, she saw that the other boat had reversed engines and was coming back around.

Bullets cored through the canal behind Elle. She paused and frog-kicked, holding her position beneath the water's surface. She kept her calm with some effort.

With the houseboat burning nearby, the flames ripped away some of the shadows. Gray-green streamers ignited by the light followed the bullets' trajectories.

An iron grip closed on her ankle and tugged.

Panicked for just a moment, Elle kicked out at the hand that held her. The water slowed the kick, but she still hit Joachim in the head.

He released her ankle and held his open hands up in surrender. *No*, he mouthed and shook his head. Air bubbles
escaped his mouth and nose. He motioned to her to follow
and took off swimming toward the darkness. She swam
after him.

A moment later, when she knew she could no longer
hold her breath, Elle surfaced. She'd lost Joachim in the
shadows. She floated faceup, not surfacing any more than
she had to and using only one hand.

A big hand came out of the darkness and cupped her
chin. She tensed, getting ready to fight.

"Easy," Joachim whispered in her ear. "I'm not going
to hurt you."

He cradled her against his body. She felt the heat of him,
hotter even than the flames from the burning houseboat.
Muscles in his forearm corded around her neck and she felt
the thick heaviness of his powerful chest moving easily as
he breathed. His heart thudded against her back.

He released her, and as he slipped away his heat drifted
off in the chill of the water.

A sudden burst of fire from what Elle knew to be a Kalashnikov assault rifle sounded out in the canal.

Following the familiar yammering noise to its source,
Elle spotted two boats idling out in the middle of the canal,
looking as if they'd collided. Just before one craft took off,
Elle recognized Sam at the wheel. Bits and pieces of the
speedboat she piloted plopped into the canal as sparks spat
from metalwork.

At first Elle thought Sam was going to make good on
her escape. A moment later, the other boat came around.
The pilot idled for just a second to allow a man in the water
to clamber aboard. Then he powered up again and shot
across the water in Sam's wake.

"She's not going to make it," Joachim said. "That boat's too fast."

Elle's mind raced. Panic threatened to disrupt her control. *Help Sam.* Rusland Street wasn't far away. Once she made it there, she could cut across to Kloveniersburg-wal Canal and attempt to ambush the boat following Sam. But she needed a rifle rather than the handgun she had now.

Hurried footsteps rushed to the canal's edge above her.

One of the hunters appeared through the darkness and leaned over the canal's edge. His head and shoulders hunched together, forming a tight frame around the assault rifle he held. The man saw Elle and sighted the rifle at her.

Before the man could fire, Elle shot for his face. He pirouetted around and dropped bonelessly to the ground.

Elle swam to the nearest landing and climbed up to the street. She stopped at the man's body, took the AK-47 and ran her hands along his pockets to turn up two fresh magazines for the assault rifle.

Police sirens cut through the night air.

Elle couldn't tell if the sound came from within the city or out on the canal. Police would be coming from both directions.

Another man, this one dressed in a long coat, came at her from the houseboat wreckage. The twisting flames illuminated his features. He carried a pump-action shotgun that he lowered into position.

Cradling the AK-47, Elle swung around and feathered the trigger, unleashing a deafening three-round burst. The bullets stitched the man from hip to shoulder, staggering him. His shotgun blast struck the pavement and ricocheted in all directions. Some of them must have struck his own feet because he flopped to the ground.

Joachim freed two pistols from the first man's shoulder

holsters. For a moment, Elle held him in her sights. He looked at her, his dark eyes unworried and calm. Pocketing the pistols, he searched the dead man for extra magazines.

"If you're going to shoot, you'd better hurry," he said calmly. He thrust the magazines into his pockets, then took the pistols back out.

Which mistake are you going to make? Elle asked herself. *Shoot him and discover he's innocent? Or let him live so he can shoot you in the back?*

Chapter 7

Turning from Joachim, Elle sprinted toward Rusland Street. She cradled the assault rifle in close against her body to minimize its visibility and to better balance the weight.

Joachim ran after her.

When the flip-phone rang in her pocket, Elle took it out and answered, thankful that the technology and hardware were so durable. "Riley?"

"Yes."

"Call Sam. Tell her to go north on Kloveniersburgwal."

"Where's that?"

"The canal east of my position. Have Sam take the two next left turns. That will put her north on Kloveniersburgwal. I'm going to try to get over there to intercept her pursuers."

"Affirmative," Riley said.

Elle closed the phone, put it away and saved her breath for running. Her wet shoes pounded the pavement.

Revelers and late-night tourists gave her ground immediately once they saw the assault rifle.

Joachim ran beside her. Like a wolf, he loped, making
the effort he expended look too easy.

As she closed on the canal, Elle glanced to the right.
Several boats moved along the turgid water. Two slalomed
dangerously at the edge of control—Sam's boat and the
pursuit vessel. In just the short amount of time that had
passed, the pursuit boat had almost managed to catch up.

Elle reached the midpoint of the bridge over Kloveniersburgwal. She knelt at the low wall, resting on her left
knee. Automatically, she flipped the Kalashnikov's tripod
down, pulled the stock into her left shoulder and kept both
eyes open as she sighted on the pursuit boat. From her
vantage point, she had a clear view of the canal.

The pursuit boat tried to pull alongside Sam's port.
Steering into the other craft, Sam shouldered the boat aside
and pulled hard to starboard. They split to go around a large
pleasure boat hosting a wedding reception.

A chunk of stone broke from the bridge near the Kalashnikov's barrel. Stone splinters struck Elle's unprotected
right cheek and made her eye water.

Joachim cursed and returned fire with his pistols.

Elle didn't take her attention from the pursuit boat as it
sped around the pleasure boat. The wedding guests milled
around in confusion. She set her finger over the trigger, targeting the gunman's head and shoulders. The distance was
almost three hundred meters. And the target was moving.

"I've got your back," Joachim said.

Elle felt the heat of him up against her, providing a
living shield over her body. That was more distracting than
being shot at.

"Take the shot," Joachim told her.

Using the open sights, knowing that even if she'd had a sniper scope she wouldn't have been able to use it on the careening boat, Elle let out half a breath. Then she fired the rifle on single-shot mode, steadily squeezing off each round.

The third round jerked the gunman around as the boat closed on Sam's vessel again. The fourth or fifth bullet knocked the gunner down and left him sprawled. Grimly, Elle turned her attention to the pursuit boat's pilot. She fired faster now.

Ultimately, she didn't know if she hit the man or not, but the boat suddenly pulled hard to starboard. Out of control, the craft slammed into a moored yacht, lifted out of the water, and flipped onto dry land. The hull shattered against a group of trees. If the boat pilot survived the wreck, he wouldn't be going anywhere soon.

More bullets struck the bridge where Elle was. Throwing herself from her sniper spot, she went prone on the ground. Lifting the Kalashnikov, she took aim at one of the gunmen, suddenly visible as a crowd of frightened pedestrians split around him. Before she could squeeze the trigger, Joachim opened fire and put the man down.

Scanning the street and the nearby buildings, Elle spotted another downed gunman. That accounted for the four they had spotted during the original attack. If there weren't any backup teams on-site, they were in the clear.

Police sirens screamed.

Elle got to her feet, panting, her mind still running at warp speed. She turned her attention to Joachim. "Who were those men?"

Joachim hesitated.

Elle shifted the assault rifle in her arms. "I intend to have an answer."

A confident smile twisted Joachim's handsome lips.

The effort lost some of its bravado as blood seeped from the cut over his eyebrow.

"All right." Joachim pocketed the pistols and took his empty hands out. He stepped closer to her, taking away the distance.

Stubbornly, Elle stood her ground and looked up at him.

"They belonged to a man named Arnaud Beck."

Elle knew about Arnaud Beck. The man was muscle-for-hire and had an international reputation. "What did Beck want with you?"

Joachim shook his head. "Not me. You or your sister." He paused. "From the way you both move and shoot, I don't get the impression that you're simply tourists here."

Elle didn't reply.

"I followed them to the train station and noticed they were watching your sister," Joachim said. "Since you didn't spot them tracing you from the train station, I assume they didn't trail you long."

"They knew where we'd end up," Elle said, figuring it out.

Joachim nodded. "You have to ask yourself how they knew that."

Elle didn't respond, but she knew it was true. Sam's Athena Academy friends had sent her on this mission. They were the ones with the leak. Even Riley hadn't known where Sam was going, so the leak couldn't be blamed on the CIA.

The police sirens sounded louder and nearer. A group of spectators filled both ends of the bridge.

"How do you fit in to this?" Elle demanded.

Still holding his hands at his side, Joachim took another step into her space. He cupped her chin in his hand and offered that mocking smile again.

"I fit in anywhere I want to," he told her. Then he kissed her.

Elle knew she should have shoved him back with the Kalashnikov. Or maybe even knocked him down or out with a swipe of the rifle butt. But she didn't. She kissed him back, feeling the crazy chemistry bouncing around inside her head—and other places.

Before she was aware of it, her hand curled in his black T-shirt, pulling him even harder against her. His mouth opened and he kissed her more deeply. His hand slid from her chin to the back of her head, holding her tightly.

Then he broke the embrace, the kiss and the magic of the moment.

"I don't know who you are," he growled in German, "but you're good."

Good? What the hell does he mean by that? Elle stared at him.

His eyes, even the partially closed one, took on a hard glint. "Are you waiting for your friends from the CIA to close in?" He glanced around.

"I don't have any friends at the CIA," Elle said, growing a little annoyed with his behavior.

"What about Riley McLane?"

Oh. That friend. "He's not a friend," Elle said. "He's my—" She stopped herself. *"Sister's boyfriend" is definitely not the answer to go with here.*

"Too bad," Joachim said. "Getting to know you might have been interesting." Without another word, he turned, placed one hand on the edge of the bridge and vaulted over the side.

For a moment, Elle felt certain he'd lost his mind. She rushed forward just in time to see Joachim land on top of a yacht passing under the bridge. He stood, glaring back at her, the long, wet coat whipping around his legs.

By the time it occurred to her that she could jump as well, the yacht was out of reach.

Elle's cell phone rang. She answered it.

"The police are converging on your position," Riley said. "Unless you want to answer a lot of questions, you'd better get out of there."

"Where's Sam?"

"I've made arrangements for a safe house over on Recht Boomssloot."

"Near the Armenian church," Elle said, feeling irritated with herself as she watched the night mask Joachim from her sight. "I know the place."

"You know about the safe house?"

"Yes." Elle tossed the Kalashnikov into the canal and followed it with the pistol Sam had taken at the sex shop. "But don't worry, Riley. The CIA has maintained a few of its secrets."

A police boat appeared from the north. The lights flashed over the canal and other boaters hove to, clearing the way.

Elle closed the phone, cutting off whatever response Riley might have made, and ran east. She wanted to see Sam. Her sister had a lot of questions to answer.

Suwan, Berzhaan

Vasilios Quinn stared at the television footage coming out of Amsterdam. Rage filled him, but it was the panic he felt at the situation that he struggled to control. Rage was an old friend. Helplessness was something he'd never gotten used to and seldom experienced.

On the television, the Dutch-speaking woman reporter stood in front of a blazing pyre that had once been Tuenis Meijer's houseboat. Fireboats worked in the background, hosing the flames with water cannons.

"What happened?" Quinn demanded.

Arnaud Beck answered from the speakerphone. "I was wrong about the woman."

Quinn struggled to remember the woman's name. "St. John? The CIA agent?" The phone connection was encrypted and scrambled.

"Yes. She had help I wasn't expecting."

"Who?" Quinn sat in front of his computer.

"A man named Joachim Reiter."

"German?"

"Yes. He's one of Günter Stahlmann's top lieutenants."

Quinn knew Stahlmann. *Had known*, he reminded himself. But that had been in the other life. The one that he struggled to keep buried.

"How is Stahlmann involved in this?" Quinn asked.

"I don't know."

Quinn sat back in his chair and thought about it. "Perhaps Stahlmann has business with Tuenis Meijer as well."

"Perhaps."

"Did you kill Meijer?"

Beck was quiet for a moment. "Unfortunately, no. Both the women and Joachim Reiter escaped."

"What of Tuenis Meijer?"

"Gone as well."

Quinn pushed up from the chair. If they'd had the chance to talk to the computer hacker, if they'd backed up his files, they couldn't live. "Find them, Beck. Wherever they go, whatever they do, find them and kill them."

Amsterdam, The Netherlands

Elle seethed inside. "You're not listening to me, Sam." She spoke in Russian. Over the past year they had discovered they seemed to communicate better in that language. Elle felt certain it was because they had heard that language as babies and perhaps somehow communicated with each other before they were separated.

However, communication wasn't easy now.

"I am listening." Sam's tone was flat, neutral. She stood on the other side of the living room area in the CIA safe house near Amsterdam's waterfront.

Losing patience, Elle paced. "Your friends have a leak in their intelligence network."

"If my friends had a leak," Sam insisted calmly, "they would know it."

"Okay." Elle sighed. "Okay. Let's agree—for now—that they would know. That doesn't mean they would tell you."

"If not knowing meant my life," Sam stated, "they would have told me."

"If you believe that, you're a fool. They *do* have a leak. They *didn't* tell you."

"Those men could have been following Joachim," Sam said. "Not me."

"He said no."

Sam arched an eyebrow. "And you believe him?"

The question, asked so baldly, put Elle on notice. Did she trust the man? She remembered how he had guarded her back on the bridge as Arnaud Beck's men had closed on them. She also thought about the fact that he hadn't killed her when he could have. Twice.

"I do," Elle said.

"I've known my friends a lot longer than a five-minute conversation in a crowded train station," Sam countered.

Ah, so you do have claws, sister, Elle thought.

Located in the basement of the safe house, the room

they were in was small, but Elle felt as if an impassable void existed between Sam and her. The closeness that had been so natural over the past year and a half now seemed to hang by a fragile thread. The living room furniture in the center of the room didn't match the cutting-edge computer equipment that lined one whole wall.

The basement doubled as a sound studio that specialized in special effects noises for video games. The man who lived in the safe house, and was currently upstairs, drew checks in that capacity from several computer gaming companies. Of course, the soundproof room on the other side of the thick glass window doubled as a holding cell. Tuenis Meijer sat inside the room on a stool under the boom microphone. He didn't look happy.

"We need to make a plan," Elle said.

"I have one," Sam replied.

"You're going back to Athena Academy?"

"Riley will help with transportation out of this country and to the United States," Sam said. "He's working on it now. We'll be safe with him. And if you choose not to go, I'll be safe with him."

Finally acknowledging that she wasn't going to get anywhere with her sister, nor be able to actually argue the point, Elle nodded. "Okay. Fine. We'll do it your way."

"You don't have to go," Sam said.

That only made Elle angrier. "Do you really think I'd leave you right now? When you don't even know what we're facing?"

"I don't know."

Elle wanted to explode. That was the course of action she would have taken with one of her sisters in the Petrenko family. They were always up for a fight, and it used to drive her father insane.

"You know what," Elle said coldly, "I think I need a breath of air." Without another word, she left. As emotional as she was, there was only one person she wanted to talk to.

Chapter 8

Leaning into the pay phone down near the dockyard a few blocks from the safe house, Elle used a prepaid phone card to dial the number.

Night had come to neon life in the second tier of the city behind the dockyards. The warehouses and shipping companies were mostly closed for the evening, but taverns, adult shows and restaurants competed for the wages of the cargo handlers and sailors.

The phone was answered on the second ring.

"Hello?" Colonel Fyodor Petrenko's voice was thick with sleep. He had always gone to bed early and started his mornings before the dawn with a cup of black coffee and rolls that Mother made fresh from the oven. But Mother had died five years ago and there were no more homemade rolls in the mornings, except when Elle or one of her sisters was home. Those times weren't often these days.

"Father," Elle said.

"Elle?" Concern echoed in his voice. Springs creaked and she knew he was checking the time on the old clock by the bed. "Are you all right?"

"I'm fine, Father," she replied.

"It is late," he observed.

Elle almost laughed at the habitual remonstration that stained his voice, and the feeling felt as good as she'd known it would. His words carried both a query and a mild rebuke. It was almost like being a teen again, getting home after curfew.

"I know it's late," she replied, "but I wanted to hear your voice."

"You could have heard my voice in the morning. At a more reasonable hour."

"I wanted to hear it now."

Her father was silent for a moment. "Something is wrong."

Elle's first impulse was to lie, but she didn't. "Yes. Something is wrong. It's complicated."

"I see." He paused for a moment. A hiss and a soft crackling sound reached her ears and she knew he'd lit his pipe. That was another thing that had changed with her mother's absence. As long as her mother had been alive, her father hadn't been permitted to smoke in the bedroom. "I thought you were supposed to be with your sister."

"I was. I am. Sort of." Elle turned and scanned the surrounding street.

Drunken sailors weaved down the block. Prostitutes working the corners tried to solicit business. Shills for the peep shows called out for attention.

"That is rather an oblique answer. Perhaps you could share a few details."

Quietly, quickly, Elle relayed the evening's events.

"You say this is not a CIA mission?"

"No. Agent McLane seemed as surprised to learn that Sam was here as I was when she first told me."

"Then whom is Sam working for?"

"Her friends at the Athena Academy."

"What interest would they have in Tuenis Meijer?"

Elle hesitated then. The problem with spreading a confidence was that once spread, it was gone from her control. Spycraft was all about controlling assets as well as damage. Both of those things came from information.

"There has been some kind of incident at Athena Academy," she said. "Evidently there was more to Senator Marion Gracelyn's murder than clashing political beliefs. While searching for her mother's killer, Allison Gracelyn uncovered a computer file concerning an individual known as Spider."

Her father remained quiet. He'd learned from the SVR and his wife when it was proper to ask questions.

Elle went on. "I don't know yet, but I suspect that the Spider file they uncovered might be connected to the file the SVR has on Madame Web."

"Did you mention this to your sister?"

"Of course not. Madame Web is a problem for the SVR."

"Madame Web is a ghost," her father said. "Her existence has never been proven."

Elle knew that. According to some, Madame Web was a figment of an overactive and paranoid imagination in the intelligence community. Supposedly, Madame Web had the ability to crack into any Web site, no matter how secure, and ferret out whatever information she wanted. In the past, a few Russian politicians and businessmen had claimed to be blackmailed by her.

"But many suspect that she does exist," Elle said.

"How does Madame Web connect to Tuenis Meijer?"

"I don't know," Elle answered. "But someone was concerned enough about it to attempt to kill Sam."

"So why did you call me?"

Elle thought about that for a moment. "I'm angry with Sam. She—she *frustrates* me."

"Because she won't take your advice?"

Elle grew a little irritated with her father then. "Yes."

"She's proposing taking Tuenis Meijer back to her friends at Athena Academy?"

"Yes. For all she knows, her friends leaked information and nearly got her killed tonight."

"And for all you know, they didn't."

Elle supposed it was possible. But she did so with reluctance.

"You have to remember that your sister is not you, Elle," her father said gently. "She wasn't raised as you were. From everything you said, she wasn't given a home when she was little. Family…is new to her."

"She froze me out." Elle remembered the vacant stare Sam had given her. "Like I wasn't even there."

"Do you know how many times I sat in my office or at the dinner table and listened to you fight with your sisters?"

"What does that have to do with anything?"

"You learned to fight with your sisters, Elle. You learned to fight with your brothers. Mostly, it was over inconsequential things. Territorial rights to the bathroom. Borrowed clothes. Hurtful comments uttered in the heat of the moment. And boys." Her father chuckled. "I seem to recall many fights over boys."

"She's my sister. We should be able to talk."

"Yes. You should. Who walked out of the conversation?"

Elle thought about that. She hated it when her father was right. "She wasn't listening."

"And the best way to get someone to listen is to stop talking," her father said. "Your mother taught me that."

Elle remembered all the years spent in the Petrenko household. She had always been one of Fyodor Petrenko's children. She'd shared the table, the chores and a bedroom, until she was grown and off to university. Then, when she came home on weekends, the usual pecking order resumed.

"She chooses to believe her friends over my choice of caution," Elle said.

"Yes. From what you say, they are the only family she's ever truly known."

For a moment Elle's heart went out to Sam. In her own home, she'd had two older and three younger sisters. She'd dressed the younger ones, combed out their hair and washed their faces when they were little. As they'd gotten older, Elle had given them advice on what to wear, what boys were like and how to conduct themselves around others. Her older sisters had done that for her.

No one did that for Sam.

"I've made a mistake," Elle said quietly. Sadness chewed at her.

"A small one," her father agreed. "Nothing that can't be fixed."

"I'll keep that in mind when I talk to Sam." Elle took a deep breath. She felt better. She'd known she would after talking with him.

"Good. Now you should go and smooth things over between your sister and you."

She smiled and some of the night's chill seemed to dissipate. She told him he was right, of course, then thanked him for his time and hung up after promising to call every time she was able.

Feeling a little better, Elle went in search of chocolate.

It was one of the things she always used to break the tension with one of her sisters. But she went with her hand on a pistol inside her jacket and carefully watched the shadows. Whatever had started tonight, she was sure, was far from over.

Sam was sitting quietly in the dark in a chair against the wall in the basement when Elle returned. Sam had changed into jeans, a green knit long-sleeved shirt, tennis shoes and an empty shoulder holster, all supplied by the safehouse. The SIG-Sauer .40-caliber was in her right hand.

Elle stopped at the foot of the stairs, prepared to duck for cover around the basement wall if Sam shot first and thought after. Under the circumstances, it was possible. *Maybe I wouldn't even blame her.*

"Sam? Are you awake?" Elle asked.

"Yes." Her voice was soft and wary.

"Mind if I turn on a light?"

"Whatever."

Elle didn't let the passive-aggressive stance Sam had adopted bother her. She hadn't returned to the safe house to fight. She wanted to be with her sister. And there was the matter of Madame Web.

She turned on the light. "I took a walk."

Sam didn't respond.

"Cleared my head. Called my father."

"Oh?" A note of suspicion sounded in Sam's voice. She knew that Fyodor Petrenko was an SVR agent, too.

"He said that you were right and I was being bullheaded. I think he enjoys that. I've heard it often enough from him." Elle sat at the table and opened a bag, revealing a half gallon of ice cream. "He reminded me that I am not the only one in the espionage game, that you have your system and your backups in place as well."

"I do."

Elle pried the lid off the ice cream. The scent of chocolate and almonds seeped into the room. "You're still mad at me."

Sam hesitated only for an instant. "Yes. I don't like being told what to do."

"I know. I should have realized that. I didn't, and I'm sorry." Elle looked at her sister. "Getting to know each other, even if we weren't in the line of work we're in, would be hard, Sam. Something like tonight—" she shrugged "—can make getting to know each other almost impossible. The good thing is that we're both still alive. We've lived to be mad at each other at some other time. But I'm through being bullheaded and angry tonight. This is your mission, your decision. However you want to do this, I'm there for you."

Sam said, "All right," but she didn't sound convinced.

"Now, this is chocolate-almond ice cream," Elle said, adopting a lighter tone. "One of my personal favorites. I've already carried it for a while, so it's melting. We can continue being mad at each other until it completely melts." She produced a pair of spoons with a magician's flourish. "Or we can eat. Which do you prefer?"

"That's one of my favorites, too." Sam slipped the pistol into her shoulder holster and brought her chair over to the table. "I could go upstairs and look for bowls. I'm sure there are some."

"No," Elle said. "We eat it straight out of the carton. It has fewer calories that way."

Sam smiled a little at that. "Are you sure that's true?"

"Cross my heart. My mother told me that."

For a second, sadness tracked Sam's face, but then it was gone and she was smiling again. "Then let's eat."

Chapter 9

Phoenix Sky Harbor International Airport
Phoenix, Arizona

Lean, hard and deadly looking around the eyes to anyone trained to see such things, Riley McLane was the kind of man who left an impression when he didn't take pains to fade into the background. There was something predatory that lingered around him, a wolfish quality that made an impact even on Elle.

Today he wore jeans and cowboy boots, a loose Western shirt unbuttoned over a white T-shirt and wraparound sunglasses. With his tan, most people would take him for a local. Elle had seen him look just as at home at a political function.

He waited for them on the other side of the security area. So far, he hadn't noticed them.

Sam quietly took Elle's hand and held her back. "Wait," Sam said.

Curious, Elle asked, "For what? Everything looks safe enough." She'd been concerned on the way back. Even with the straight flight to Phoenix out of England on British Airways, there was a chance one of their adversaries had caught up with them. But they seemed to be safe now.

A blush tinted Sam's cheeks beneath her sunglasses. "Just to…to watch him. I like to watch him when he doesn't know I'm there."

Elle smiled and shook her head. "And you always come across so serious. I swear, Sam, you do surprise me."

But a pang of envy touched Elle, too. Despite all her amorous adventures, she'd never met anyone who turned her head quite like Riley did Sam's. Although she had had several entirely too intimate curiosities about Joachim on the long flights out of Amsterdam. She almost blushed herself, remembering how his hard body had felt against hers.

"Why do I surprise you?" Sam asked, grinning. "Riley brings something out of me that I've never before experienced."

"Then you're lucky."

Sam shook her head and the grin diminished somewhat. "Maybe. But it's scary, too."

"Why?"

"What if…one day it just goes away?"

Looking at her sister, Elle saw the real fear in her then. She dropped an arm around Sam's shoulders. "That's not going to happen. Riley is crazy in love with you."

"I hope so."

He saw them then. Elle knew it from the way Riley's stance changed. He became eager and wary at the same time. The airport was a big area to try to cover.

Sam let go of Elle then and hurried over to Riley. They kissed briefly, but with enough passion to draw stares, a few shaking heads and a few chuckles from passersby, who were surprised, dismayed or reminded of their own feelings.

"Come with me now," Riley said as Elle joined them. "I've got a couple men in baggage claim to get your luggage. They can bring it out to Athena Academy for you."

"What about Tuenis Meijer?" Sam asked.

At Riley's insistence, the computer expert had flown in on a separate flight. So far the CIA had seemed more enamored of having Meijer in custody than with reprimanding Sam. Thank goodness.

"He'll be here this afternoon." Riley led the way through the airport. Sam stayed at his side and they moved so in step it seemed as if they'd been practicing for years.

Elle remembered Joachim as she watched her sister and prospective brother-in-law. Aboard the houseboat with the rocket streaking toward them, they'd moved together, too. Even in the water and on the bridge they had shared... something. She turned her thoughts away from that. Thinking about Joachim was an easy distraction.

Hopefully she wouldn't see him again. If she did, and he was on the wrong side, she might have to kill him. That was an uncomfortable possibility.

"Director Stone agreed to let Alex Forsythe interview Meijer," Riley was saying as he hustled them out into the sweltering heat of the hot June summer. "Sloan is allowing it as a courtesy. Allison Gracelyn is pulling strings—and she's also protecting you two. Personally, I think Alex will find she's beating a dead horse. Those old files they found are worthless."

"Marion Gracelyn might have been killed because of those files," Sam said.

Riley shook his head. "It doesn't scan. Those files are nine years old, Sam. Some of them are older than that."

"Maybe," Sam agreed. "But Allison Gracelyn was able to track some of the communications back to Tuenis Meijer."

"I still don't understand that," Riley said.

"She explained it to me," Sam said. "It has something to do with the coding of the utilities that Meijer was using then. Computer coders leave the equivalent of fingerprints behind when they write programs and utilities. The ones scripted into the e-mail exchanges and firewalls were definitely Meijer's work. When she checked through his prison records and CIA files, Allison correlated the connection."

Riley opened the passenger's door of a sleek black Suburban parked at the curb. Two CIA agents held the vehicle under observation and disappeared at Riley's nod.

"Geek police," Riley growled, referring to the computer experts.

"Without them, we'd never be able to do our jobs," Sam said.

Elle silently agreed as Riley let her into the second seat back.

"I know," Riley admitted with a sigh. "It's just that I'd feel better knowing how they do what they do instead of just taking them on faith sometimes."

"Allison is money in the bank," Sam said. "When it comes to computers, she's one of the best."

"That's why she works for the National Security Agency." Riley went around the car and climbed in behind the steering wheel. "At any rate, Alex—and you—get Meijer for a couple days. Then the CIA gets him for a host of charges regarding threats to American security."

Elle sat in the backseat and gazed out at the White Tank Mountains. During her talks with her sister, Sam had told

her a lot about the Athena Academy for the Advancement
of Women. She was looking forward to seeing the school,
but she really doubted that Tuenis Meijer would offer much
information. Still, it would be an interesting visit.

Dream Motors
Leipzig, Germany

Metal sanders screamed as Joachim walked through the
large garage. Cutting torches sliced through metal bodies
and created geysers of sparks that danced against the
concrete floor.

Two days had passed since the encounter in Amsterdam.
The swelling in his nose had gone down, but he'd taken six
stitches above his left eye and it was still black. He wore
black clothing—his work clothes. Black slacks, black
jacket cut to conceal his double shoulder holster rig, a
black turtleneck and good shoes.

He always wore good shoes when he went to see Günter
Stahlmann after a problem had occurred. When things started
to go wrong, one of the first things Günter did when he called
a guy on the carpet was to point out that he—meaning
Günter—put shoes on that man's feet. If they weren't good
shoes, things went worse for the guy he was talking to.

Nearly two dozen men worked at different bays in the
garage. All of them were doing restoration work on
vehicles. Some of the vehicles were American, Japanese
and British, but most of them were German. All of them
were sports cars or luxury cars.

Dream Motors was one of Günter's latest "legitimate"
business ventures. The garage did mostly legal work restor-
ing cars, but some nights cars stolen from Berlin or Munich
rolled through and became different cars with different

sets of papers before morning. They were shipped to other lots in eastern Europe and sold for a considerable profit that was never reported either.

Günter stood by a sleek, dark blue automobile. The car's lines made Günter's wide body seem even wider. At six feet tall, he was four inches shorter than Joachim, but Günter was broader and built like a truck, wide and low to the ground, a monster once he got started full tilt. His hair was dark black, but the color came out of a bottle these days. He was fifty-three years old and still healthy as a horse. A cigar stuck out of the center of his mouth. He wore expensive Italian suits as a trademark.

"Hey, Joachim," he called in a gruff, friendly voice.

Good, Joachim thought. *He doesn't sound too upset.*

But that wasn't totally relaxing. Joachim had seen Günter take a baseball bat to a man one night and literally beat his face off, leaving only a gaping hole surrounded by stumps of broken teeth for a mouth and a bloody pit where the sinus cavities had been. Günter hadn't seemed upset that night, either, before or after the beating.

Günter puffed on his cigar. "Have you been to see your family?"

"Yes."

"Good. Good." Günter waved to the car. "Do you know what this is?"

Joachim scanned the car and read its name. "Jaguar. XKE." He didn't know the car model by heart. He preferred bigger cars that were innocuous in traffic and could take some considerable damage before folding up.

"This is a serious car, Joachim." Pride glowed in Günter's voice. "In a car like this, a man could have his pick of women."

"If you say so."

Günter touched his nose, a purely wiseguy move he'd

adopted from the American Mafia movies. "I know so. I don't merely say it." He patted the car affectionately, then paused. "Have you heard anything more from the woman?"

"No." Secretly, Joachim was glad. It was one less lie he had to weave.

"You would tell me if you had been in touch with her."

"Of course."

"I'm glad, Joachim." Günter smiled happily. "I don't want anyone or anything to come between the two of us." His eyes stared into Joachim's. "You have truly been like a son to me. I don't tell you that enough."

Joachim had to steel himself against the emotions that flooded through him. Guilt stung him like a lash, followed immediately by anger at Günter because it had been his machinations—just like those in Amsterdam—that had ultimately left Joachim exposed to prosecution from the BND, Germany's intelligence agency. Günter liked to play his own games, and sometimes that meant losing people.

But Joachim was afraid, too. He'd been witness several times to the victims of Günter's wrath. Joachim didn't fear his own death nearly as much as his family's, and he was certain Günter would make them pay the price as well.

"You don't have to," Joachim said.

"Ah, but I feel that I do." Günter squeezed the back of Joachim's neck, then cuffed the back of the younger man's head. "I like you, Joachim. I have always liked you." He took a puff off his cigar. "That's why the business in Amsterdam was so disheartening."

Joachim said nothing. He had already apologized for Amsterdam.

"I am hoping the woman will call back and talk to me again," Günter said. "We have done a lot of business together. I would like to do more."

Joachim wanted to know the nature of that business. Schultz and the BND were anxious to know, and they weren't telling Joachim why, either.

"I have looked into this man Beck." Günter knocked ash from the cigar. "He is a very dangerous man. Did you know he was originally from East Germany?"

"Yes," Joachim answered. Over the last two days, he had spent time investigating Beck. Nothing in any of the information he had been able to find offered a clue as to where he might find the mercenary.

"Twenty years ago, he was a common criminal in the streets. A very violent man." Günter breathed out a blue stream of cigar smoke. "For a time, I knew him. We were competitors for the same business." He shrugged. "In those days, Beck got more business than I did. He worked for the *Stasi.* You're too young to remember how bad the East German police were. Very corrupt. Someone conducting criminal enterprise could do very well for himself...if he had the price or was willing to do dirty work for the *Stasi.*"

"Beck was successful."

"Yes. Sometimes if an East German citizen was successful in climbing the Berlin Wall or was spirited away by the Americans or the British, Beck was sent after them. During several of those occasions, he killed those people as well as Western secret agents. Then, one day he simply disappeared."

"Why?"

Günter shook his head. "I've never been able to find out."

"I was told the *Stasi* might have killed him," Joachim said.

"There was a story that Beck assassinated a man named Klaus Stryker, a *Stasi* agent who ranked high in the East German espionage hierarchy, but it was never proven."

"I'd heard Beck and Stryker were partners."

Günter favored Joachim with a measured glance. "Partners, sometimes, are like the wind. Things change. This man, Stryker, had many enemies. Perhaps one of them paid Beck enough to reconsider his partnership." He smiled and clapped Joachim on the shoulder. "I know such a thing could never happen to us."

"No," Joachim replied. "It never could."

"I'm going to have to wait to see how things play out with the woman." Günter sighed unhappily. "I have no control over that. In the meantime though, we have to work."

Joachim knew that Günter meant *he* had to work.

"Do you know Paul Krieger?" Günter asked.

Joachim did. "Krieger owns a clothing store here in the city."

"That's right. This season, he has done well for himself. So well, in fact, that he has obviously forgotten the debt he owes me. I covered several of his gambling losses to keep his company solvent. I need you to remind him that he owes me."

The price of failing in Amsterdam was going to be a demotion, a return to the old days when Joachim served Günter as an enforcer. Relief unlocked some of the tightness in Joachim's stomach. The work was ugly, but his family was out of the line of fire and he would live.

"How *hard* do you want me to remind Krieger?" Joachim asked, dreading the answer and knowing of no way to get out of this assignment.

"I don't want Krieger hurt. He's an old man." Günter shrugged. "Several men half his age couldn't keep up with the number of mistresses he maintains, either financially or physically. Somehow Krieger manages to do both." A broad smile crinkled his eyes. "For that alone, I would respect him." He opened the Jaguar's door, reached inside and brought out a thin manila envelope.

Joachim accepted the envelope, then lifted the flap and shook the contents out into his hand. A dozen color 35-millimeter pictures filled his palm. Two people, a man and a woman, were featured predominantly. Both were young and looked affluent.

"That's his son, Christian, and his favorite mistress, Marina. Remind Paul that I don't want to hurt him because that would keep him from paying his debt. However, his son and mistress are expendable."

Remembering again why he wanted to get away from Günter and why he was willing to betray the man to get it done, Joachim shoved the pictures back into the envelope and put the envelope inside his jacket. "All right."

Chapter 10

Athena Academy for the Advancement of Women
Outside Athens, Arizona

"It's bigger than I thought," Elle said as they crested the foothills of the White Tank Mountains and she saw Athena Academy for the first time. The approach view from Script Pass, the road that led out of Athens to the school, was breathtaking with the four-thousand-foot-tall mountains in the background. "Even after your descriptions and the courses you said you took here, I never imagined the school would be this big."

"It's big," Sam agreed. "But part of that is because the campus is spread out."

Mesmerized by the school, Elle studied buildings. What Sam said was true: the campus was spread out and nearly all of the buildings were only a single story tall.

"The main building holds twenty classrooms in the middle section," Sam said. "We'll be meeting Allison and Alex in one of the offices on the right side of them later." She pointed out the two-story auditorium on the far end.

In addition to the classrooms, the campus included a horse stable with an accompanying riding ring, several athletic fields, and tennis and basketball courts.

"The gymnasium is incredible," Sam went on. "Growing up here after all those foster homes was like being forced to live at Disney World. I love the horses and the pool. I spent most of my free time there. And in the dojos."

"Tory told me that the school administration had to recruit instructors to teach Sam different disciplines," Riley said. "Then she became an instructor. She still conducts specialty classes."

Elle heard the pride in his voice.

"She learns martial arts quickly," Riley said. "In fact, she picks up a lot of muscle memory techniques fast."

Was the double entendre in that claim intentional? Elle wondered.

Sam colored but didn't say anything.

Oh, yes. Elle saw Sam glance at her self-consciously in the mirror and smiled sweetly. *That was intentional.*

Riley drove blithely, as if he were totally innocent.

If it weren't for the mystery involving Tuenis Meijer and the parents she and Sam had never known, Elle would have enjoyed her sister's discomfiture even more.

"Before Athena Academy was a school," Sam said into the silence that suddenly filled the Suburban, "it was a health spa."

"By that," Riley put in, "Sam means that the rich and famous came here or sent family members here for detox or psych evals and treatment."

"That was a long time ago," Sam said. "This is a school now. There are a lot of new buildings and facilities."

As she scanned the surrounding foothills, Elle saw horseback riders in the ring and students playing tennis on the courts and walking between the buildings.

"Farther up in the hills," Sam said, "there are rifle ranges and combat pistol courses."

"Is that a challenge?" Elle asked.

"For me, yes." Sam grinned. "For you, I'll reserve some time at the dojo."

Riley followed the road into the circular drive in front of the main buildings. They took one of the few parking spaces out front.

Gratefully, Elle climbed out of the Suburban and stretched her legs. After two days cooped up, first in the safe house and then on the airplane, she felt tense and tired. She needed to run and stretch.

A large, beautiful fountain occupied the middle of the driveway circle. Students worked the huge flower beds that exploded with riotous color and greenery.

"Landscaping class?" Elle asked, joking.

Sam nodded. "As well as horticulture, botany and chemistry. Students who work on the flower beds not only learn how to lay them out, but also how to grow them, hybridize them and break them down for homeopathic remedies and poison. They also use them in forensic studies."

"I wouldn't have thought so many subjects could be covered in a flower bed," Elle responded.

A jeep marked with the Athena Academy colors drove over to them. A young woman in shorts and a rugby shirt climbed out from behind the wheel.

She was pretty, possessing an angular face and dark tan that spoke of an Indian heritage, but blond-streaked hair the color of straw. Wraparound blue-tinted sunglasses hid her eyes, but not her warm smile. Tall and slender, she looked all of sixteen or seventeen. Her cross-trainer tennis shoes were blindingly white.

Stopping in front of them, she came to parade rest, her hands behind her. "Special Agents St. John and McLane, Agent Petrenko."

They replied in the affirmative.

"On behalf of Athena Academy, I'd like to welcome you to our campus," the young woman said. "Special Agent St. John, I was instructed to welcome you back home."

"Thank you." Sam smiled.

Watching her sister, Elle saw an ease in Sam that she'd never seen before. *She is home*, Elle realized. *Home isn't that apartment in Virginia. Home is here.* That surprised Elle.

When she'd grown up in Moscow and gone off to university, she hadn't liked leaving home. For her, home had been the Petrenko residence, in the middle of her brothers and sisters, buried in chores and arguments and noise. She'd never felt that way about any of the schools she'd gone to.

"I'm Teal Arnett," the young woman said. "I'm a student here, but one of my duties today is to oversee the arrival of guests. Ms. Gracelyn has made one of the staff bungalows open to you. The professor is currently off with his class on a field trip to New Mexico on an archeological dig, so the house is available to you. You can stay in Athens, but Ms. Gracelyn thought perhaps you might want to stay on-site."

Sam hesitated. "Special Agent McLane has an interest in our project. I know Ms. Gracelyn hadn't planned on his presence—"

"Ms. Gracelyn said to assure you that the invitation extends to Special Agent McLane as well." Teal smiled.

"The bungalow has two bedrooms. She said to use them as you see fit."

"Thank you," Sam said. Bright spots of color showed on her cheeks.

"No problem. You know the way to the bungalows?" Teal asked.

"Yes."

"It's number six. Is there anything else I can help you with?"

"Our bags will arrive later," Riley said.

Teal nodded. "I'll see that they find their way to you."

"Did Ms. Gracelyn tell you when we're supposed to meet with her?" Sam asked.

"At three forty-five," Teal answered. "She wants you to make yourself comfortable." She nodded to Elle. "She suggested perhaps giving Agent Petrenko a tour of the campus. Make use of any of the facilities you want. While you're here, I'll be your liaison." She produced a card with a quick flip of her hand that looked like a magic trick. "My cell number is on that card. Please don't hesitate to call for anything at all."

Sam thanked her.

"I'll need a secure line," Riley said.

"All the lines in your bungalow are secure, Special Agent McLane. If you want them scrambled or coded so they don't appear to come from the campus, you'll find a code on the card Special Agent St. John has. Dial it before you dial your number."

The bungalows were located in the woods to the left of the dorm building. Each house had a private driveway off the circular road that lay like a hangman's loop. The buildings were small and modest, under the heavy boughs of trees. The manicured lawns warred against encroaching brush. Gray squirrels and rabbits leaped through the trees and sprinted across the road, disappearing almost immediately. Colorful songbirds flitted everywhere.

It was, Elle had to admit, a lot different than the Moscow neighborhood where she grew up.

At number six, she took the smaller bedroom, leaving Riley and Sam the master bedroom without taking a vote. It was obvious they wanted to be together, though both of them seemed equally reluctant to tell Elle. Instead, Elle announced that, after being crowded in the safe house, the plane and the airport, she wanted to have some alone time and hoped that Riley and Sam could put up with each other.

That, apparently, was no problem. Their carry-on bags contained a change of clothing. Sam and Riley had a private bath in their bedroom and quickly availed themselves of it.

In fact, they availed themselves of the privacy in the bathroom so loudly and enthusiastically that Elle had to turn up the radio in the other bathroom to drown out the sounds of passion while she showered.

Obtrusive thoughts of Joachim Reiter bounced through Elle's head, and she didn't know where those came from. The shower turned out not to be so relaxing. Knowing what Sam and Riley were up to in the other bathroom increased Elle's frustrations and irritability.

When Elle finished her shower and retreated to the bedroom, she used the television to mask any noise in the other room, giving Riley and Sam more privacy. She took the time to look around her temporary quarters.

Whoever the professor was, he obviously had two daughters. Elle gathered that from the twin beds and the obvious separation in the closet. Both of them were teens and took lots of pictures that they shoved up under the frame of the vanity mirror. Post-it notes in a rainbow of colors adorned the computer and the bulletin board.

With the realization of what Sam and Riley were doing, Elle suddenly couldn't get Joachim out of her mind. How he'd looked in the train station and then—so menacing, so…sexy—in the darkness of Meijer's boat. When she closed her eyes, she could feel his heat against her, in the water on the bridge….

She and Joachim had unfinished business. Against all good sense, she hoped they would meet again.

Gradually, thoughts of Joachim still teasing her mind, Elle managed to drop into a light sleep.

A light knock on the door woke Elle. Out of habit, she reached for the pistol and knife she often carried while on a mission. Neither was at hand. At the same time she grew aware of that, she realized where she was.

The door opened.

Sam stuck her head in. "Want to sleep? Or do you want to see the campus?"

It was obvious to Elle that Sam wanted to show off the academy.

"I'd love to see the campus," Elle answered. "Are you certain you're up to it?"

Sam's brows knitted. "What do you mean?"

"I mean, this is a walking tour you're suggesting, right?"

"Yes."

"After all the…*showering*, I thought maybe you might not be able."

"For your information," Sam retorted, "I'm quite capable of a walking tour. Or of further…*showering*."

Elle lifted a skeptical eyebrow.

"I'd be *showering* now if Riley didn't have other obligations."

Elle sat up. "You left him alive? He's still able to move?"

"Yes," Sam said smugly. "He's more resilient than you might think." She folded her arms over her breasts and leaned against the door frame. "Well?"

"Let's go."

Hours later, nearing exhaustion but happy, Elle decided that out of everything she had seen, she loved the horses most of all. She had seen them in other countries, but had never gotten to spend time with the big animals. They were fascinating.

She and Sam stood inside the barn grooming the horses they had ridden for the last hour. It had become immediately evident that Sam knew every riding trail around the school.

During the ride, Sam had shown Elle the campus from different spots throughout the White Tank Mountains. Elle had witnessed students at work in the rifle and archery ranges and the outdoor combat handgun simulation. Other students had been learning to fly fixed-wing aircraft from the small runway and helicopters from the landing pad. The obstacle courses stayed full, and Elle was certain the pool and gym remained busy as well.

"With all the training that goes on here," Elle said as she ran a currycomb across the mare's flanks the way Sam had demonstrated, "Athena Academy could field a small army."

She spoke in English because she didn't want to draw the attention of students in the barn who were caring for other horses.

"We're not an army," Sam said. "We're just…everything we can be. As close to being everything we want to be that's possible."

"You wanted to be a CIA agent, Sam?"

Sam didn't meet Elle's gaze. "I don't know. I'm good with languages. I'm good with computers." She paused. "Some of my counselors suggested I think about intelligence work."

"Because you're bright and capable, or because you like being alone?"

"Maybe a little of all those things. Being alone is…was…easy."

"Not so easy now?"

"With Riley?"

"Yes."

Sam worked at brushing out the horse's coat for a while.

Elle couldn't stand thinking that Sam was uncomfortable. "Hey, forget I asked. I was just making—"

"Riley…complicates things," Sam said.

"Men you want to hang on to have a tendency to do that." For a moment, Elle flashed on the men she'd been involved with. Some had been boys she'd grown up with, some were agents in the SVR, and some were men she'd met while out in the field in a dozen different countries.

Like Joachim Reiter.

Get him out of your head, she told herself. *This is stupid.* But she couldn't.

"When I was growing up in those foster homes," Sam said, "I didn't have anybody. For a while there, I didn't even have myself." She kept brushing, but her voice was quiet and cold. "I didn't know how to be me. I didn't even know I was supposed to be me. I didn't even know who I was."

Elle didn't know what to say.

"Then I came here," Sam said. "I met my friends. It was hard. Learning to trust them was hard. In the end, I did. I missed them when they were gone."

"When were they gone?"

"We have trimester classes. Three months at school, a month away."

"Only you didn't have anywhere to go," Elle said softly, understanding. "You stayed here."

Sam glanced over her shoulder and smiled. "Yes. I liked it, though. The horses never went anywhere, either." She resumed brushing her mount. "After a while, I learned to trust my friends. Sometimes I got to go with them for visits. Then, after graduation, we all went our separate ways."

"So you were on your own again," Elle said.

"For a time." Sam combed out the horse's mane, concentrating on the task. "I got through it. Then I found out we still shared a lot. Rainy's death last year brought us all back together in ways we hadn't expected. We'd always been there for each other. We're just more so now."

"After you've had your own mortality thrown in your face."

"I suppose."

Elle left the mare and walked over to Sam. She turned her sister around, holding her by the shoulders and looking her in the eye. "You've got great friends, Sam. I don't know them, but I can see what they mean to you. It's good to have friends like that. But you've got me now, too. I'm family. Nothing is ever going to pull me out of your life."

Fiercely then, Elle hugged her sister, pulling her as close as she could. Tentatively, Sam wrapped her arms around her and held her back.

"I'm not going anywhere, Sam," Elle said. "I swear that I'm not."

Elle watched CNN on a plasma screen television in one of the main building's offices. A glance at her watch told her it was 2:57 p.m. Alex Forsythe and Allison Gracelyn still had three minutes to put in an appearance.

Elle and Sam's luggage had caught up to them, courtesy of Riley's agents. Elle wore business attire—slacks, blouse and a jacket—as well as a pair of Italian shoes she liked. The only thing missing was her pistol.

Seated in another chair, Sam waited patiently.

Then footsteps sounded out in the hall. A moment later, Allison Gracelyn entered through the door.

In her mid-thirties, Allison stood five feet six inches tall and was solidly built. Her dark brown hair was long enough to sweep her shoulders. She peered at Elle, then at Sam with her dark brown eyes. She wore a dark blue business suit with a skirt.

"Sam?" Allison asked finally.

"Here," Sam said.

Despite the tension radiating from her, Allison smiled a little. "I've seen pictures of the two of you together and I knew you were identical twins, but seeing you here together in the flesh, I don't think I could tell you apart without talking to you."

Sam made the introductions.

Elle shook hands with Allison, who continued to look a little ill at ease.

"Isn't Alex coming?" Sam asked. "I thought she would be here, too."

"Actually," Allison said, "we're having the meeting in one of the conference rooms."

"Why didn't you just have us meet there?" Sam asked.

"Because that conference room is now in a restricted area," Allison said. "Only people who need to go there can go there. Neither of you is on the list without a chaperone."

Sam walked out into the hallway after Allison.

Elle followed.

"Agent Petrenko," Allison said, "I would like to ask that you wait here."

Caught off guard, Elle paused. She had to check an immediate impulse to demand explanation. *You're in someone else's house,* she told herself. *You'll play by their rules.*

Sam wasn't inhibited, though. "Why?" she asked.

Allison was forthright. Elle grudgingly gave the woman points for that.

"Because the information we have to share with you is hard, Sam," Allison answered. "Alex and I would prefer if we only dealt with one of you at a time."

And how much of that has to do with the fact that I'm an agent for the SVR? Elle wondered.

"Sam," Elle said quietly. "It's all right. I don't mind waiting for you. I'll meet you back at the bungalow when you're finished." She wasn't going to cool her heels in the office under the scrutiny of security.

"All right," Sam said. She looked troubled.

But she still went with her friends.

Chapter 11

Krieger's Creations
Leipzig, Germany

Joachim sat in one of the overstuffed chairs in the waiting room outside Paul Krieger's office. Soundproofing protected the room from the roar of the sewing machines out on the factory floor, where seamstresses labored to produce Krieger's line for the upcoming season.

The receptionist was a young woman with punk-cut red hair who took care of the phones via an earpiece she kept on. She also kept track of Krieger's e-mail, dealing with each piece as soon as it came in on the computer monitor in front of her. When she wasn't busy dealing with those things, she divided her time between watching a television soap opera she had open in a window on the monitor and imagining Joachim naked.

At least, that's what Joachim's sister had told him women were doing when they looked at him like that. Long ago, Joachim had decided that sisters gave their brothers far too much information about the opposite sex. Personally, he liked a little bit of mystery to cling to a woman. Just as he preferred to undress them himself, layer by layer.

That thought struck him and he immediately thought of the blonde he'd met in Amsterdam. All he had to do was close his eyes and he could imagine her wrapped in silk scarves that only partially revealed tantalizing shapes and curves through the thin material. He had yet to pick a favorite color for her, though he had tried several hues. At the moment, pale electric blue—like that of her eyes—was his favorite.

His mind had been preoccupied with those images since Amsterdam. Suddenly uncomfortable sitting there, Joachim checked his watch. He'd been kept waiting for eight minutes. Dressed in black and without a briefcase or PDA or wireless cell phone earpiece, he definitely didn't look like someone who fit in at Krieger's Creations.

He stood, drawing the receptionist's attention from the soap opera. Hands in his pockets, he walked to Krieger's ornate door. A simple bronze nameplate announced Paul Kreiger, CEO.

"Hey," the receptionist called, "you can't go in there." She twisted in her chair but didn't leave it.

However, Joachim could go into the office. The door wasn't locked. He twisted the knob and followed the door inside.

Krieger lounged in a massive chair behind a huge glass-and-steel kidney-shaped desk. The surface gleamed as if it had been freshly shined.

Krieger wore a phone headset that plugged into the desk. His hands were steepled in front of him. Although in his sixties, Krieger was a big man—broad shouldered and lean. His hair was light ginger and carefully cut, matching the daring goatee. He wore a shirt and tie with diamond cuff links and a large Rolex.

His dark brown eyes roved restlessly over a bank of at least twenty monitors built into the wall on the other side of the room. Built-in shelves held hundreds of fabric books like the one lying on the gleaming desktop.

A thick-necked man in his early thirties sat on a long couch at the end of the room near the picture window that looked out over Leipzig's downtown. He cradled a Play-Station video game in his huge hands. Someone might as well have stamped "hired muscle" on his low forehead. Maybe he wore one of Krieger's suits, but his history in the streets was engraved in scars and calluses, and the cold hard stare in his narrow gray eyes.

The bodyguard tossed his video game device to the couch and stood, awaiting orders.

"Hold that thought, Emily," Krieger said as he looked up at Joachim. "I need to put you on hold for just a moment." Then he punched a button on the earpiece. "Who the hell are you?"

"Günter sent me," Joachim answered.

"I don't give a damn who sent you," Krieger exploded. "You don't just walk into my office unannounced."

"I was announced. I've been waiting outside." Joachim kept his hands in his pockets and made no overt threat. He was too professional for that. Also, he didn't like threatening unless there was no recourse.

Krieger was tough. He hadn't survived in the garment industry without being tough. Fashion was a hard business and made for harder players.

"Then if you've got any sense, you'll walk back to the door

and wait until I'm ready to deal with you." Krieger leaned back in his chair as if the matter were finished. He tapped the earpiece again. "Emily? No, no, I'm ready to talk. I just had a momentary distraction, that's all. I've dealt with it already."

Joachim leaned over the desk and pulled the phone cord out of the plug.

Red in the face now, Krieger pointed to Joaquin. "Irwin, throw this bastard out of my office. Now!"

Irwin closed on Joachim without a word. Dropping his head down as close to his shoulders as he could, the bodyguard held up his massive fists and began circling to Joachim's left.

Joachim didn't protest. It would have done no good. Both of them were seasoned veterans operating under orders.

"Who gave you the black eye?" Irwin taunted.

Raising his open hands to shoulder height in front of them, Joachim replied, "A woman. About half your size."

Irwin laughed. "Whoever sent you should have had his head checked. I'll ask you once, nicely, to leave. So I don't have to mess up your looks any more."

"I appreciate that."

Irwin shrugged. "Professional courtesy."

"I'm staying, but I'll offer you the same chance."

When Irwin attacked, it was just as Joachim figured it would be. A man Irwin's size grew used to using his height and weight against the opponent. He was a street boxer, employing only techniques he had picked up bouncing in bars and busting heads down on the docks as part of a private security team.

Using his hands and forearms, Joachim fended off the first few blows, turning them away from his head and body. He knew that if he gave Irwin the chance, the man would hurt him or Joachim would be forced to put him into the hospital to stop him.

Surprised by Joachim's skill, Irwin withdrew slightly. Joaquin followed at once, throwing a series of fist blows designed to bring Irwin's hands up. Once Irwin's chest was exposed, Joachim drove a snap-kick into the center of his opponent's stomach that sent him stumbling backward. Before Irwin could recover, Joachim launched a side kick into the middle of the big man's face.

Irwin dropped as if he had been poleaxed. Stubbornly, though, he forced himself to his hands and knees, and stood again, swaying this time. He attacked Joachim, firing a punch right off the shoulder. Joachim slipped the punch and threw a right cross into Irwin's face that left him sprawled unconscious on the floor.

Joachim turned to face Krieger.

The garment king sat calmly behind his big desk. He took a cigarette from a gold case, tapped the cigarette on the back of his hand and lit up with a gold cigarette lighter. "You're good. Irwin's no pushover."

Silently, Joachim agreed.

"You're just better than he is." Krieger's eyes danced. "But tell me this. What would you do if I pulled a pistol from this desk?"

"Kill you," Joachim replied.

Some of the humor left Krieger's eyes, but he kept the smile. "I don't think Günter would like that."

"Probably not, but I would mind being dead a lot more than I would mind having Günter mad at me for a while." Joaquin walked back toward the desk. "Besides that, you don't have a gun in the desk. At least, not one you're willing to use in this occasion." He took the envelope containing the pictures from his jacket, then spread them out on the table like playing cards.

Krieger studied the pictures but did not touch them. "So these are the stakes, then?"

Joachim met the man's eyes without flinching from the scorn and fear that he saw there. "Günter wants his money. Call him. Now. Make the arrangements."

For a moment more, Krieger held Joachim's gaze. Then the old man gathered the pictures with a trembling hand. "All right."

Feeling sick and disgusted with himself, Joachim left Krieger's office.

Outside, Joachim stared at the leaden sky and the hard faces that filled the sidewalks. He wanted out of this business. He'd had more than enough. Pitor Schultz was going to have to make good on his promise to get him clear.

Doing the enforcement work for Günter hadn't been so bad when Joachim had gone after criminals who had robbed Günter and welshed on deals. Or men who had tried to kill Günter. There were no innocents among them.

Trudging back to the ten-year-old sedan he was currently driving, Joachim wanted a drink. Anything to take the taste of what he had just done from his mouth. His hand was already swelling and his forearms would be bruised for days.

One of the phones in his pocket vibrated for attention. From the position in his jacket, he knew it was the cell phone he kept for Pitor Schultz.

When he got the phone out, he saw that he'd received a text message: Meet me at Heidahl's. 9:00. I have news.

Athena Academy for the Advancement of Women
Outside Athens, Arizona

Controlling the outrage that stirred within her, Sam sat at the conference table across from Alex Forsythe and Allison Gracelyn.

"I know you're angry, Sam." Alex spoke softly, in her professional voice, and that irritated Sam more.

At five feet eight inches tall with long, curly red hair and blue eyes, Alex was a hard woman to miss in a crowd. She grew up in a family fueled by Old Money. The original Forsythes had come over on the *Mayflower* and set about making their first million in short order.

Charles Forsythe, Alex's grandfather, had helped found the school and believed in its objectives. After finishing at Athena, Alex had gone on to study forensic science and was now one of the top practitioners in her field. Currently, she lived in Washington, D.C., and worked for the Federal Bureau of Investigation.

"You're right," Sam said in a controlled voice. "I'm angry. I had a vacation planned with my sister. A quiet time where we could get away and get to know more about each other. Instead, I ended up in Amsterdam, in an area that is an absolute zoo and freak show where people sell their freedom and self-respect for cash," Sam continued. "As if that wasn't bad enough, Elle nearly gets blown up capturing the man you two wanted to question, and now, after she's risked her life to help me with a task I still don't even know the reason for," Sam said, "you two turn her away like you don't trust her. You bet I'm angry."

"We have a reason for talking to you without Elle at the moment," Alex assured her.

"Oh, really?" Sam stared at her friend. She couldn't ever remember being so pissed at Alex. Or any of the Cassandras, for that matter. "What?"

"I can't tell you yet."

Abruptly, Sam stood to leave. "Then I can't stay." She turned and headed for the door. She was so mad she was shaking. She couldn't remember the last time she had been this angry or this near to being out of control. The realization scared her. Without control, she was a victim, and victims had to go along with whatever happened to them. She'd learned that in the foster homes.

"Sam," Alex called. "Please don't leave."

Pausing at the door, Sam turned to face the other two women. "You've known me for a long time. Both of you. I've never asked for much. From either of you. Or from anyone. I gave you help on this without ever asking why or what it was about. Elle gave me that same thing. Simply because we're family. Something I thought you of all people would understand. You hooked me with the possibility that what we were doing had something to do with my parents."

Alex fixed her with an open, honest gaze. There wasn't a hint of deceit in her blue eyes. "This *is* about your parents, Sam. That's why it's so hard. The answers you want are complicated. We're still dealing with them ourselves. Please be a little more patient."

"Why couldn't Elle be here?" Sam asked. "My mother and father were her parents, too. That's what this is about, right? My parents?"

"Yes," Alex said, "and no."

Sam blew out an angry breath.

"I told you it was complicated," Alex said.

"You're aware that your mission was initiated by an investigation into my mother's death," Allison said calmly.

For the first time, Sam saw that Allison looked frayed around the edges. In her days at the academy, Allison and Rainy had been rivals. Allison had mentored a group called the Graces, while Rainy had mentored the Cassandras. The rivalry had continued up until the time that Marion Gracelyn was murdered. Rainy had returned to the school to help Allison deal with her loss and the resulting investigation, which hadn't turned up a murderer. After that, they had become good friends.

Until Rainy's death last year.

Sam said nothing. She couldn't be influenced by whatever pain and confusion Allison was going through. The quickest way to lose herself was to become overly concerned about someone else involved in the situation.

"We sifted through a lot of old evidence while looking for Marion's murderer," Alex said. "We also turned up several e-mail communications from someone who only signed the messages 'A.' Most of those communications were fragmented and hidden in code we believe Marion created herself. We have been able to decipher some of them, but not all."

"I'm still working on it," Allison said. "But, it seems, my mother was even more clever than I had known."

Curiosity nibbled at Sam's anger. Mysteries had always appealed to her.

"My mother was being blackmailed," Allison said. "Months before she died, she began making weekly payments of five thousand dollars cash. We believe it was to protect you."

Chapter 12

"**M**arion Gracelyn was blackmailed because of *me?*" That surprised Sam. She had graduated a few years before Marion Gracelyn had been murdered, and she was certain that the woman hadn't known her. While at Athena, Sam had only seen the senator in the hallways a handful of times.

"Whoever this 'A' is," Alex said, "he or she was threatening to expose your parents."

"Marion Gracelyn knew who my parents were?" Sam couldn't believe it. "And she never mentioned it to anyone?"

"No," Allison said.

"Why?" Sam's voice was hoarse with restrained anger. Although knowing the identities of her birth parents hadn't been a pressing need for her the way it was for some foster children, she'd still wanted to know.

"Anya and Boris Leonov were dead," Allison said. "I

suppose my mother thought it would have been better if you weren't burdened with that. She wanted to protect you."

I would have liked to have a chance to decide that for myself, Sam thought.

"More than that, Marion wanted to protect you from international repercussions," Alex put in. "Your right to stay in this country as an American citizen would have been questioned. Marion believed that you had been through enough and that pulling you out of the Athena environment would have been debilitating to you."

Sam hadn't thought about that. Truthfully speaking, she'd been born a Russian citizen and had been brought to the United States as a baby through some illegal means. Sam still didn't know how that had happened. Or why whoever had brought Sam over hadn't provided her with a family like Elle's.

"If she had told someone, I could have met my sister before now."

"Sam," Allison said, "Mother believed your sister was dead. That was in her notes. The blackmailer sent case files from the CIA and MI-6 that documented your parents' assassination. Those reports listed both daughters as victims of the explosion as well."

"But Elle—" Sam started.

"There was no mention of her surviving. Both of you were listed as casualties."

Sam was quiet for a moment, trying to get around it all. Silently, she returned to her chair.

"My mother liked you, Sam," Allison said. "She saw great promise in you. She didn't want to lose you if she could prevent it." She paused. "But there was more to the story than your nationality."

Sam waited.

Alex looked at her and let out a breath. "The rest isn't easy, Sam."

"It hasn't ever been easy," Sam replied.

"There's something you don't know about your parents."

Sam laughed bitterly. "There's a lot I don't know about my parents. They were Russian agents doubling as British spies. They were desperate to get out of Russia so they made every deal they could with the British, got every secret they could from the Russians and pressed their luck past the breaking point. When they were trying to get out of Moscow ahead of an execution squad, someone killed them with a rocket launcher. End of story."

"No," Alex said. "That was just the beginning of an even bigger story. According to the files we've managed to decipher—"

"Files even my mother couldn't decipher back then," Allison added.

"Your parents were in possession of a deadly nerve gas when they were killed," Alex finished.

Sam looked at them. "I don't understand."

"Under international agreement at the 1972 Biological and Toxin Weapons Convention, none of the superpowers were supposed to work with nerve toxins," Alex said. "The American government knew that Russia was. That fact has been in the news quite often lately because of the events going on in Iraq and Berzhaan."

Since her career had started with the CIA, Sam had been aware of biological threats. She was familiar with the agreement, and with the CIA's attempts to locate secret Russian labs charged with designing illegal bioweapons.

"The Soviet Union had a dedicated program to design and produce biological weapons through the 1990s," Allison said. "Dr. Kenneth Alibek testified to that in a 1998 statement to a joint congressional committee. He was a First Deputy Director of Biopreparat in charge of those efforts, That was the civilian arm of the bio-weapons development. He revealed that the research that had been going on involved over forty facilities and thirty thousand employees."

"Okay," Sam said, holding up a hand. "I'll agree that Russia had been involved in making bioweapons until that time, but what does that have to do with my parents? How do you know they were carrying a nerve toxin?"

"It's in the documents my mother had," Allison said.

"I checked through the CIA's files on my parents," Sam said. "The CIA hacked into MI-6's files. There was no mention of a nerve toxin."

"Why did the CIA have a file on your parents?" Alex asked.

"Because Anya and Boris Leonov were suspected spies and double agents," Sam said. After she'd learned of her parents, she had explored the CIA's archives looking for more information. She'd been disappointed with how little there was.

"The files my mother had possession of suggested that the Leonovs were selling the nerve toxin to a third party," Alex said. "Someone in East Germany. A man named Stryker was named in the documents. He was an East German *Stasi*. The *Stasi* were—"

"East German police," Sam interrupted. "I know. They were supposed to be very corrupt. But why would my parents work with the *Stasi*?"

"Britain may have been willing to grant them asylum, but evidently the Leonovs didn't trust the British to take care of their financial needs."

Overcome, Sam sat quietly. *My parents? The bad guys?*

"They were scared, Sam," Allison said. "They were defecting from their country, going to a place that wanted them only for what they knew at the moment. They had two beautiful baby girls. They just wanted everything to be all right."

Stunned, Sam didn't move. Didn't breathe. Even with Allison's blessing, the possibility of her parents being involved in wrongdoing just seemed...wrong.

"Do you see the problem we have if we choose to tell Elle?" Alex asked.

Sam focused on her friend. "No. I don't."

"My mother's files almost constitute an accusation," Allison said.

"How?"

"The nerve gas is named in the documents."

"How did the blackmailer get all that information?"

Alex shook her head. "We don't know. We're still investigating."

"Who's investigating?" Sam asked.

"An agency we have friendly connections with," Allison said. "I've done work with them for years. Believe me, you can trust them."

Sam believed Allison's earnestness. But other thoughts bothered her. "You can tell Elle."

Alex leaned back in her chair. "We can. But what happens then?"

"What do you mean?"

"One way or another, Russia is still culpable for the creation of that nerve agent," Allison said. "We have proof of that. It was code-named Lenin's Lullaby. If it's used, we have enough of the chemical makeup on record to match it to them."

"'If it's used'?" Sam echoed.

"That's one of the problems," Alex said, "Lenin's Lullaby is still out there. We just don't know where."

Heidahl's Coffee Shop
Leipzig, Germany

Although not as posh as the Starbucks coffee shops Joachim had seen, Heidahl's coffee shop maintained its own elegance. The décor was Old World German. Bookshelves lined the walls, filled with old leather-bound books. Color-stained glass filled the awning over the front of the building and created a design in the main windows that depicted a coffee percolator and steaming cup of coffee.

Joachim left his car parked at the side of the building and went inside. He scanned the interior out of habit. Several men and women with phone headsets sat at tables with notebook computers open before them, doing business around the world.

Pitor Schultz sat in the back at a small table with an inlaid chessboard. He was reading a paper. In his forties, small and shaggy looking, he was a man who would be overlooked in most occasions out on the street or in a crowd. Gray tinted the hair at his temples. His nose was too large for his face and, combined with the thick mustache that looked like a fat caterpillar, lent him a homely look that made him appear unthreatening to most women and vulnerable to most men. He wore a trench coat and a suit.

After getting a cup of coffee, Joachim joined Schultz at his table.

Schultz put the paper away and looked up expectantly. "Well?"

"What?" Joachim asked.

Folding his hands patiently, Schultz said, "You called this meeting."

"No," Joachim said, more calmly than he felt. The walls were closing in on him. "*You* did. I got a text message."

"So did I." Schultz pushed himself up from the chair. His eyes surveyed the room.

"I tried calling you to confirm." Joachim stood. Every survival sense inside him was screaming to get moving. "Your line was busy."

"So was yours. I don't like walking into a situation unprepared." Schultz jerked his chin to the rear of the coffee shop. "There's a back entrance we can—"

Suddenly, Schultz jerked backward, half turning as a high-powered bullet hit him in the left side of his chest. Time slowed down for Joachim as his brain leaped into overdrive. Blood spilled out from Schultz's chest. Pain filled his blocky face. He fell backward, arms flung out to the sides. He grabbed hold of a nearby chair and spilled a man in a suit from it.

Then the sound of the rifle shot invaded the coffee shop. Everyone in the neighborhood knew what the sound was. Screaming and cursing, patrons dived to the floor.

Joachim ripped his pistol free of the shoulder holster under his jacket and knelt beside Schultz.

The BND agent coughed and wheezed once, then shivered and went still. His eyes took on the thousand-yard stare Joachim had seen so many times before.

He's dead! Joachim screamed to himself. He tried not to remember that Schultz had been a family man. He couldn't remember if the agent had two small children at home or three. *Move!*

Staying low, the pistol held out at the ready, Joachim headed for the back door.

Athena Academy for the Advancement of Women
Outside Athens, Arizona

"Lenin's Lullaby?" Elle asked.

Sam nodded.

They were back in the bungalow Christine Evans had made available to them. The school's principal had even sent over a care basket filled with jams, crackers, chocolate and fruit.

Elle had rummaged through it already, unable to simply sit and wait for her sister's return. Now she was irritated with herself for having delved into the basket. It was a weakness, and she hated being weak. However, normally she had a cause-and-effect relationship with situations she found herself in—she was used to taking action instead of being on hold.

"That's what the nerve agent was called," Sam said. "*Is* called, I suppose I should say."

"There's no doubt our parents were the ones who sold this nerve toxin to the East Germans?" Elle said.

"Yes. To two men." Sam seated her iPAQ into the cradle that connected the device to her notebook computer. "Alex and Allison gave me their files."

"Awfully kind of them." Elle still felt the sting of the rejection she'd unexpectedly faced. She didn't want to acknowledge it, but the feelings kept surfacing.

Sam turned to her, looking somewhat put out. "Elle, I don't agree with what they did. You had as much right to know about this as I do, which is what I told them."

"But they didn't want you to, Sam," Elle said. They spoke in Russian.

"No," Sam agreed. "So do you want to deal with that or with the nerve toxin issue?"

"Both." Elle sighed. "But it's too late to deal with your friends."

Sam concentrated on the computer. "This is Klaus Stryker."

Elle studied the harsh face on the screen. Stryker had a broad forehead and deep-set eyes. Black hair framed his fleshy face. His thin-lipped mouth had a cruel set to it.

"Who is he?" Elle pulled a chair over and sat in front of the notebook computer.

"According to the files Alex and Allison got," he was the man who supposedly brokered the deal."

Quickly, Elle read the thumbnail biography. Twenty years ago, Klaus Stryker had been thirty-two years old. He'd joined the *Stasi* at eighteen, then worked his way up through the ranks by being brutal and efficient, and delivering whatever his commanding officers wanted. Eventually he had become a go-between for espionage deals.

When he'd been paid the right amount of money and there was little risk involved, he'd escorted defecting East German scientists and spies through Checkpoint Charlie and the Berlin Wall. Unfortunately, he had shot four of the people he'd been paid to escort when they were discovered escaping while he was nearby. No investigation by his people had ever found him guilty of wrongdoing, but the suspicion was there and he had been closely watched. The CIA had a file on him, too, and they had considered him a risk to deal with.

An investigation by a *Stasi* junior officer had turned up information about the nerve toxin purchase. Boris and Anya Leonov had approached Stryker to set up an arrangement. For other parties to purchase the bioweapon.

"Where did the toxin come from?" Elle asked.

"A facility outside of Odessa."

Elle knew the Odessa area. Located on the Black Sea,

Odessa had started life as an outlaw town filled with pirates and shady deals. It remained so to this day. "Transportation through Odessa could have been easily arranged."

"I know," Sam said.

But you're working on secondhand information, Elle thought irritably. *You've never been there.*

"Our parents were killed outside of Moscow," Elle said.

Sam flipped through the photo archive and showed the file pictures of the twisted wreckage of their parents' car. The vehicle had taken an almost direct hit from a rocket launcher.

For the first time since she'd heard about her parents' murders, Elle realized how brutal they had been. Boris and Anya had never had a chance.

"It was an execution," she whispered.

"Yes," Sam said. "And we're going to find the person responsible.

Elle nodded. Given who they were, that was a certainty.

Chapter 13

Downtown Leipzig, Germany

Cold rain swept the city, pouring down from the dark clouds that filled the night. Neon signs from taverns, restaurants and office businesses that kept late hours reflected against the wet street. Tires of the passing cars whickered through the water. Passersby were few and far between, usually young people and determined tourists out to soak up the nightlife.

Collar turned up against the wetness, Joachim leaned into the public phone outside a convenience store whose windows were filled with paper advertisements.

Krista answered on the first ring. Her voice was tight with fear and excitement.

"There's not much time," Joachim said.

"The police have been by," his sister said. "They're saying you killed a man."

"I didn't. I was set up." Suddenly, the enormity of everything that faced him hit Joachim. His family, whom he had struggled all his life to keep out of harm's way, was suddenly on the firing line and he couldn't get to them. Anger and nausea whirled inside his stomach. His hand holding the phone shook.

"What happened?" Krista asked.

"There's no time," Joachim said. "The police have already tracked this phone connection. They'll be here in minutes. I've got to leave."

"All right."

"Remember when we set up your escape route?"

"Yes."

"Do that," Joachim said. "Now."

"But the police—"

"The police are the least of our worries." Joachim was lying and hoped that his sister couldn't hear that in his voice. "I was set up by someone else." He still had no clue who. "Someone who won't hesitate to kill you."

"Joachim, the police said if you would just turn yourself in—"

"If I turn myself in or get caught by the police," Joachim interrupted, "they'll kill you."

"But—"

Joachim made his voice cold and hard. "They will kill Brita. Do you want to see your daughter dead? Have you got a tiny coffin picked out for her?"

Krista exploded then, cursing him violently in German and English.

The words dug into Joachim and hurt him deeply. Even if he could somehow fix this situation, his mother and sister would never forgive him. "Go," he said hoarsely. "As far and as fast as you can."

"Take care of yourself, Joachim," Krista said. "Come back to us when you can."

"I will," he promised. Then he made himself hang up the phone and got moving.

Athena Academy for the Advancement of Women
Outside Athens, Arizona

"Stryker went to Russia under an assumed name with all the proper identification and documentation," Sam said. "Getting forged papers in those days wasn't hard, just expensive."

Elle knew that. Those days were not actually far away. "Stryker traveled to Moscow to kill our parents?"

"Yes."

"Who found that out?"

"The Moscow police department." Sam moved on to more electronic documents that included handwritten and typed reports in Cyrillic. All of them were on Moscow police department stationary. "After the fact. Although they didn't have his name. They weren't able to penetrate the false ID. But look at the pictures."

Elle watched the monitor as Sam split the screen and put the ID pictures side by side. There was no doubt that they were the same man.

"How did the Moscow police identify Stryker's false ID?" Elle asked.

"An informer's tip." Sam grimaced. "As it turned out, the CIA had a loose tail on Stryker because they'd caught a whisper of the nerve toxin exchange. Stryker was supposed to be one of the players. The agent followed Stryker into Moscow and was on hand when he killed our parents. That's where the pictures come from."

Elle didn't ask Sam why she hadn't looked up the file years ago. Until nineteen months ago, Sam had had no clue who her parents were.

"The CIA agent didn't try to stop the murder?" Elle asked.

"The agent stated in his report that there wasn't time to act without betraying his cover," Sam said.

"This," Elle said, "is some kind of business we're in, isn't it?"

"I know. I tell myself it's better now. Riley tells me that, too. But, some days, I don't know."

"Do we know where Stryker is? We could pay him a visit."

"Stryker's dead," Sam answered.

That surprised Elle and made her feel curiously hollow. "How?"

"Only days after he killed our parents, Stryker was killed by Arnaud Beck."

"Beck? You're sure?" The sudden turn caught Elle off guard. She had just learned the name of her parents' murderer, had only started thinking about revenge, and already the opportunity to avenge them had slipped through her fingers.

"I'm having Riley check on it for me, but I think he's only going to confirm what Alex and Allison have found out through their sources."

Disappointment and frustration vibrated inside Elle. "Why did Beck kill Stryker?"

"The story was put together after the fact and might all be conjecture. Maybe there was another reason. Stryker made plenty of enemies. Beck was believed to be Stryker's silent partner in the nerve toxin purchase. Evidently Stryker tried to cut Beck out of the deal. Beck killed him in retaliation. He burned Stryker to death in a car while people watched."

"Do we know where to find Beck?"

"Not yet."

"Not *yet?*"

Sam looked uncomfortable. "Allison and Alex would like me to follow up on this," Sam said. "But I'm not going to do it without you. Unless you don't want in."

"Aren't you worried that your friends might get annoyed if I tag along?"

"You're my sister. Boris and Anya were your parents, too. Arnaud Beck is a homicidal maniac. A very smart, very vicious homicidal maniac." Sam let out a breath and unconsciously squared her shoulders. "Do you really want to fight when I'm on your side?"

Stated bluntly, Sam's question took away some of the angry edge Elle was feeling. "No. I don't want to fight." She looked back at the screen. "You've told your friends that I will be accompanying you?"

"Yes."

"They were in favor of that?"

"No."

Elle smiled. "I didn't think they would be."

"This investigation is sensitive," Sam said. "It's hitting close to home. Whoever this 'A' person is—"

Madame Web, Elle thought, and realized she had no right faulting Sam for being reticent when she wasn't being exactly straightforward herself.

"—he or she is good at covering tracks."

"They didn't get any information from Tuenis Meijer?"

"He confirmed that he did the work, but he didn't know who he was working with. Then or now."

"He's still working with the blackmailer?" That intrigued Elle.

Sam regarded her quietly. "Yes. He is."

"You said there was a second man involved in the toxin transaction." Elle focused on the notebook computer.

"Yes. His name is Alexi Zemanov." Sam tapped the keyboard and brought up a picture of a man with light brown hair and gray eyes. In his late fifties, he looked tan and fit, but a thin scar sliced from the corner of his left eye to his jawline.

"He's Russian?"

"Yes. He was a member of the Biopreparat stationed at the Odessa lab. According to the intel, Boris and Anya stole Lenin's Lullaby from under his nose and he was sent to Siberia for allowing the theft to happen."

"How did our parents do that?"

"They were friends with Zemanov."

Elle studied the man's face. Her adoptive father had never mentioned the man. Fyodor Petrenko had talked a lot about Elle's parents when they were alone and she'd had questions about them. She remembered, and had met, other friends of her parents, but she didn't recall Zemanov's name being mentioned. Were her parents the kind of people who betrayed their friends?

"Where is Zemanov?" Elle asked.

"We don't know," Sam admitted.

Elle sat and quietly contemplated everything she'd learned. "What are you going to do?"

"Lenin's Lullaby may still be out there," Sam said. "Either it was destroyed, or someone took possession of the nerve agent after Stryker was killed."

"You think it was Beck?"

"He was there."

"If he had tried to sell it on an international market, then someone would have known about it."

"I know," Sam said. "The CIA was already watching the action going on around the bioweapon. Beck killed Stryker that night, then set up business in the Caribbean. Since then he's moved around a lot. Somewhere between that night and now, Lenin's Lullaby disappeared."

"If it ever existed at all," Elle said.

Sam glanced at her sharply. "What do you mean by that?"

"Our two countries are presently at peace, Sam, but that doesn't mean they don't have their disagreements. Oil, economics and world presence still divide us on several fronts."

Sam spoke carefully. "The United States government is trying to do what it thinks is necessary around the world."

"Necessary for who?" Elle asked. She shook her head. "You've been indoctrinated in this country's schools and culture too long to get a proper view of it. If you truly want to see what the United States is like, you'd have to live elsewhere and look at this country through someone else's eyes."

Frowning, Sam leaned back a little. "I believe in my country, Elle."

Elle waved to the bungalow around them. "If I had been schooled in this place, taught to look at things the way you've obviously been taught to regard them, maybe I would feel the same way."

"Another argument?" Sam asked.

"Another point of view," Elle responded. "I believe in my country, too, and I don't believe it has any more faults than your own." She paused and felt bad about the tension that had sprung up between them again. "Life has more than one answer. That's all I'm saying."

"We chose careers that deal in absolutes."

"Only if that's how you want to deal with it." Elle shifted gears. "So you believe Beck is the answer to this?"

"He's the only one left alive who might know the whole story."

Elle nodded. "Finding him sounds like a good plan. A

dangerous one, though. Beck very nearly killed us in Amsterdam."

Sam smiled. "I know. But you'll be there with me. And this time we'll be hunting him. He can't escape both of us."

In spite of her mood, Elle grinned. There was a lot, she'd decided, that she and Sam had in common. A certain amount of fearlessness and tenacity, and cockiness. Both of them, it seemed, also had a penchant for the adrenaline afforded from their respective careers.

"All right then," Elle said. "We'll hunt Beck." She offered Sam a chocolate.

Sam took the candy then looked through the basket Christine Evans had sent. "Don't tell me you ate all the white chocolate."

Elle feigned innocence. A love of white chocolate was another thing they shared. "There weren't many of them. They were gone before I knew it."

Before Sam could deliver whatever scathing remark had occurred to her, the cell phone in her pocket rang. She answered it, brightened immediately and said hello to Riley, then turned somber as she listened. She told Riley goodbye and put the phone away.

"Don't tell me Riley has already found Beck?" Elle said.

"He hasn't," Sam said. "But he knows where Joachim Reiter is."

Involuntarily, Elle's heart skipped a beat. She grew irritated with herself. She really needed to get that man off her mind.

"Well?" Elle pressed.

"He's on the run in Leipzig," Sam said. "For the murder of a German BND agent."

Elle tried not to react, but something must have shown.

"I'm sorry," Sam said.

Waving the apology away, Elle said, "We both knew he

was a criminal." Riley's reports on the man had ascertained that. "It's not a surprise."

But it was. Elle couldn't imagine what could prompt Joachim to murder a BND agent. Remembering him the way he'd been back in Amsterdam, the way he had covered her back through the worst of it, she just couldn't imagine Joachim as a murderer. *What the hell happened in Leipzig?*

Chapter 14

The Velvet Kitten
Leipzig, Germany

Trying not to appear haggard and worn, Joachim stood outside the nightclub and surveyed the entrance. It occupied a corner spot on the first floor of a six-story walk-up in one of the impoverished areas near the warehouse district downtown. A sandwich shop, now closed, and a tattoo parlor festooned with neon lights that worked late into the night flanked the club. Industrial music slammed into the alley as the breeze outside the building stirred up fast-food refuse.

Joachim had never been to the Velvet Kitten, but he knew one of the women who worked there. Both of those things had drawn him to the nightclub. Whoever was looking for him—police, BND and the mysterious sniper who had killed Schultz—wouldn't go there to find him.

Ingrid was from the old neighborhood and had been one of his sister's friends. Almost ten years ago, Ingrid had fallen on bad times and gotten in trouble with the drug scene. Her boyfriend at the time had ripped off the dealers and left Ingrid to hang in the wind. They'd focused on Ingrid, threatening to sell her to a white slavery ring to recoup part of their losses.

Ingrid had gone to Joachim's sister, and Krista had begged him to intervene. Both of them had been teens then, but Ingrid had been living well beyond her years, stepping directly into the roughest side of life.

Joachim had used Günter's connections to track down the AWOL boyfriend, brought the man back from Munich, delivered him and what were left of the drugs to the dealers.

Joachim had never found out what the dealers had done with the man, but they'd left Ingrid alone. Now he hoped that she would be willing to help him, and would be clean enough to do it. He'd called her earlier, making arrangements to borrow her car to get clear of Leipzig. He had a safe-deposit box in Berlin, as well as papers in three other names. He hoped it would be enough.

A hulking young man guarded the club door. Joachim paid the cover charge and walked through the metal detector without setting an alarm off, feeling exposed without his weapon.

Inside, the club was filled with smoke from cigarettes as well as marijuana. The music that outside had seemed too loud was now deafening. A huge mosh pit formed out in the center of the floor. Dancers threw themselves against each other with reckless abandon. The band performed on a small stage to the left.

Cocktail waitresses in skimpy clothing circulated the floor. The crowd in front of the bar was three deep, and harried bartenders kept the liquor flowing.

"Can I get you something?"

Joachim glanced around at the young waitress who stood with a server tray balanced on one hand and her other hand on her hip. She wore knee-high boots, a pullover top that emphasized her breasts and a skirt so short it barely covered her modesty.

"I'm looking for Ingrid," Joachim said.

"She's here." The waitress turned and glanced around. She pointed across the room. "There. Do you see her?"

Joachim did. He shoved a few deutsch marks into the young woman's tip glass. "Thanks."

"Anytime." The woman gave him a smile. "If you don't get any satisfaction from Ingrid, let me know."

"Sure," Joachim said. He crossed the room and took Ingrid by the elbow.

The last time Joachim had seen Ingrid, she had been blond. Tonight she had ice blue hair cut square with her shoulders. She was slim hipped and had a girlish figure that she'd used to her advantage ever since she'd been a teenager. Despite her misadventures, nothing had ever happened to her natural beauty, "either from the drugs" or from harsh dealings at the hands of others. She wore the same boots, skirt and blouse as the other servers.

She yanked her elbow from Joachim's grasp.

"Keep your hands to yourself!" Ingrid exploded angrily as she turned to face him with a bottle of beer drawn back to slam into his face. Then she saw who it was and the anger went away. She smiled a little blearily as she replaced the bottle on her serving tray. "Hey, Joachim."

"Ingrid." Joachim tried to mask his disappointment. *She's still using.* His anxiety levels rose.

"I've seen you on television," Ingrid said, passing beers

out to a table of young men. "Didn't know you'd be so famous one day."

"I don't have a lot of time," Joachim said, barely loud enough to be heard over the crowd.

Ingrid gathered the money from the young men, thanked them, then walked away with an exaggerated hip sway.

"I tried calling Krista," Ingrid said over the roar of the crowd.

Joachim didn't comment. The less Ingrid knew, the better.

"All I got was the automated answer." Ingrid stopped by the bar and told the bartender she was going to be off the floor for a moment. She took Joachim by the arm and clung to him, molding her body against his as she guided him to the rear of the club. "So?"

"So?" Joachim repeated.

She pouted. "Did you kill that guy?"

"No. If you thought that, why would you help me?"

Ingrid showed him a gamin's grin. Life had always been a game to her, not worth living without some kind of risk. She trailed a hand suggestively over his chest. "You know me, Joachim. I've always had a thing for dangerous guys."

Joachim kept silent.

"Plus, I'm Krista's friend." Ingrid wrinkled her nose. "And I owe you something for that help you gave me."

"I never said you owed me anything," Joachim said.

"I know." Ingrid laid her head against his arm. She didn't even come up to his shoulder.

Joachim looked at her and tried to handle the unexpected situation the best that he could. She ran her hands over his chest and quickly headed south, still smiling. He caught her hands in his.

"A lot of bad people are chasing me," Joachim said.

"They're not here." Ingrid tried to free her hands.

Joachim kept hold. "The thought that they're out there somewhere is…distracting."

"Another time?" Hope showed in Ingrid's peppermint-swirled eyes.

"Not tonight," Joachim agreed. *Not ever.* But he didn't say that. Even if he didn't need her help, he wouldn't have hurt her with his blanket rejection.

She laid her head against his chest for a moment, her hands still trapped in his. He felt the warmth of her against him, but more than anything he felt the clock ticking away.

Just before he could say anything, Ingrid asked, "Have you got the money?"

"Yes." Joachim stepped back from her, then reached inside his jacket and took out the ten thousand dollars he'd promised her for the car. The car wasn't worth that much, but Ingrid had quoted the price and he hadn't wanted to argue the amount.

Ingrid took the money, riffed through it, then shoved it down inside one of the knee-high boots. She smiled. "Thanks, Joachim."

"Thank you," he replied.

Pulling a key chain from her other boot, Ingrid dangled the keys from a forefinger sporting an electric blue fingernail that was long enough to rate as an edged weapon.

Joachim took the keys, then followed Ingrid through the back door.

A weak yellow light illuminated the narrow concrete stairs that led down into the alley. The pool of light barely made it out to the streetlight, leaving much of the alley cloaked in shadows.

Ingrid pointed. "The Cabrio convertible at the back."

The car was a ten-year-old, rusted-out pit. Under the streetlight, Joachim didn't know what color the vehicle had originally been or was supposed to be now. Graffiti covered the sides, all of it pertaining to industrial metal bands.

"Not exactly inconspicuous," Joachim commented.

Crossing her arms over her breasts, Ingrid said, "I don't want to live an inconspicuous life. That's just not me."

Joachim headed for the car. He was halfway there when Ingrid called out to him. He turned to face her. Something sharp bit into his leg. When he glanced down, he saw a feathered tranquilizer dart jutting from his flesh. Drugs flooded his nervous system, turning his muscles to jelly and his brain to mush. He tried to move and almost fell. Helpless, he looked back at Ingrid.

With the light behind her, she stood silhouetted on the steps. "I'm sorry," she said.

Before Joachim could respond, rubber shrieked against pavement. Three vehicles roared into the alley, filling it at once. Their headlights splashed over Joachim. He moved, but it was in slow motion. They surrounded him at once.

Athena Academy for the Advancement of Women
Outside Athens, Arizona

"Where are you going?"

Standing at the bungalow door, Elle glanced back at Sam. Her sister peered from behind the door in the other bedroom.

Elle was dressed. There was no denying that she was leaving. "Riley just got in. I thought maybe you could use some quality...*alone* time." She smirked. "Although you might want to keep it down a little. You do have neighboring bungalows, you know."

"I know." Sam smiled a little. "Are you sure you're okay?"

"I'm fine." Elle shrugged. "I slept too much this afternoon. Maybe I'll catch a movie."

"There's a theater in Athens."

Elle showed Sam the MapQuest pages she'd printed out. "Found it. And I've got a map of the city on my iPAQ." She touched the device.

Sam didn't appear reassured. "Athens isn't big and there's hardly any trouble there with Kayla Ryan on the police force. If you have any trouble—"

Holding up her cell phone, Elle said, "I'll call."

"Be careful."

Elle grinned. "You, too. I hear a lot of accidents can happen in the bedroom."

Riley's laughter, deep and rich, came from behind the door.

Sam looked a little embarrassed. "Thanks."

"No problem. I'll be back in a few hours. Maybe you'll be exhausted by then." Trying not to feel guilty, Elle left.

She walked to the jeep parked in the circular drive. Air-conditioning noises warred with crickets chirping. Leaving the top down, her hair pulled back into a ponytail, she started the jeep and drove back to the main campus area, then down the access road to Script Pass.

Elle turned right on Olympus Road and headed south into Athens. The town was small and compact, another small pool of community formed by the ever-expanding Glendale/Phoenix metro area. Although part of the larger city, Athens maintained its own police, fire and rescue services, which were subsidized from larger entities.

Traffic was heavy, mostly teens out looking for something to do and packing the fast-food and pizza chains.

Elle pulled into the parking area of a convenience store and went inside. A tall twentysomething clerk was hitting on a young woman, both of them enjoying the flirting.

A sign over a back hallway announced the phones and bathrooms.

Interrupting the clerk, Elle purchased a pre-paid phone card, then retreated to the bank of pay phones. She punched in the prepaid number, then dialed the number of the Russian consulate in New York City. When the call was answered, she spoke a password that got her directly into the intelligence service.

"You are not on a secure line," a pleasant male voice said.

"I know," Elle responded. That meant that anything she said could be intercepted. She assumed that it would be. "This is important."

"Of course. How may I assist you?"

Elle gave three more passwords to each cutout along the line. The United States government's spy network would be hard-pressed to keep up with the phone connection as it split and split again.

In less than four minutes, Fyodor Petrenko was on the line.

"We are on an unprotected line," he said gently when he answered.

"Yes." Elle hesitated.

"What is wrong?" Concern sounded in her adoptive father's voice.

"I have come across some information that is disturbing."

"What?"

"Lenin's Lullaby," Elle said. "Men named Klaus Stryker and Alexi Zemanov." She listened to her father breathe in silence for a time.

"We need to speak."

"I agree. Arnaud Beck is part of this, but that was never mentioned when we spoke."

"That was my choice. Perhaps I was mistaken. Can you get away?"

The question sounded innocuous, but Elle knew it was intended to be taken literally. "Of course."

"Then do so. Let me know where to meet you."

"I will."

"Take care of yourself," her father said. "The affair you're looking into has many old and dangerous twists. A number of people and agencies wouldn't want any of this to come to light."

"I understand."

The click of the connection breaking sounded grim and final. Elle held the receiver for a moment, then carefully cradled it. Getting out of the United States was going to be hard. Since 9-11, security had tightened up to the point that it was almost impossible to do anything without someone knowing. Her saving grace was that she wasn't trying to hide anything and wasn't a fugitive.

Yet...

When she walked back out to the jeep, Elle found an Athens police car had pulled in behind her, blocking her way.

A uniformed female officer stood with crossed arms and a hip leaning on the car. Her dark brunette hair was long and pulled back. American Indian heritage showed in her honey complexion, high cheekbones and warm brown eyes. Her uniform was neat and carefully pressed. Lieutenant's bars shone on her collar. She wore a pistol high on her hip.

Her name was Kayla Ryan. Elle knew her from the description Sam had given. Kayla was one of the Cassandras, one of the young women that Sam had grown up with. After graduating from college, Kayla had returned to Athens to be a police officer and to raise her daughter, Jasmine, who was now thirteen and in attendance at Athena Academy.

"Hello, lieutenant." Elle stopped out of arm's reach.

Kayla's smile faded, and Elle noticed the wariness in the

woman's eyes. "Hi. You're not Sam, so you must be Elle. There's nothing wrong. I just saw the Athena jeep and decided to stop to see who had come into town. I graduated from Athena. My name is—"

"Kayla Ryan," Elle said. "Yes. Sam has told me a lot about you."

"I see." Kayla shook her head. "You look just like her."

"I get that a lot."

Kayla laughed. "I'll bet you do. I mean, I'd heard the two of you were identical, but I hadn't known *how* identical until tonight."

"She would love to see you."

"I'm planning to stop by tomorrow. I usually see Jazz on my days off. That's my daughter. She's at the Academy now."

"Make sure it's not too early," Elle suggested. "When I left her, Riley had just gotten in."

"Oh."

"Big *oh*," Elle said. "Sometimes it's embarrassing hanging around the two of them. I thought maybe I could make myself scarce for a while."

"I understand."

"Sam mentioned there was a club where I could get a drink."

"There's no shortage of them," Kayla agreed. "What were you looking for?"

"Something relaxed but safe. Live music if possible." Live music generally meant a larger crowd.

"You might try Bogart's over on Saguaro," Kayla suggested. "They've got live music. Tonight they're featuring a singer called Lauren Holly. She's a recent graduate of Athena Academy trying to make a go of her musical career. She's got a big voice and does a lot of torch singer and jazz tunes." She added directions.

"Sounds good. I may try that."

Elle clambered back into the jeep and pulled out of the parking lot after Kayla. The police car turned left but Elle turned right, following the directions she'd been given. She breathed deeply, knowing that next time she and Kayla met, the policewoman would likely not be so friendly.

When she reached Bogart's, Elle found the parking lot full. The club was somber and dark, trusting reputation and not neon to bring in the clientele. A simple marquee advertised Lauren Holly.

After making sure there were no Athens PD cars around, Elle got out of the jeep, walked through the lines of cars, found an older Mercedes and used a Swiss Army knife to break into it. In less than five minutes, she'd hot-wired the car and driven off the lot.

In less than an hour, she was at the airport and on the first available flight.

Chapter 15

Sunbright Cleaners
Leipzig, Germany

"Wake up, Joachim. Come on now. I don't have all night."

Blinking, Joachim struggled through layers of pain-filled fog. Fear was a distant throb somewhere deep inside him, but he knew he should pay attention to it. Instead, he thought he'd go back to sleep.

"Get his attention," a rough voice said.

Burning agony suddenly flooded Joachim's face. It took him a moment to realize he'd been hit. The coppery taste of blood filled his mouth. He forced open his eyes.

Someone had tied him to a chair. His hands were numb behind him.

"Joachim," Günter called.

Focusing on the hulking figure in front of him, Joachim

shook his head in an effort to wake up more. That was a mistake. His skull suddenly felt as if it were going to splinter.

After a moment, Joachim realized where they were. Although he hadn't been there often, there was no way he could forget the basement of Sunbright Cleaners. The Laundromat was one of Günter's legitimate businesses. It also had open access to Leipzig's sewers. The new pollution standards hadn't caught up to the entire city. Joachim had been there the night Günter had taken an ax to an ex-lover and tossed her body into the sewer.

The basement air was stale and dank with mold. The stench of detergents and bleach clung to the walls. During the day, when the big industrial-size machines grinded and whirled, conversation was almost impossible. On the plus side, no one could hear screams or cries for help, or the gunshots that ended, either.

"Are you awake this time?" Günter demanded. He sat in a straight-backed wooden chair. He looked pallid in the weak fluorescent light.

"Yes." Joachim's tongue was dry and thick. Warm blood ran down his chin.

"Good. Because we've got some things to discuss." Günter leaned forward. His cigar glowed violent orange, then he breathed out a plume of blue-gray smoke that coiled against Joachim's face. "Why did you sell me out?"

"You gave me no choice," Joachim said.

"Me?" Günter's eyes widened in surprise. "What the hell did I do?"

"You sent me after Leitner last year."

"Jacob Leitner stole from me." The man had been an accountant for some of Günter's enterprises. During his tenure, he'd stolen over ten million dollars. Günter had caught the man a step after he was gone. Joachim had tracked him down before he could get out of Berlin.

"Leitner was one of theirs," Joachim said. "He belonged to the BND."

"An agent?"

"An informant."

"Like you." Günter sneered.

"The BND squeezed me," Joachim said, "because you didn't catch your mistake soon enough. They saw me kill Leitner."

At the time, though, Joachim had been acting in self-defense. Leitner had resisted Joachim's efforts to take him alive and had pulled a pistol he'd never before carried.

"You could have come to me," Günter said.

"And gone down with you?" Joachim shook his head and regretted it.

"Law enforcement agencies have been after me for over twenty years," Günter said defiantly. "They haven't put me down yet."

"They will. You're too big to simply slip away. You've gotten more greedy than you should have."

Günter backhanded Joachim, rocking his head back on his shoulders.

"I won't tolerate disrespect," Günter said when Joachim's head stopped reeling.

Joachim said nothing.

"If the police or the BND could have gotten me," Günter stated proudly, "they would have done it a long time ago. Nothing sticks to me. They can take down some of my operations, sure, but they can't touch me." He puffed on the cigar. "If you had come to me, Joachim, I could have gotten them off you as well."

Quietly, Joachim thought about all the violence and

killing he'd done at Günter's instruction. Joachim had never killed an innocent man or woman. He hadn't wanted the BND off him; he'd wanted a way out and away from Günter that would leave his family protected. The only way to do that was to be part of a successful effort to bring Günter down.

"Ah well, it's too late for that, isn't it?" Günter asked. "Your friends at the BND no longer trust you without your sponsor standing for you."

Realization flashed into Joachim's mind. "*You* killed Schultz."

Bringing up his leg to rest on top of the other, Günter rounded his cigar ash on his heel. "I had him killed, yes. I also knew you would be blamed. In case there was any doubt, I had informants advance the theory that you set Schultz up for the assassination. After all, your message was found on his answering service."

"Why didn't you kill me?"

"Because," Günter said, smiling, "I still have a use for you. I only needed to sever your connections to the BND." He paused. "I have."

Joachim stared into the eyes of the man who had been like a father to him. He had no doubt that Günter would kill him if he chose to.

"Amsterdam cost me business," Günter said. "The woman has evidently elected to pull back her offer. However, I know what she wants. You can't stay alive in a business like mine and not learn things."

Joachim waited. Günter had a use for him. As long as that was true, he would live. Staying alive meant he had time to think and plan. Günter was not infallible.

"She wanted Tuenis Meijer because of his connection to a blackmailer. A person whom I had believed to be a myth.

The woman I'm dealing with wants Beck's employer, a man this blackmailer is supposed to be pressuring."

"Why?" Joachim asked.

"According to the myth, this blackmailer has been quietly spinning devious little webs for years, snaring and releasing information that has built and toppled careers and kingpins. All for a price." Günter lifted an eyebrow. "A list like that would be worth millions. Maybe billions. On regular installment plans. It would make a nice retirement plan in exchange for the business you are going to cost me." He smiled. "That's worth killing for."

Joachim waited quietly, not daring to think a minute into the future.

"I have to admit, until I started dealing with the woman and found out all the resources she had, I hadn't believed the blackmail myth, either." Günter shook his head. "No one could possibly have the amount of information the blackmailer is supposed to have." He took a drag on his cigar and smiled. "Remember the pretty blonde you ran into in Amsterdam who was searching for Tuenis Meijer?"

Joachim's thoughts flew to Elle. Staring death in the face, he couldn't help feeling angry and frustrated that they'd never see each other again.

"I identified her through an associate," Günter said. "She was part of a CIA task force that took down Konrad Steiner."

Joachim remembered that. For a time Günter had been concerned the fallout from that operation would affect him. Günter had maintained a few dealings with Steiner.

"Her name is Samantha St. John," Günter continued.

Sam, Joachim thought.

"I assume the other woman you mentioned was her

sister," Günter said. "St. John was a graduate of Athena Academy for the Advancement of Women. Are you familiar with it?"

"No," Joachim replied truthfully.

Günter nodded. "Neither was I. However, it appears Tuenis Meijer was somehow connected to Marion Gracelyn. Have you heard of her?"

Joachim shook his head automatically. The pain wasn't as severe this time.

"She was a United States senator," Günter said, "and she was largely responsible for the creation of the Athena Academy. I'm willing to wager that St. John knew Marion Gracelyn."

You've been busy. Joachim was amazed. Günter had put considerable time and money into digging up information. But, of course, he was looking for a big payoff.

"Gracelyn was murdered years ago," Günter said. "Her murderer was only recently caught, but her name came up in connection with the blackmailer."

"The senator was being blackmailed by this mythical person?"

"According to the information I've received, her name was on the list."

"Why was St. John after Meijer?"

Günter grinned. "Because Meijer supposedly worked with the blackmailer."

Joachim was quiet, trying to put it all together in his head despite the painful throbs that kept erupting. "The woman you were talking to is looking for this mythical blackmailer?"

"I believe so."

"You intend to find out the identity of the blackmailer and give it to her."

Günter nodded, smiling like a teacher pleased with a

prized pupil. "Or, if I'm able, use the information myself to establish an alternate revenue stream. Your compliance with the BND is going to cost me. I don't know how much yet, so I choose to be prepared. I'm already moving assets out of the country."

"What do you want me to do?"

"Find Beck. Someone employed him to kill Meijer. When you find Beck, I want you to find his employer. Once we have him, we can find out the identity of the person blackmailing him."

"Perhaps he doesn't know."

"And perhaps Beck will know the blackmailer's name and you won't have to go any further than that."

Joachim thought about that, realizing it was true. Whoever employed Beck trusted him. Maybe the employer had told Beck the identity of the blackmailer.

"Don't think that you can run after I release you," Günter cautioned. His eyes took on a hard, cold gleam. "I won't go after you, Joachim. I'll go after your family. And I'll get them. You can't take them far enough or fast enough." He paused. "I'll get you when you come for me, when you have no other reason to live."

Sickness twisted through Joachim's stomach.

"Do we have an understanding?" Günter asked.

"Yes," Joachim answered, knowing he had no choice.

"Good." Günter stood. "These men have been given instructions to release you after I'm gone. They'll give you papers under another name and safe passage to Prague. After that, you're on your own."

"Where do I find Beck?" Joachim asked.

"Greece."

"What makes you think Beck is there?"

"Because I know Beck," Günter said. "From the old

days. We've got a score to settle. Both of us have stayed away from it, but now it's time. He's often at Mykonos Town on the island of Mykonos."

"How do you know he's there?"

Günter winked but there was no mirth in the effort. "Maybe you pulled the wool over my eyes for a while, kiddo, but I know a lot more than you do. I know Beck. He has certain…'appetites' that haven't changed. Once you know a man's appetites, you know the man." He fixed Joachim with his cold, harsh gaze. "I know you, too, Joachim. You've done everything for your family. You can't run out on them. And if you do, I'll kill them. I know that about you, and you know that about me."

Knowing Günter wouldn't leave until he admitted it, Joachim said, "Yes. I do."

"Then we have an agreement. Stay in touch. You'll be given numbers." Günter turned and walked up the stairs leading to the first floor. "Wait an hour. Then get him to Prague and set him free." He paused at the door and looked back. "Joachim, don't let me down. Don't let your family down. We're all depending on you."

Joachim sat quietly in the chair. He struggled to keep a grip on the fear that raged through him, but it was a losing battle. The clock was working against him. He needed to be out and running, hunting down Beck.

Breathing in, Joachim centered himself and held on.

Phoenix Sky Harbor International Airport
Phoenix, Arizona

Until she saw the Athens Police Department patrol car in the parking lot, Sam kept hoping that everything she'd learned in the past two hours had been a bad dream.

"There," Riley said, pointing. He sat in the Athena jeep's passenger's seat.

"I see it," Sam snapped, cutting the wheel to drive toward the cruiser.

That morning Sam had gotten up and found out Elle hadn't come home.

Sam pulled the jeep to a halt behind the cruiser. She released a pent-up breath. "I'm sorry," she apologized. "This isn't your fault."

"No prob," Riley said.

Gripping the steering wheel in both hands, Sam wanted to bang her head against it. "This is my fault."

Riley dropped a big hand across Sam's shoulder. Normally his touch would have been welcome. Even after an all-night session like last night. Most of the time, Sam was pleased and surprised to discover that she never grew tired of his touch.

Now she shrugged his hand off. "Don't," she said.

"This isn't your fault."

"I should have been there for her."

"You were."

"I wasn't last night." Sam felt confusion looping through her stomach like razor wire.

"She chose to go alone," Riley said.

"We weren't…exactly open to company. She was being polite."

"No." Riley talked calmly. "She'd already made up her mind to leave."

Sam looked at him. "Why do you say that?"

"Because she left."

Anger sparked inside Sam. Sometimes the calm, self-assured way Riley handled things annoyed her. On other days, like now, the annoyance rose to honest irritation. *Riley McLane does not know everything.*

"If she was planning on leaving, she would have taken her things," Sam insisted.

"If she'd taken her things, don't you think that might have been a tip-off to you? Not taking her things was just proof that you weren't supposed to know."

Sam ground her teeth. He was right. This was one of those instances when she hated that.

Riley sighed. "To give you—and her—the benefit of the doubt, maybe she didn't plan on leaving last night."

"What do you mean?"

"Maybe she was told after the fact. While she was making the phone call to Russia."

Sam stared at the police cruiser. The officer watching over the Mercedes Elle was suspected of stealing from Bogart's had turned his attention to Riley and Sam's Athena jeep. He clicked the walkie-talkie clipped onto his shoulder and spoke briefly.

They knew about the phone call to the Russian embassy because Allison had managed to pull the phone records. After Kayla had mentioned that she'd seen Elle at the convenience store, checking the outgoing calls had been common sense.

Elle left last night so she could use the phone, Sam knew. *She called to check in, and to get orders.* Seated quietly behind the jeep's steering wheel, Sam wanted to scream. She forced herself to be calm.

"She's all right," Riley said.

"How do you know that?" Sam demanded.

"Because I've seen her in action. Elle's good. One of the best field agents I've ever worked with."

"You only worked with her once." That had been on the joint operation to save Sam from the Cipher.

"Once is all it takes sometimes," Riley replied. "And

I've seen her files. She's one of the best a lot of people have ever seen and/or worked with. If something happened to her, a lot of evidence would have been left behind."

Sam took a little solace from that. Riley wouldn't offer her platitudes. He knew better than that. "Then where has she gone?"

Riley shifted uncomfortably in the seat.

Watching him, Sam knew how much she loved him. She felt it resonate through her. Over the past year, the emotion had gotten so big it seemed to fill her to bursting. She couldn't remember how it had felt not to love him. And if that love were ever taken away, how much of her would be left? That scared her.

Don't go there, Sam told herself. *Elle leaving so unexpectedly has triggered that fear in you. That's all. You're just rewinding those old tapes from all those foster homes. Focus on what is in front of you. Deal with that.* She worked to concentrate on what Riley was saying.

"—went wherever they told her to," Riley told Sam.

"But where would they send her?" Sam persisted.

"I don't know."

"Why send her now?"

"Something could have come up that doesn't have anything to do with this. Or with you."

Sam thought about that for a moment, then shook her head. "No. If that had happened, she'd have said goodbye." She paused. "She left because of something that happened here."

"Elle didn't know about the nerve toxin until she got here?"

Sam shook her head.

"Lenin's Lullaby never surfaced," Riley said. "The Agency thought maybe it was all blue smoke and mirrors.

A rumor without substance. Maybe Russian intelligence felt the same way."

"My parents were killed because of that nerve toxin." Sam kept her voice flat.

"Maybe they were killed because it never existed," Riley said. "You've got to remember the time, Sam. Russia was in turmoil. The whole country was about to fall apart. The cold war had pressed the Communist government past its financial ability to keep up. The Agency was following up on Lenin's Lullaby, trying to find it, but what if your parents were just playing a part?"

"Creating a diversion?"

"Dividing manpower out in the field is always a chief directive when you're wanting to find out what the opposition is up to. If you run an operation thin, it gets ragged, more exposed."

"But why were my parents killed?"

"It could have been revenge. Maybe it was a scam run by Russian intelligence. Maybe this guy Stryker had a buyer who fronted half the money. Things like that have happened."

"Then why would the SVR call Elle in?"

"I don't have a clue, Sam," Riley admitted.

Dissatisfied, Sam got out of the jeep and met the uniformed police officer.

"This is a restricted area, ma'am," the policeman said.

Sam flipped out her CIA ID. "Yes," she agreed, "it is."

He took in the ID behind his mirrored sunglasses. "Agent St. John," he said, "until I hear otherwise from the chief, this is our crime scene."

Before Sam's anger got away from her, Kayla Ryan drove up in a cruiser. She wore her uniform and sunglasses. As she got out of her car, she took in the situation at a glance.

"Stand down, Tony," Kayla said.

"Yes, ma'am. The CSIs are on their way over."

"I heard." Kayla pulled out a pad and briefly consulted her notes as she peered as the Mercedes's license plate. "This is the stolen vehicle." She looked at Sam. "Your sister as good at the spy biz as you?"

"Yes," Sam said.

"Then the CSI team is going to be wasted effort."

"Bet on it," Riley said.

"On the way over, I checked with the airport. Elle secured passage on a British Airways flight under her name early this morning. She was gone shortly after midnight. At the moment, she's somewhere over the Atlantic Ocean."

"Even if we could convince the British government to detain her, the Russian embassy in London would have her free before we arrived there," Riley said. "Even if we found enough proof to make the theft of the car stick, which I doubt."

Kayla studied them. "Do you know why she left in the middle of the night?"

Meeting her friend's gaze, Sam crossed her arms over her breasts. "Did you just happen to come by the convenience store when she was there last night?"

"No," Kayla answered without hesitation. "The campus security department called me to let me know that you or Elle had left the school. With Riley in town, I guessed it was Elle."

"You were following her?" Sam couldn't believe it.

Kayla shook her head. "If I'd been following her, I'd have seen her boost the car at Bogart's. I just wanted to make contact."

"To let her know she was being watched?"

Kayla didn't flinch from Sam's anger. "Yes."

"Why?"

"Allison and Alex—all of us—felt it would be better that way. Just a reminder that she wasn't on her home turf."

Sam didn't know what to say.

"We didn't know you were bringing her, Sam," Kayla said. "The investigation surrounding Marion Gracelyn's death, the blackmail list, this is scary stuff. You haven't seen the names on that list Marion compiled. If it's all true, and Alex and Allison believe it is, some major power brokers in the political arena as well as movers and shakers on Wall Street are going to be affected."

"You don't trust Elle," Sam said.

"We don't know her," Kayla said gently. "*You* don't know her. You're only now getting to."

"She's my sister."

"She's a Russian agent."

Sam sighed and nodded to concede Kayla's point. A jet screamed by overhead. The vibration of the big engines shook the concrete beneath Sam's feet. She felt exhausted, physically and emotionally, but those things were old companions. She knew how to deal with them. *Just shut down,* she told herself. *Put up the walls till you get a handle on things.*

Unfortunately, all the programming she'd provided herself with as defensive skills no longer helped. In the past she'd been able to contain her emotions. There had only been her to worry about. Her life now was more complicated. She had Elle to worry about. And Riley. And the Cassandras. All of them—all of the people she cared about so much that she couldn't just turn those feelings off—seemed to be working at cross-purposes.

Riley stepped over to her and put his hands on her shoulders. "Sam, Elle didn't leave because she felt like no one trusted her. The trust issue was a given and she's pro enough to know that. She left because she had a job to do."

Automatically, Sam pulled her hands together and drove

them upward, breaking out of Riley's gentle hold. "Don't," she rasped. "Just…don't. I need to think."

Hurt showed in Riley's eyes. He pulled his hands back and folded them under his arms. His mouth turned flat and hard.

Without a word, Sam turned and walked back to the jeep. She crawled behind the wheel and drove away. Neither Kayla nor Riley made an effort to stop her.

As she drove, Sam's thoughts whirled. She didn't know what she was going to do. The threat of Lenin's Lullaby hung in her mind. Someone would be sent after Elle, and Sam had the feeling that Riley would be involved with that. He knew her and he sometimes served as mission control.

Elle wouldn't have just left on a whim because her feelings were hurt. She'd have stayed and fought. That was what she was about. Sam would have left as long as she'd had a way out of the confrontation and no reason to stay. She knew that was one of the differences between them.

So Elle's departure meant what? That someone had called her into action. But why would the SVR do that? Because Lenin's Lullaby was real? Because after twenty years it was still out there?

No matter how Sam chased the possibilities, she kept coming back to the same conclusion. Lenin's Lullaby, in whatever form, had been real and still existed as a threat, and Russia wanted it cleaned up.

And Elle was stepping into the line of fire.

Old Arbat
Moscow, Russia

Elle walked through the early afternoon rain along Ulitsa Arabat and watched the street musicians and artists gathered in front of tiny boutiques, small antique shops and souvenir places that catered to the Western trade.

The rain was gentle and cold, a Russian rain that came upon the city without warning. Dark clouds shifted and drifted over the onion-domed buildings in the center of the metro area.

Fatigue ate into Elle's body. For the last twenty-three hours she had been on planes. From Britain she had flown to Paris, then Munich, hopscotched to Prague and finally made the jump into Moscow along Eastern Europe. She'd catnapped on the flights, but her thoughts were never far from Sam. Her sister would be confused and hurt by the unexplained disappearance.

"Umbrellas," a young man called out from a pushcart loaded with umbrellas and rainwear. He called out his wares in Russian and English. "Umbrellas for sale or rent."

Elle smiled at the young man, thinking of how capitalist Russia had turned just during her lifetime.

The young man smiled back at Elle. "For you," he said in English, "I will make a special price."

"No," Elle said. "Thank you anyway."

"But a lovely girl like yourself shouldn't be out in the rain."

"I love the rain," Elle responded in Russian. She always had. Even as a little girl she'd refused to come in just because it was raining.

"I'm sorry," the man replied, putting a hand over his heart. "I'd thought you were American."

"No," Elle said. *I'm Russian, and I'm proud of that.*

Only a short distance ahead, standing in front of a small bistro and holding an umbrella over his head, Fyodor Petrenko waited for her.

Her father wore a black trench coat over a plain blue suit.

Despite the rain, the creases in his pants remained sharp. His face looked like a hatchet, angular and sharp, blunted a little by the thin iron gray beard and mustache. He was trim and neat, only a few inches taller than Elle, not a man who would draw attention in a crowd. Crow's-feet stood out in the deep olive complexion, but it was his eyes that drew people in. They were large and dark, brimming with feelings and passion.

He dropped his cigarette to the wet sidewalk and crushed it out underfoot. "Elle," he greeted.

"Hello, Father." Despite her father's reluctance for public displays of affection, Elle hugged him tightly. There was never a shortage of hugs in the Petrenko house, though. After a moment, he wrapped his free arm around her and hugged her fiercely.

"Are you well?" he asked as she stepped back. Concern fired his eyes.

"I am."

"I know they sell umbrellas at the airport."

"I wanted to walk in the rain."

He shook his head. "You will never change."

"I get that from you, you know. That desire to have everything in its place, to do everything a certain way."

"You keep talking like that and your nose will grow."

Elle laughed. It felt good to be back home. *Pinocchio* had been her favorite movie as a child. The Petrenko children had worn out several black market VHS tapes her father had gotten over the years.

"You love excitement and adventure," her father said, "and the promise of new experiences."

"I do," Elle admitted.

"I was told you had no trouble with your flights."

"You had someone watching?" That surprised her. She had seen no SVR agents.

Her father shrugged and smiled a little. "But of course. For all I knew, the CIA might try to spirit you away."

"They didn't, but I think they came close in Munich." Those Elle had seen, all of them courtesy of Riley McLane, she felt certain.

He nodded. "Not close enough. The agents I had there were set to intervene, but they didn't have to."

"I was trained by one of the best at evading a tail."

"Yes, you were." Her father gestured with the umbrella. "Walk with me."

Elle stood close to her father, accepting the presence of the umbrella though she longed to be free. "Lenin's Lullaby was a real nerve toxin?" she asked.

"It appears so. At least, that is what I have been told this time."

"Were Boris and Anya involved with it?"

"They were."

"In what capacity?"

Her father hesitated. He did that, she knew, when he had to contemplate an answer he truly did not care for.

"You did not ask me to come all this way to keep the truth from me," Elle said.

"No. Of course not." He sighed, and it was a Russian sigh, filled with generations of perseverance and a quiet hope that simply would not die. "Your parents were working as double agents for Britain."

"I know that." She hadn't learned that for a long time, though.

"Many of my colleagues—*our* colleagues," he corrected himself, "fault them for that."

"You have never said what you felt," Elle said.

Her father shrugged. "There were a few hard feelings at first, after I found out, but they were dead by then and I had recovered you. Now that I am older, I truly believe they did not see the change coming that would render Russia different. None of us did."

Elle walked quietly with her father, easily matching his long stride.

"I think they only wanted what was best for you and Natasha."

"Her name is Samantha," Elle put in.

"Of course. But I only knew her as Natasha. I was a friend to both your parents. I knew the two of you as babies."

"What happened with Lenin's Lullaby?"

He glanced up at the sky, toward the Kremlin. "In those days, the Communist government believed they had to keep the United States on a short leash. Korea remains an issue, but Vietnam was not so long ago. The cold war was very vicious. Russia did not have the resources or technology that the Americans did. They invented new and better ways to kill and arm their troops in the field. Also, the Communist leaders felt certain that the United States was continuing work on bioweapons as well. In politics, Elle, everybody lies. It's just a matter of to what degree. To whom. And for what reasons."

Elle took her father's arm as they walked.

"Lenin's Lullaby was concocted, as so many of the other nerve agents were, in a small lab under exacting conditions," he said.

"Outside Odessa."

"Yes. Boris and Anya discovered this, and the fact that the American Central Intelligence Agency was aware of the lab."

"The CIA was involved?"

He nodded. "They felt the British were dragging their feet about getting Boris and Anya out of the country. And, in truth, MI-6 was. The Russians began a quiet investigation into their background, one that would have certainly proven them guilty of treason to our country."

"You've never mentioned this."

"It wouldn't have made any difference in your life."

Elle accepted that. The Petrenko parents had only told their children what they had needed to know. Her father had only told them their mother was ill when they had exhausted all medical help and the symptoms were becoming apparent. They hadn't wanted any of their children to agonize with them.

"Boris made a deal with the CIA to get all of you out of Russia," her father went on. "He was going to force the hand of the British."

"The CIA wanted Lenin's Lullaby."

"Exactly. Boris and Anya gained the confidence of Alexi Zemanov. He was the director of the bioweapon lab in Odessa. Unfortunately, Zemanov had made an agreement with a *Stasi* agent named—"

"Klaus Stryker." Elle interrupted.

Nodding, her father said, "The American intelligence agencies know more than we gave them credit for."

"Sam's friends at Athena do," Elle acknowledged. "But that was only because of the files they uncovered." Quickly, she outlined the story she had of the investigation into Marion Gracelyn's murder and the resulting surprise blackmail history.

"Fascinating," her father said when she had finished. "Madame Web, do you think?"

"The e-mails were signed with the English letter *A*."

"No mention of anything beginning with that letter exists in our files. You're familiar with the Madame Web files?"

"I am."

Her father shook his head. "Such a treasure trove of knowledge that woman must have. Millionaires, billionaires, politicians, religious leaders. If everything is true about her, she possibly has enough secrets to upset the balance of power in some nations."

"What happened to Lenin's Lullaby?" Elle asked.

"Zemanov agreed to sell samples of Lenin's Lullaby as well as the chemical formula to the *Stasi* agent, Klaus Stryker."

"Why would Stryker want it?"

"It was believed that he was merely acting as an agent for someone else."

"Who?"

Her father shook his head. "No one ever had a clue. It died when Stryker was killed."

"How did Sam and I get separated?"

"Your parents put you with two different families. Possibly because if anyone started looking for the two of you, they would be looking for twin girls. After the explosion, the family that had you turned you over to me." His voice turned tight and grew hoarse. "I couldn't believe you were still alive. Seeing the remains of that explosion that night, I'd held out no hope. If you'd been with Boris and Anya—" He didn't finish the possibility.

"What about the family Sam was with?"

"We found them by going through your parents' lists of contacts and friends. Three days later. It wasn't so much that we went to them after discovering them, but because they were murdered."

"Murdered?" The announcement started Elle. Neither she nor Sam had known anything about this.

"They were," her father said gravely. "The mother and father, and three of the children."

"Why?"

"To this day, no one knows."

"How did Sam end up in America?"

He shook his head. "Again, Elle, those are questions I can't answer."

They walked on in silence. The rain thinned out to mist, then finally went away altogether and allowed the sun to shine. The humidity soaked into Elle's skin and thickened the air.

"Why did you ask me to come here?" she asked.

"Because Lenin's Lullaby must be found," her father answered. "We are going—as the Americans seem so fond of saying—outside the box on this one. Intelligence wants you to find Lenin's Lullaby and control the situation."

"How? Everyone connected with the investigation is dead or has disappeared. Stryker. My parents. Zemanov. I don't know where to find Arnaud Beck."

"Beck is a hard man to locate. We have another avenue for you to pursue." Her father looked at her. "We know where Alexi Zemanov is. You will begin with him."

Elle stopped, bringing her father to a halt. "What do you think I should do?"

Sighing, he folded his umbrella and hung it from his arm. "The CIA is searching for Lenin's Lullaby."

Meaning Sam is looking, too, Elle realized. And if Sam were looking, she would be in the middle of the action. Without her. Elle knew she didn't truly have a choice.

"I think," her father said, "that you should be careful." He leaned over and kissed her forehead. "Very, *very* careful."

Chapter 16

Criminal Detention Center
Siberia, Russia

Everyone in Russia talked about being shipped off to the Siberian wasteland. From the stories most people told, they each had someone in the family or a friend who knew someone who had been exiled to Siberia under the Communist leaders and had never come back.

To Elle's way of thinking, tainted by her exposure to Western culture, it was Russia's own brand of six degrees of separation from Kevin Bacon.

Siberia was still used as a threat in some circles, but not nearly so much as Chernobyl. Elle had never seen Siberia, but she had been to Chernobyl chasing after black marketers with international connections. Chernobyl was bleak and filled with death, burnt and twisted buildings and landscape, and wildlife filled with tumors and gross mutations. She'd had to wear a radiation counter the whole time she'd been there.

The military helicopter cleaving the wind above the detention center struggled to its destination. Elle didn't like flying in Russian military vehicles because they had a tendency to drop from the sky. Maintaining the army, even after the acknowledgement of capitalism, was no easy task. Government hadn't gotten any richer for doing away with Communism, though crime now paid very well.

The detention center sat exposed on a somewhat flat surface amid the mountains and crags. Men and women transported to the detention center were sent there to be forgotten until they died or killed each other.

The compound was a rough rectangle, enclosed by high fences topped with looping lengths of razor wire. Snow covered most of the ground, but it was so cold the precipitation just piled up and didn't stick. Blotches of hard gray rock showed through the white mantle.

The pilot took the helicopter down, landing at a partially concealed helipad west of the small parking lot that contained trucks and jeeps with four-wheel drive. The landing was bumpy as the crosswinds caught them.

A waiting jeep pulled next to the helicopter as Elle stepped out. Dressed in a greatcoat that allowed the tan and red colors of the Russian military to be seen, the driver got out of the vehicle and stood at attention. He carried an AK-47 on his shoulder.

The passenger clambered out as well. He was smooth shaven and wore sunglasses. "Agent Petrenko?"

"Yes," Elle answered, going forward.

"I am Colonel Lutikov." The colonel tucked his chin briefly. "I am commanding officer at the detention center."

"I appreciate the personal attention, Colonel," Elle said, "but I assure you it wasn't necessary."

"It's my pleasure." Lutikov gestured to the passenger's seat. "You see, we don't get many visitors up here."

Elle sat in the passenger's seat and closed the door, grateful that she was out of the wind. The few short minutes she was exposed to the unforgiving cold had left her feeling frozen to the bone.

The colonel gestured to the driver, assigning him to the back while sliding behind the steering wheel. Without a word, the driver climbed onto the rear deck and hunkered down. Almost nonchalantly, the colonel put the jeep into gear and eased out on the clutch. He drove confidently over the hard-packed ice.

"No one mentioned who you were here to see," Lutikov said.

"They were given instructions not to."

"Yes. But sooner or later, I will know. Curiosity won't kill me, but I will admit to some discomfort."

Elle laughed. "Alexi Zemanov."

A frown tightened Lutikov's face. "You were told that he hasn't spoken to anyone in twenty years, weren't you?"

"He will speak to me," Elle replied.

The colonel regarded her with heightened interest. "Really? I don't even know why he's here."

"I'm afraid," Elle said, "that's something you'll have to remain curious about."

Mykonos Town
The Cyclades Islands, Greece

Sweltering afternoon heat baked into the harbor and made the brine and the fish odors stronger. In the shaded comfort of the *taverna* overlooking the fishing and tourist boats tied up in the docks, Joachim sat at a table and drank a bottle of flavored water. Beads of sweat ran down the bottle and dampened the coaster.

Colorful plastic orange lobsters, purple squids, pink fish and green crabs lay in nets hanging from the ceiling. A swordfish hung on one wall over a small saltwater aquarium that held a seahorse, a few fish and a deep-sea diver bubbler. That was the only effort the *taverna* made at décor. An awning blocked some of the afternoon sun. The small, round bar occupied the center of the room.

Tourists walked along the harbor, ducking into the small restaurants and curio shops. Taxi boats plied their trade, calling out to passersby and offering their services. Fishermen ignored the tourists who snapped their pictures, working on their nets and boats now that their catch had been put away. The fishing boats put out into the Aegean Sea hours before dawn to cast their nets for red mullet, Dover sole, prawns, red sea bream, swordfish and baby squid.

Joachim stared out at the sea. For three days, since his arrival from Prague, he'd kept watch over the harbor. Greece consisted of one major land mass and fifty-six islands. According to Günter, Arnaud Beck lived in seclusion on one of them. But Beck favored the nightlife in Mykonos Town, which offered a mixture of locals as well as tourists from around the world.

The trick in hunting a man was in knowing where to look and what to look for. Günter had known about Beck's proclivities regarding young women. Beck didn't buy them because he preferred to win them over with charm and wealth. Mykonos, known for its nightlife, was the obvious place to set up watch.

"Would you care for another, sir?"

Glancing up at the server, Joachim nodded. She took the empty bottle away and brought a fresh one. She was young and pretty, her black hair a mass of wild ringlets that tumbled nearly to her waist, and she liked to flirt.

Joachim paid her for the water and added a generous tip.

She stood with a hand on her slim hip, poised and confident. "You spend a lot of time looking out that window or one like it." Her English only carried a light accent.

"Does my sitting here bother you?"

"No. It makes me...curious."

Joachim just smiled at her.

"What are you watching for?" she asked.

"I don't know. Should I be watching for anything?"

A frown knitted her dark eyebrows. "Where are you from?"

"Germany." Joachim didn't hesitate about answering. Beck would have no reason to worry about anyone coming from Germany.

"I've never been to Germany."

"I've never before been to Greece."

"Do you like it?"

"Yes."

"There is much to do and see."

"So I've been told." Joachim sipped the flavored water.

She gazed at him again, taking in the lightweight khaki pants, the boaters and the sea green silk shirt. He looked young and successful and bored, an image he'd deliberately cultivated. The last few days' exposure to the sun left him reddened.

"My name is Adriana." She offered her hand.

"Joachim." It was a common enough name. He took her hand.

"Do you like to party, Joachim?"

"If it's a good one."

Mykonos Town was known for its parties. The Greek mainland had more to offer, but the islands weren't policed as well and the ocean afforded a veritable treasure trove of escape routes.

"It will be. This is a very private one. Invitation only."

Joachim didn't get his hopes up. Arnaud Beck was supposed to be a partygoer in the islands, but that didn't mean he'd attend this party. Still, starting to make the private party scene was a step in the right direction.

"Are you staying in Mykonos Town?" Adriana asked.

"Yes. I've rented a room at a house near Cavo Tagoo." The hotel was only five hundred meters inland from the harbor. Joachim gave her the address.

"Be ready tonight at eight. I will pick you up."

"All right."

Adriana turned then and walked away. She rolled her hips suggestively.

Joachim turned back to the sea. Arnaud Beck had a yacht somewhere out there as well. Joachim kept hoping to see it come in to harbor.

In the meantime, he was cultivating local black market connections. Beck was known to buy and sell things on the black market.

Waiting was painless for the most part. Günter would do nothing to his family as long as Joachim kept in touch every day.

If Beck hadn't come to Mykonos Town for days, what was keeping him?

Criminal Detention Center
Siberia, Russia

Cold filled the detention center. Walking down the quiet hallway, which was covered in dingy white paint that needed attention, Elle doubted that the building ever truly warmed. At least eighty years old, the detention center lacked a furnace that would provide adequate heat. Even Colonel Lutikov's office had been cold.

Her footsteps and those of the two security guards that accompanied her echoed through the hallway. A final turn put her in the wing where Alexi Zemanov had been kept for the last twenty years.

The first door on the left bore the number 49D.

One of the guards stepped forward and slotted a swipe card to release the locks. He had to do it twice before the locks grudgingly disengaged. He started to go in.

"No," Elle said. "Wait here."

The guard looked over his shoulder. "I should be there to protect you."

"He's seventy-six years old," Elle said. "Surely I can defend myself."

"Some of these inmates can be very dangerous," the guard insisted.

Elle fixed him with a withering glare. "All right. Have it your way. Come in. Then when I'm finished talking to this man, I'll shoot you where you stand."

The man scowled. "I'll be at the door if you need anything." He stepped back and allowed Elle to pass.

Alexi Zemanov lay huddled on a narrow bed covered with threadbare blankets. A small light flickered on the wall to Elle's left. The rhythmic rise and fall of his thin chest told her he was asleep.

In years past, Zemanov had been a robust man. The pictures in his personal file showed that. But the intervening twenty years had leached most of the life from him. Tangled snarls of iron-gray hair fanned out on his pillow. He'd lost weight till he was nothing more than loose, wrinkled flesh over bone. He slept like a child, his hands together beneath his bony chin to hold on to the blankets.

Elle stopped at the foot of the bed and felt sympathy for the old man. Even as she steeled herself to wake him, he roused.

His eyelids fluttered open and he stared at her with red-rimmed eyes filled with quiet desperation. He remained still, reminding her of a mouse caught in the baleful glare of a predator.

"I am Elle Petrenko." She spoke slowly and calmly, not at all certain if Zemanov still remained in control of his faculties. Her father could have been wrong. "You knew my parents, Boris and Anya Leonov."

Continuing to stare at her, Zemanov said nothing.

"I am here at the request of my adoptive father," Elle said. "Fyodor Petrenko. I believe you knew him, as well."

Slowly, after thinking about how to react, the old man nodded.

"Like my adoptive father, I am an agent for the SVR," Elle said. "I was sent here to ask you about Lenin's Lullaby. I have been given instructions to offer you a pardon for your treason."

A long moment passed in the chill of the room. It was so cold Elle could see her breath. *He will, of course, believe you are lying,* her father had told her back in Moscow. *Back in those days, he trusted people who shoved him into the compound and promptly forgot about him.*

Moving with arthritic slowness, Zemanov waved her forward with a hand.

After only a brief hesitation, Elle moved forward. She had her pistol snugged in shoulder leather beneath her jacket. Once she was at the side of the bed, she stopped.

Zemanov studied her with his rheumy eyes.

"Did you hear me?" Elle asked.

The old man nodded.

"I need to know about Lenin's Lullaby," Elle stated. "And the night Boris and Anya were killed. Cooperate with me and I can get you out of here."

"You," Zemanov wheezed in a weak voice that had wasted away after over twenty years of disuse, "look very much like your mother. God rest her soul." He smiled a little. "She was a...very beautiful woman."

"I've always heard that. I've seen her pictures, but I never got to know her.

"That is...most unfortunate. You have missed out on...an amazing opportunity. Your mother was kind...and vibrant. She loved flowers. Your father was a good man, as well." Zemanov smiled sadly. "What you've said...it's true?" His voice sounded thinner and weaker as he used it. "About the pardon?"

"Yes."

His eyes searched hers suspiciously. "What do you wish to know?"

"Why were you locked away?"

Lifting his thin shoulders slightly, Zemanov attempted a shrug. He didn't quite make it. "I betrayed my country. By rights, I should have been put before the firing squad."

"But you weren't."

"No. I still had friends within intelligence. They got me sent here." He rolled his eyes around the room. "Though several times over the past years I have felt certain they did me a great injustice."

"You helped—" Elle hesitated. She'd almost said *Anya and Boris* instead of *my parents*, then caught herself. She wanted to remind the old man they had both lost something. "You helped my parents get Lenin's Lullaby."

"Yes. As I was instructed."

That caught Elle by surprise. "You were instructed to give them the bioweapon?"

"Yes. By my superior. General Shekhtel."

Elle remembered the name from the mission briefing her father had given her. Shekhtel had never been accused of anything to do with Lenin's Lullaby. In fact, the general had retired and lived on his pension—and some black market dealings—until his murder three years ago by a jealous husband.

"Shekhtel told you to give my parents the bioweapon?" she asked.

"Yes. At his instruction, I gave them a sample as well as the process for making it."

"Why would he order that?"

"At the time, the Berlin Wall hadn't fallen. East Germany yet remained within Russia's influence. General Shekhtel believed that Lenin's Lullaby was going to be used by a terrorist group within West Germany to spread disease throughout Berlin and Munich. The terrorists planned for it to encompass Europe before it was eradicated."

A cold fear even deeper than the chill of the room touched Elle. "That's madness."

"Perhaps. But General Shekhtel knew what dire straits Mother Russia was under. He wanted to strike a final blow." Zemankov drew in a rattling breath. "Your parents knew this. That was why we set up the plan to double-cross Klaus Stryker."

"The East German *Stasi* agent."

"Yes. He and another man—"

"Arnaud Beck," Elle said.

Zemanov smiled. "I see you know much about this."

Elle nodded.

"Klaus Stryker and Arnaud Beck were the go-betweens for the German terrorist cell. Boris, Anya and I knew what Shekhtel intended, and we were opposed to unleashing such a weapon upon innocents. So we chose to double-cross Stryker and Beck. Boris negotiated an arrangement with the American CIA. A man code-named Stone Angel. In return for us handing over the bioweapon and Stryker, your family was supposed to get safe passage from Russia."

"That's not what happened."

"No. At the exchange, the CIA agents did not show up. Your parents were left alone with Stryker. He tried to escape once he saw that the trap was not going to spring. Stryker took the bioweapon and nearly killed Boris and Anya. They fled back to Moscow, hoping to get you and your sister from the city. But they knew they had been betrayed. By that time, Stryker had also betrayed the German terrorists."

"He didn't give them Lenin's Lullaby?"

"No." Zemanov shook his head. "Stryker kept their money and the bioweapon. I was told Beck killed him for his trouble. The German terrorists also withheld their payment to General Shekhtel, which angered him greatly. By this time, he'd somehow learned of the CIA involvement that was supposed to take place. Before he could reach your parents—"

"Stryker killed them."

"Yes. No one even knew Stryker was in-country." Zemanov studied her. "I had feared you and your sister were dead as well. I didn't know. Shekhtel's men took me into custody. In those days, a trial wasn't necessary to send you to a hell such as this. I was out of town, spirited away by General Shekhtel's handpicked squad, the very night your parents were killed."

"You never talked about Shekhtel's involvement."

"No. It would have been suicide. If I had said anything against him, he would have had someone kill me inside this place." Zemanov looked around. "I'd always hoped to get out one day." He focused on her. "I truly hope you are not lying to me about the pardon."

Elle was touched by the quiet fear and desperation she saw in the old man's gaze. "I'm not." She paused. "My father said that you were a man who always knew more than he told."

Zemanov tried a small shrug and almost pulled it off. "I always tried. Knowledge is power. You can't buy power. Not truly. You must earn it. Or learn it. But what I know, young lady, is what your father learned."

"My father?" That surprised Elle.

"Yes. The money he was paid came from a German bank, but it was paid into a Swiss account your father set up. The day your parents were killed, that Swiss account was drained of all the money in it."

"By who?"

"By the man who killed them. Klaus Stryker."

"Stryker killed them for the money," she whispered.

Zemanov nodded. "I think so. Your father gave me the number of that Swiss account." The old man tapped his forehead. "I memorized it. If I give you the account, then perhaps you can find out what happened to the bioweapon Boris and Anya sold. Am I right?"

"You are." Excitement flared through Elle. Maybe she couldn't catch and punish Klaus Stryker for the murder of her parents, but she could go after the people who helped orchestrate it.

Chapter 17

Ftelia
Mykonos, Greece

"You don't enjoy the water?"

Seated on the warm sand beneath an umbrella thrust into the sandy beach, Joachim shook his head. "No."

Adriana smiled at him. "You are a strange man."

"How so?"

"To come to this place where you are surrounded by water and not enjoy getting in it."

"I enjoy looking at it, though." Joachim nodded toward the white-crested waves rolling into the beach. "You don't see something like this in Leipzig."

"Someday," the young woman said, "I shall have to go there. To see if it's truly as bad as you say it is."

Joachim knew he was supposed to suggest that he show

it to her at that point. But he didn't. During the last three days, Adriana had made it apparent that she was attracted to him.

If Joachim hadn't been there on business, with the lives of his family hanging in the balance; if thoughts of the blond woman didn't plague him, and if he didn't *need* her to help him move through the local environment, maybe he would have been more inclined to let nature take its course.

Lying on the beach towel only a short distance away, dressed in a crimson bikini that barely hid anything, Adriana was a sexual buffet waiting to be taken.

So far, there had been no sign of Arnaud Beck. Although he checked in with Günter every day, the crime boss's patience was at an all-time low.

Lying back on his elbows, Joachim watched the afternoon sun settling into the ocean to the west. Out in the bay, windsurfers rode their boards across the waves, taking to the air on occasion. Small boats hauled water-skiers and parasails.

"There is another party tomorrow night." Adriana rolled over on her stomach and undid her top so her bare back would tan evenly. Her breasts pressed into the sand and proved distracting to Joachim.

"Who is having this one?"

"Sapphira Quinn."

"Who's she?"

Adriana folded her arms under her chin, deliberately flashing the side of her breast at him, and smiled. "Sapphira Quinn is the only daughter of Vasilios Quinn."

"Never heard of him."

"Vasilios Quinn," Adriana said, "is a very rich man. He lives on his own private island."

"How do you know Sapphira Quinn?"

"I don't." Adriana pouted. "But I have a friend who does."

"Will it be a big party?"

"One of the biggest." Adriana paused. "Of course, if you're busy—"

"Never too busy for a party." Joachim smiled.

An elegant yacht sailed into view, coming into the harbor. It was a trim motor sailer, capable of navigating the sea by sail or by diesel engines.

Joachim's attention riveted onto the man piloting the big craft. Though Arnaud Beck hadn't been in sight during the attack in Amsterdam, Joachim had gotten familiar with the man's features from the files Günter had provided.

Beck was a tall man, six feet three inches, only an inch shorter than Joachim. But the man outweighed him by at least forty pounds, all of it dense, hard muscle from body-building. He wore his dark brown hair long, hanging in a ponytail just past his shoulders. Mirrored sunglasses masked his eyes. Dressed only in swim trunks, his deep tan shone in the sun. His head swiveled as he called out orders to his crew.

The boat, *Dionysius*, came to sharply. The crew furled the sails as Beck effortlessly changed to diesel engines. Several of the crew were young women dressed in bikinis, all of them hard bodies.

"Do you know him?" Adriana asked.

"He looks like someone I should recognize," Joachim replied cautiously. "A rock star, perhaps. Or an actor. Some kind of celebrity."

"He's neither." Adriana's tone was heavy with disapproval. "He's just rich."

A couple men dressed in swimwear jumped to the dock. The bikini-clad women threw mooring ropes that were quickly tied to the cleats. *Dionysius* came to a gentle stop. Beck kissed the women, stepped into a white windsuit and Top-Siders, then stepped onto the dock. Three men wearing fanny packs and hard ways about them followed Beck.

Joachim knew the fanny packs carried weapons from the way the men moved.

"His name is Ross Andros," Adriana said. "He's a party animal here in Mykonos Town. And the emphasis is on animal. He likes picking fights, and he likes hitting on women in the company of their husbands."

"Which leads to hitting the men," Joachim said.

"You see how it works, then."

Joachim knew how it worked. While Beck had been with the East German *Stasi*, he'd had a reputation as a womanizer. Several rape charges had been brought against him as well. In no few instances, the women who had brought those charges mysteriously disappeared.

Beck walked across the sand talking on a cell phone. As Joachim watched, the man started hitting the *tavernas*, calling out to people he knew. For a mercenary with an international reputation, Beck didn't keep a low profile. Of course, no one had ever before found his base of operations.

Joachim stood.

"Where are you going?" Adriana reached up hurriedly and fastened her bikini top.

"For a walk."

"Want company?"

"Not at the moment." Joachim felt guilty about the hurt look in her face. "Adriana—" Words failed him. This was truly one of the times he could have used his sister's advice. Usually the women he knew wanted something from him. Walking away from them was no problem.

Adriana held up a hand. "It's all right. I promise. You're a nice guy. You never once led me on." She smiled, but it took effort. "Catch up with me later. I still enjoy the company."

"I will." Joachim turned, feeling like a heel, and tried to catch up with Beck without being obvious.

Novokuznetskaya Metro Station
Moscow, Russia

All Elle knew about the man she was to meet was one name: Ashimov. She didn't believe it was his real name.

Ashimov was thin and nervous, in his late forties or early fifties. Gray streaked his black hair. His beard was neatly trimmed. He wore a business suit and coat that allowed him to blend into Novokuznetskaya Metro Station's bustling evening crowd, but she had seen him in jeans and an American concert T-shirt on occasion. Today he wore wire-rimmed glasses.

He smiled a little when he saw her, but his eyes darted to the left and right, checking for anyone who might be lurking in the shadows.

The metro station's green interior and baroque style, with its many edges and hallways, left plenty of lurking room. The place was one of Elle's favorites.

When she'd been a little girl, she'd accompanied her father here several times. She'd always believed it was for the nearby ice-cream vendor. It hadn't been until years later when her father was training her that she'd realized Fyodor Petrenko went there to meet associates.

"Ah, Miss Petrenko," he greeted.

"Mr. Ashimov," Elle responded.

"I do not see your illustrious father." Ashimov stopped in front of her. A small notebook computer case dangled at the end of his right arm. A fiber-optic cord ran from a box on his belt to the computer.

Over the years, people had tried to take Ashimov's computers. No one ever had successfully captured one. All of them were booby-trapped to self-destruct once out of his possession. Later, Elle had learned that Ashimov kept nothing on the computers he carried with him once wireless Internet had become available.

"My father isn't here," Elle said. "This is my contract."

"I see. Do you have the money?"

"Of course." Shifting carefully, with the skill of a street pickpocket, Elle slipped him the envelope containing the agreed-upon amount.

"Walk with me." Ashimov started forward.

Elle fell into step beside him, but not too close.

Ashimov removed the envelope from his coat pocket and ran an experienced thumb along the edges of the bills. "American dollars." He smiled at her as he put the envelope away. "I love American dollars. They spend so easily."

"I know."

"You said you wanted to know about an account at a Swiss bank."

"Yes." Elle knew they both deliberately did not use the bank's name.

"As it happens, I do have a few back doors into some of those banks. The bank you're interested in is just such a bank."

"I want to see where the money went on an account twenty years ago."

"Twenty years?" Ashimov shrugged. "It's not impossible. The Swiss keep very good records, you know. They just try to keep them so…*secret*." He grinned and his eyes flashed behind his lenses. "Of course, they can't keep them secret from me. You have the account number?"

Elle handed him the slip of paper containing the number. Ashimov walked forward again, coming to a stop in one of the hallways that led to Pyatnitskaya Ulitsa outside. Cars and buses passed in the street. He popped the computer open on one of the window ledges. Quickly, he opened an Internet connection through a wireless source.

The notebook computer was partnered to a satellite dish on a nearby vehicle. A couple of times, the Moscow police had caught Ashimov's accomplice, but there was no crime against having a satellite dish on a vehicle.

Once he started, Ashimov concentrated solely on his efforts at the computer. Minutes ticked by as he tapped keys in rapid syncopation.

"Twenty years is a long time," he said. "And the Swiss are very good."

"If you can't do it—" Elle suggested, knowing her mention of the possibility would prick his pride.

"Nonsense." Triumphantly, Ashimov turned and showed her the computer screen. "I only had to go a few layers deeper to get into the bank's archived files. I should have charged you more, but—" He shrugged. "Having the account number instead of searching for a name was immensely helpful." Pausing, he studied the information on the screen. "Twenty years ago, the money was transferred from this account to another."

"At the same bank?"

"Yes. That fact makes it easier, but I still could have done it."

Elle peered at the screen.

The documentation was in German.

"The other account was held in the name of Klaus Stryker."

"So the money is still there?"

"No. That money was transferred within a few days to still another account. Again at the same bank."

"Someone else was listed on Stryker's account?"

Ashimov stared at the screen. "No. Stryker is the only depositor of record. He requested the transfer."

"Over the phone?"

After a moment, the computer expert shook his head. "In person."

"That's impossible."

Ashimov gestured to the screen. "There it is. Just as plain as the nose on your pretty little face."

"Klaus Stryker was killed in East Germany by a man named Beck."

Smiling, Ashimov said, "They also say that security at a Swiss bank in impenetrable. Getting information is difficult, true, but possible. Stealing funds? More difficult still. And in many cases impossible without being on-site. Twenty years ago, such a thing would have been even harder." He tapped the screen. "I suggest to you that the reports of Klaus Stryker's death are greatly exaggerated."

Elle thought about that. If what Ashimov was suggesting were true—and now that made sense and would explain what had happened to Lenin's Lullaby—then Stryker had double-crossed everyone.

The possibility that Beck had been in Amsterdam not to ferret out Marion Gracelyn's blackmailer but to protect one of his own made more sense to Elle. What good would it have been to blackmail a dead woman? But to blackmail a living one? Or to protect one that he was in a partnership with? That definitely made more sense.

"Can you follow that money?" Elle asked.

"Not," Ashimov said, "if the depositor employed someone more skilled than me to hide it." Arrogantly, he chuckled at the suggestion of the possibility. "I've never found anyone that good."

"Follow the money," Elle said. "Let me know who ended up with it and where that person is now."

Ashimov sighed. "Regrettably, such action was not covered by your initial payment."

"Do you trust me for more?"

The computer expert closed his weapon of choice and spread his hands. "But of course. I love doing business with you and your father."

"Get it done. Then get back in touch with me." Elle thanked Ashimov, then strode off, thinking that her parents' murderer might still be out there somewhere running free. The possibility made her queasy—and hopeful for vengeance.

Chapter 18

The Petrenko home
Moscow, Russia

"Elle."

She woke instantly at her father's quiet voice. Only after she had her eyes open did she realize her hand had snaked under her pillow where she kept her pistol. Feeling a little ashamed, she released the weapon.

Her father stood in the doorway of the bedroom where she'd slept as a little girl with her sisters. Only a few years ago, when her youngest sister had left, had the room been made over into guest quarters.

The room was dark. The sound of the radio, tuned to a station that played American jazz, sounded in the distance.

"How long have I been asleep?"

Her father shrugged. "Nine, ten hours."

Elle got out of bed. She still wore the clothes she'd laid down in, when she was only going to rest her eyes. "I never sleep that long."

"You do," her father said, "when you are very tired." He waved to her. "When you are ready, we can talk in the kitchen."

"Did Ashimov find Klaus Stryker?"

"He did. It is an interesting story. And one with certain...*liabilities* that were not foreseen."

"Give me five minutes," Elle said.

Nine minutes later, dressed in American jeans and a pullover she'd bought from a black market dealer, her hair damp from the shower and pulled back in a ponytail, Elle joined her father at the small kitchen table the Petrenko family had crowded around for meals for so many years.

"Sit," he said, waving to a chair. "I have made toast. I have a few oranges. If you want something more substantial, there is a little café I frequent not far from here. The price is reasonable and the food is good."

"But it isn't Mother's." Elle sat.

"No." Pain showed in her father's eyes for just a moment.

"I've been so busy these past few years." Elle glanced around the kitchen. "I didn't think about how you have to get up every morning and face this."

"What? Your mother's absence?" Fyodor shook his head. "When I am here by myself, looking at this kitchen where she spent so much of her time, she is with me. Conversations we had while you children were still abed or after you had gone to bed, they are here with me."

"But don't you get—" Elle stopped, unable to go on.

"Lonely?" Her father smiled. "Of course. Some days I am even angry with her for leaving me. I know it wasn't her choosing, but the anger is still there. But I truly loved your mother. A love like that—" He shook his head. "It doesn't end."

Reaching across the table, Elle took her father's hand. "I want you to be happy."

"I know. I am. Love always brings a quiet sadness with it. At least, that's the way it is here in Russia." He tapped the notebook computer in the center of the table. "Ashimov sent this for you."

Elle opened the computer.

An icon blinked at her, demanding a password.

"You've seen the file?" Elle asked.

"When I met with Ashimov, he showed it to me. I'm familiar with it, but it needs to be studied. As soon as I got home, I woke you."

"Does he know anything of Lenin's Lullaby?"

Her father hesitated. "I think he does. Ashimov is a very crafty man. He has a back door into the SVR files as well. Were he not a true Russian, I would fear him. Maybe enough to have him eliminated."

Elle typed in the password he gave her. The file opened immediately. An index of all the documents contained within appeared first, all neatly numbered and tagged with a note that said the numbers were suggestions of viewing order.

The first document was an overview of the information Ashimov had compiled.

"Have you read this?" Elle asked.

"Yes. Klaus Stryker faked his own death in East Germany. Then he showed up in Switzerland and transferred the money he'd stolen from Boris as well as the East German terrorists into another account. Ashimov was very tenacious, but even he admitted that if he hadn't had the original account number and had a hint of what to look for, he might have lost the trail."

"Stryker is still alive?" Elle asked. She sipped the tea her father had poured for her, then picked up a piece of toast.

Her father pushed a jar of orange marmalade at her. It was fresh, unopened. He'd remembered her favorite. "Yes. He's now going by the name Vasilios Quinn, a wealthy Greek resident. Over the years, Quinn has done very well for himself. But lately, given all the disruption in the aggressive stocks he was trading in, he's suffered a certain reversal of fortune."

Elle flipped through the file. "He's hurting for cash."

"Yes. He's also being blackmailed."

Scanning the index, Elle found a document labeled Blackmail Possibility. She opened it and quickly read through the contents, looking at the bank statements Ashimov's investigation had unearthed.

Every month, for the last twenty years, no matter what account Stryker/Quinn had used, a steady drain on his assets had taken place. The sums were large, but not too large. For the last few months, though, since Quinn's business losses, those payments had become devastating.

"Blackmailed by who?" Elle asked.

"A good question. I asked Ashimov. I even offered to pay him for the information. Do you know what his reply was?"

Elle waited.

"Ashimov insisted that no matter what he did, he couldn't find the owner of the accounts Quinn paid his monthly payment to."

"Do you believe him?"

Her father considered for a moment. "I believe Ashimov is afraid. I think he was reluctant to give me the information he did concerning Quinn. Maybe, if he had known at the onset that his investigations would have revealed the blackmailer, he wouldn't have accepted your assignment."

"Do you think Quinn's blackmailer is Madame Web?"

"It's possible. Something led Quinn to send Beck to Amsterdam. The man your sister was after, this Tuenis Meijer, was connected to Madame Web."

And she could be the mysterious "A" Sam and her friends are searching for, Elle thought.

"Is it possible Stryker or Quinn or whatever he calls himself still has Lenin's Lullaby?" she asked.

"The bioweapon has never surfaced," her father said softly. "It has to be somewhere. At one time, it did exist."

Elle flipped through the files. "Quinn lives in Greece. In the Cyclades Islands." Ashimov had even provided a map marking the island that the man owned.

"Yes."

"How soon can we get a team together?"

Her father looked pained. "At present, Intelligence doesn't want to send a team into the area. Too much possibility of...*negative* publicity remains."

"Meaning they don't want to get caught with an SVR team in the area in case something goes wrong."

Nodding, her father said, "Also that they don't wish to get caught strong-arming a Greek citizen."

"He's a killer."

"Who would bring charges against him? East Germany no longer exists. The Americans wouldn't want to risk exposure to the fact that they let a bioweapon slip through their fingers. Our government doesn't want to admit Lenin's Lullaby was even made." He shook his head. "No. Until we're able to prove that Lenin's Lullaby is still out there and still a risk, we'll be given no support."

"'We'?" Elle echoed.

"I can't let you attempt this alone and unaided, Elle."

"What does General Dragovitch say about your partic-
ipation in this?"

"That I am crazy. That I am exposing myself need-
lessly. That I should stay home and be content with
becoming an old spy."

"I can—"

"Not be difficult, if you please," her father interrupted.
"Arguing will only waste time and energy for us both. I am
going, and that is final."

"All right. When do we leave?"

"I have someone making arrangements now. We'll arrive
in Turkey, then take a boat over to the Cyclades Islands. The
cover identities I've been able to arrange are good but will
not bear up under close scrutiny. We'll have to be careful."

Elle turned her attention to her toast. Despite her father's
obvious expertise, she had misgivings. Klaus Stryker, aka
Vasilios Quinn, had already proven himself a dangerous
man. It had been a long time since her father had been out
in the field in another country.

Vasilios Island
The Cyclades, Greece

"Well?" Adriana asked, smiling hugely. "Isn't it as
breathtaking as I said it would be?"

Seated in the prow of the small sailboat so he had the
best view of the small island that was their destination,
Joachim had to admit that the sight spread out before him
was awe inspiring.

The island was small but crescent-shaped, providing a
natural harbor on the lee side sandwiched between two high
stone spires. The doors of nine boat garages had been carved
into the shore, all of them painted different pastel colors.

Above the marina, a house stood tall in the uneven crags. If not for the docks and the dwelling, the island would have looked like nothing more than a rock thrust into the sea.

Nothing grew on the island naturally except for a few shrubs that fought valiantly against the hostile environment, but Vasilios Quinn had employed a small army of landscapers to import sod and trees, flowers and vines to his small kingdom. Olive trees and bougainvillea stood tall and colorful against the gray-white rock, seated in pools of imported grass manicured into interesting geometric shapes.

The house was an alabaster confection of stones two stories tall. Contoured to fit the shape and slope of the tall hill, it was an organized jumble of walls and angles contained within a high perimeter wall made of the same stones. Security cameras topped the walls but Joachim figured that the exposed systems were redundant to others that were hidden and more protected.

Vasilios Quinn was obviously not a man comfortable with taking chances.

So what relationship do you have with a man like Arnaud Beck? Joachim wondered.

Behind the house, the cliff continued to rise another hundred and fifty feet. At the top, a sleek Bell executive helicopter sat on a helipad.

"You haven't said anything," Adriana reminded. She sat in the pilot's chair, guiding the boat with a deft hand.

Four of her friends from the *taverna* manned the lines and the sails, all of them moving in smooth concert to capture the wind.

Joachim could only sit. He'd never spent much time aboard boats or ships and was at a loss to help with crewing the vessel.

"It is breathtaking," he agreed. "And expensive. What did you say Quinn does?"

Adriana shrugged slim shoulders. She wore her hair tied back, dark sunglasses and a pink bikini. "He's an investor. I've heard he's involved with pharmaceuticals, oil, the stock market."

Several other boats were already tied up in the marina. Red-jacketed valets hustled along the docks to moor the arriving craft and direct traffic.

Adriana called out commands to her crew and guided the sailboat into a slip in the marina. Joachim tossed the mooring line across to a valet, who tied the rope to a cleat and used a boat hook to pull the sailboat against the rubber tires tied along the dock to act as a cushion.

"Welcome to Vasilios Island," the valet greeted as he hung a ladder over the side. "Enjoy your stay."

"You're supposed to look like you're fishing."

Lying on her stomach in the prow of the fishing boat on a blanket and wearing a turquoise bikini, Elle said, "Fishing is your cover. As the flighty daughter of a cur-mudgeonly Russian business owner, I'm sunbathing."

Her father hesitated. "I'm not entirely comfortable with your choice of covers. In fact, you're wearing little cover at all."

They spoke in Russian. None of the Greek crew they'd hired to man the deep-sea fishing boat spoke anything besides their native language and a little English.

"I can't sunbathe and appear innocuous and flighty in a raincoat," Elle said.

"I'd prefer that you did."

Elle looked at him, enjoying her father's discomfiture probably more than she should have.

Fyodor Petrenko looked like a vacationing business-man either recently retired or on a much-delayed holiday. His khaki shorts hung to his knees, exposing his fish-belly white legs. He also wore an obnoxious flower-print shirt, sunglasses and a fishing hat festooned with flies and lures. A white sunblock protected his nose.

"You," Elle declared, "look ridiculous."

Her father smiled self-consciously. "I look the part of a tourist. I'm supposed to look ridiculous." He paused, frowning again. "If you stay up there, exposed like that, you're going to get skin cancer."

"No, I won't. I'm wearing sunscreen."

"Well, the men are ogling you. You would not believe some of the things I have overheard them say about you."

"You don't speak Greek," Elle reminded.

"I speak *those* words," her father corrected. "Even a deaf man could understand those nudges and winks and nods in your direction. And that braying, obnoxious laugh-ter—" He shook his head. "I have half a mind to find them tonight and beat them within an inch of their lives."

"Ignore them. I am." But there was a part of Elle, a small, guilty part, that took pride in capturing the attentions of men. It made her feel good. Just a little.

"I'm your father," he protested. "It's hard for me to ignore such crude commentary about my daughter."

"You're a spy," Elle replied. "A professional in your field. You've ignored much worse. Now let me work."

Grumbling, her father returned to the stern, where their hired guide was teaching him the intricacies of deep-sea fishing while the crew divided their time between watching him and ogling Elle.

A gull flew overhead, its shadow skating across the water. Elle watched the bird as it flapped lazily and rode the wind to Vasilios Island. She studied the marina and the big house atop the hill, watching the steady stream of arrivals walking up the landscaped path leading through the main gate to the gardens around the big house. The party had been set up around a huge pool. Tables and grills filled the area under lights strung from the olive trees. A live band performed rock and roll covers.

She and her father had arrived at Santorini Island from Turkey only that morning and set about hiring the boat to take them out near Vasilios Quinn's private island. The fishermen had suggested better fishing could be found in other places, but money quieted their reservations.

She picked up the nearby Canon digital camera with its heavy telescopic lens and aimed it at the marina. Through the camera lens, she scanned the boats tying up in the marina. The party area seemed set up for three to four hundred people.

Probably all close, personal friends, Elle thought sarcastically.

Many of them were young, though. While on Santorini Island, she'd caught bits of conversation about the party. It was being hosted by Quinn for his daughter Sapphira, a spoiled nineteen-year-old from all accounts.

Raking her studied gaze over the next boat in line, Elle lurched in shock. Six people occupied the sailboat. A pretty, dark-haired young woman piloted the craft, but it was the man in the prow that captured Elle's attention.

Clad in orange-and-white swim trunks, Docksiders, a loose white shirt left unbuttoned and sunglasses, Joachim Reiter stood in the prow and tossed the mooring rope to one of the valets. Then he held the ladder for the young woman who had steered the sailboat. Joachim watched her as she went up, and Elle saw that the young woman made the most of the moment by accentuating her hip roll as she climbed.

Joachim watched the young woman all the way up.

A troubling bit of anger nibbled at Elle's conscious mind. She kept remembering how he had guarded her back in Amsterdam, the way he'd smelled, the quick way he'd reacted and the hardness of his body.

If you're jealous, she thought furiously, *then you're stupid. He's wanted for murdering a BND agent in Leipzig. He's a career criminal.*

After the young woman gained the top of the dock, she turned and called back down to Joachim. She was all smiles and giggles, and in that moment Elle hated her. Joachim climbed the ladder swiftly. The muscles in his back and shoulders and legs corded and released with supple ease.

What the hell are you doing here? Elle wondered.

She would find out.

Chapter 19

"You look lonely."

Joachim turned toward the young woman's voice. He'd heard her heels click against the stone path that meandered through the exotic gardens Vasilios Quinn maintained around the house and pool area.

"Actually," Joachim said, "I'm here with someone. She went to meet a couple of friends."

Tall and elegant, her hair a mix of fiery reds and her curvaceous body encased in a white sheer gown that fit her like a second skin, the woman looked at home against the riotous color of the thick vines and foliage behind her. Like some kind of jungle predator that had just stepped from the wild.

Smiling, showing even, white teeth, the young woman said, "She's a fool to leave you alone and untended. Anyone could come along and make off with you. You're good-looking. Tall. With just a hint of danger."

"No danger," Joachim said. "I prefer a quiet life."

Stepping closer, her muscles rolling beneath the thin material of the gown, the woman reached out and traced a scar along Joachim's flat belly. "That is a knife scar." Her voice was low and seductive.

Joachim felt the heat of her touch and felt exposed. Some of his sister's friends had left him with the same feeling over the years. He didn't like it. He almost felt vulnerable.

"An accident," Joachim assured her.

"And when you turned, I saw something else." She ran her hand under his shirt and slid it back to expose the puckered scar high on the left side of his chest. Her fingertips tapped the old wound. "A bullet made that."

"Another unfortunate accident."

She let her hand wander, sliding down his body. "Have you had any other *unfortunate* accidents?"

Joachim captured her hand before her fingers reached the top of his swim trunks. He suddenly felt underdressed. "Nothing you would be interested in," he told her.

She tried to withdraw her hand but Joachim held on to it. She smiled again. "I like a man who is forceful."

"And I like women who prefer to be chased."

"English is such a demanding language, don't you think? In some ways, very limited."

Joachim looked at her.

"I mean, in English, words sound the same but have different meanings. Did you mean women who prefer to be chased? Or chaste?" She spelled both.

Before Joachim could respond, she leaned into him, molding her body against his. He felt the heat of her plastered against him. When she breathed out, he smelled alcohol on her breath.

"Sapphira," a voice barked.

A man stood on the path that led back to the pool and party area. He was tall and broad, dressed in a white tropical suit. His gray hair looked silver in the fading sunlight. The blue eyes appeared watery, but there was a cunning viciousness, like the eyes of a wolf, in them. He spoke to the young woman, but he stared at Joachim.

"Hello, Father," she greeted.

"Who's your friend?" the man demanded.

Sapphira smiled up at Joachim but made no move to disentangle herself. "Actually, we just met."

Gently, Joachim separated himself from the young woman. "I'm Joachim. A friend of Adriana's. She was invited to the party. She brought me along."

"Some friend," Sapphira said. "This Adriana left him standing here all by himself."

"I am Vasilios Quinn," the man announced.

Joachim thought he detected a hint of a German accent in the man's words and that made him curious. "You have a very nice garden, Mr. Quinn."

"Thank you. Who is Adriana?" Quinn asked.

"She works in a *taverna* on Mykonos Island."

"Not one of my personal friends," Sapphira said. "She probably got one of the invitations I had passed out."

Quinn's eyes drifted to the knife scar on Joachim's belly. "You work at the *taverna*?"

"No. I'm on holiday."

Quinn switched to German. He spoke it fluently. "How do you like the islands so far?"

Joachim responded in German. "They're beautiful." He decided in that moment that playing elaborate games with the man was too dangerous. Knowing that Joachim was of German nationality wasn't harmful in any way.

Smiling, Quinn said, "I thought I detected an accent. You speak English very well."

"Thank you." Joachim pretended not to have noticed the faint German accent in his host's speech. "You speak German fluently."

Quinn shrugged. "I've had practice. What type of work do you do?"

Joachim thought quickly. Something about him had set off Quinn's curiosity. The scar on his stomach honed that to a fine edge. "I work in…debt consolidation."

Arrogant and acting amused, Quinn laughed. "You're a leg breaker."

"Some call it that," Joachim agreed.

"I won't put up with any disturbances on my island."

"There won't be." Joachim shrugged easily. "I…had a disagreement with my employer." That was close enough to the truth that it didn't even feel like a lie.

"Oh?"

"Usually he's very forthcoming with information. Recently, though, he chose not to give me many details about an assignment. It was very risky. I decided to spend some time away and reevaluate my career."

"Daddy," Sapphira protested petulantly. "Enough with the foreign language. This is *my* party."

"So it is," Quinn said in English. Then he changed to German again. "Perhaps, at a later date, we can talk further."

"All right," Joachim said.

Quinn nodded and stepped back. "Sapphira, say goodbye to your friend for the moment. I need to introduce you and get this party underway."

Sapphira hesitated a moment. "Come with me," she said to Joachim.

"I told my friend I would wait," Joachim said.

She gave him a pouting look. "You should work on getting new friends. Ones that won't leave you stranded."

Joachim just smiled.

After a moment, Sapphira trailed after her father.

Now what, Joachim thought, *was that about?*

"The water is cold."

Seated in the prow of the powerboat she and her father had rented only hours before, Elle pulled on a swim fin. "It is," she agreed. "That's why I'm wearing the swimsuit." She popped the elastic sleeve of the black, formfitting one-piece. "Neoprene. Guaranteed to hold in heat and keep the cold out."

Her father showed her a displeased frown. "I'd feel better if I were going with you."

"Oh?" Elle looked up at him in fake surprise. "Have you suddenly learned to swim? Been taking lessons?"

He scowled. "I was in the army. We did not swim in the army. It was not required."

"Then the answer," Elle said as she finished pulling on the other fin, "is no." She stood and picked up the face mask with the miniature scuba tank affixed at the chin. At best the air supply would give her twenty minutes under water.

Night covered the ocean, turning the water wine dark. A mile away, with all the festive neon lights strung around it, Vasilios Island stood out like a multicolored jewel.

"If you get into trouble, call me." Her father held up a micro-miniaturized copy of the walkie-talkie strapped to her left bicep.

"A rescue army of one?" Elle grinned. "Doesn't sound very promising."

"It will be a very *dedicated* army of one."

Moving to the stern railing, Elle lowered herself into the water. Even with the protective suit, the sea was cold. With a final wave to her father, she launched into the long swim.

Elle chose the marina for her arrival, but security proved too thick there. She supposed it was because of all the boats, all the guests' private things that were at risk. So she swam another two hundred yards and came up at one of the private beaches just south of the main house.

Tall palm trees blunted the neon lights from the party and draped long shadows over the pale sand. Elle came out of the sea and stood, surprising two lovers who had found the stretch of beach too inviting not to take advantage of. Naked, they held onto each other and didn't look embarrassed, only startled.

"You're swimming?" the guy asked, struggling with the words enough to let Elle know he was under the influence of something. The young woman with him didn't look in any better shape.

"Lost my keys at the marina," Elle explained, knowing in his state the excuse would sound perfectly plausible. She could have told him she was catching lobsters for the buffet and he would have believed her. "They let me borrow a dive suit to look for them."

He blinked blearily at her. "Oh. Cool." He blinked. "Did you find your keys?"

"No. I've got to go get a big flashlight." Elle unzipped her suit and stepped out of it wearing the turquoise bikini. "Is it okay if I leave this here?"

"Sure."

Elle put the suit and the oxygen-equipped face mask beside one of the trees, marking the spot in her mind so that she could find them again in the dark. Then she headed for the party.

* * *

Techno music exploded over the party area, guaranteeing that all conversations were turned into shouting matches. A number of people were on the dance floor, but an equal number stumbled through beach volleyball games. Several others were held in thrall at the wet bars and the huge projection screen monitors that had been set up to show sports events.

Elle moved through them easily. However, her passage did draw the attention of more than a few of the male species and even got one guy slapped for his lack of discretion while in the company of a young woman.

Confident that the protective coating she'd applied to her fingertips would keep her prints from being identified if it came to that later, Elle picked up a drink in a tall glass from the bar. Dodging through the throng—darkly aware that she was not only looking for Vasilios Quinn/Klaus Stryker, but also for Joachim Reiter—she scored an hors d'oeuvre with pineapple and ham and kept moving.

She told herself she was watching out for Joachim only because he knew what she looked like. However, she'd never been very good at lying to herself.

Portable bathrooms had been set up outside to handle the overflow, so to speak, but guests were allowed into the main house as well. The security systems were top-flight, though, and supplemented by guards.

After a brief tour of the lower floor of the big house that showed off room after room of extravagant wealth in Italian marble tile, Old World furniture, and the latest in technological marvels, Elle knew she wasn't going to get to the upper floor by a door inside the house.

Outside again, she circled the house and decided to try her luck on the east side, the only one away from the party. That side of the house faced the island's interior, which rose steeply. The balcony of what appeared to be a master bedroom jutted out over the garden below.

The balcony was out of reach of even the tallest tree in the garden. Elle was certain that was by design. However, egress from the cliff itself was possible.

If you're desperate, she told herself.

Thinking about Lenin's Lullaby and the murder of her parents, the fact that she had hurt Sam and possibly damaged her relationship with her sister, Elle admitted that she *was* desperate. The only problem was the security camera that swept the area.

At the back of the garden, the landscaping crashed onto the broken rock of the cliff side and stopped. The cliff blocked the moon at the moment and the darkness was complete.

Breathing easily, Elle made herself wait until her eyes had more fully adjusted to the darkness. Then she sought out nearly nonexistent handholds and toeholds, leaned into the climb and went up the cliff. Even skilled as she was, she was challenged by the ascent.

Four feet above the level of the balcony, nearly forty feet above ground level and the tops of the trees fifteen feet below, Elle paused. The palm trees hid her from the security camera as it cycled slowly from side to side. Her fingers and toes ached from the effort of climbing.

Taking a final deep breath, timing the security camera, she swung her right arm out and held on with her left. Her fingers slipped immediately, more quickly than she'd thought they would. Shifting her weight as she had, pulling away from the cliff, had disrupted the fragile relationship she had with the friction of the stone and the pull of gravity.

Locked into her gamble, Elle lunged forward and pushed off with her hand and legs, throwing herself into the air. At least seventeen feet separated the cliff from the balcony. If she'd had a running start, she'd have spanned the distance easily.

She missed.

Chapter 20

Elle's outstretched hand fell short of the balcony. She felt the cool metal slide beneath her fingers. Panic detonated like an explosive through her body, adding unnecessary and unwanted fuel to the adrenaline already charging her system. She fought to remain calm.

Just when she thought she was about to start the forty-foot drop, the fingertips of her right hand brushed the bottom of the balcony. She curled her fingers and found purchase, then willed herself to hold on.

The shock of hitting the end of her arm almost tore free her grip and sent burning pain through her shoulder. *Don't look at the ground,* she told herself. *Look where you want to go.* That was a trick she'd learned in her evasive driving courses. *Concentrate on the destination, not the accident.*

Her grip on the balcony lip held. Swinging and pulling, she reached up with her other hand and caught hold of the balcony railing. Handling her weight easily, she took a moment to draw a quick breath, timed the security camera's sweep, then pulled herself up. She rolled under the periphery of the security camera and stood against the door frame, once more out of sight.

The sliding glass door featured state-of-the art security, and it was locked. Peering through the glass into the darkened room, she made out a large bedroom suite centered around a canopy bed, an entertainment center that covered a wall and a door that led to what she assumed was a bathroom.

Taking the walkie-talkie from her bicep, Elle opened the back compartment, removed the batteries, then slipped out the glass cutter hidden behind them.

Setting herself in a low squat, Elle quickly inscribed an oval in the center of the glass that stopped well short of the alarm tape. Cutting through the section had taken four different attempts with time out for the camera, but she finished. On her fifth approach, she tapped the glass with the heel of her palm and watched the oval fall inside.

She went through the hole just ahead of the security camera's sweep.

Nothing moved inside the room.

Working quickly, Elle opened the closet door and found feminine clothes. It definitely wasn't Quinn's room.

Returning to the balcony door, she paused at the glass oval, timed the security camera and ran out onto the balcony. Still in motion, she leaped up onto the balcony railing, stood and caught the edge of the roof and cautiously pulled herself up.

Once on the roof, lying flat and aware that the security measures could include pressure plates and a rooftop camera, Elle scanned her surroundings. No camera and no alarm. She figured that overall things were looking pretty good.

Working her way around the house, she invaded another room in the same way and found it filled with clothing that had been taken from luggage stored in the closet.

Vasilios Quinn's bedroom was the third she invaded. The room was huge, the size of a small house, and nearly occupied the whole front of the building, which faced the Aegean. Mediterranean-style furniture, a huge bathroom with an Olympic-size hot tub, and a home entertainment center that looked like a NASA ground control station filled the room.

A private office on the other side of the bathroom finished off the front of the home. The computer array held a dozen monitors that showed images of the party outside, the docks and the downstairs rooms.

Ship models, all of them ancient looking, filled shelves along the back wall, interspersed with shells, coins, tankards and other artifacts someone—maybe Quinn— had claimed from dives. Brass plates identified the findings and gave the date they were found.

Elle turned her attention to the computer. The soft blue-white glow of the monitor filled the room when she turned the system on.

Enter Password

The cursor blinked at her.

Abandoning the computer, Elle focused on the desk. She pulled the drawers open from bottom to top, just the way the ex-thief who had taught her to toss a room had trained her to do. Working from bottom to top meant she only had to open the drawers, not waste time pushing them back in.

She returned to the bedroom long enough to strip a pillowcase from the bed and the plastic trash bag from the bathroom trash receptacle. She stuffed the plastic trash bag inside the pillowcase. The trash bag made the makeshift container waterproof while the pillowcase was more durable.

Sorting through the contents of the desk, she tossed in all electronic handheld devices and anything that looked like an appointment book or planner. There wasn't much. She added two credit-card-size digital cameras to her haul and was turning to search the file cabinets, intending to pick them with a paperclip she'd taken from the desk, when the security monitors suddenly flickered on.

Captured on every screen, Elle stood in front of the file cabinets. Knowing the image had been relayed throughout the security system, she cursed and got moving.

She tied the trash bag, then tied the pillowcase again, front end to back to make a loop. Fisting the glass cutter, she inscribed a quick, uneven X on the floor-to-ceiling window at the front of the office. The office didn't have balconies, but the room below did. Footsteps were already sounding outside the office door. Connections chirped as someone initiated the electronic keypad.

Sliding the looped pillowcase over her head and one shoulder, Elle grabbed a bronze paperweight of a sailboat that must have weighed fifteen pounds. She spun and used her body as a fulcrum to hurl the paperweight at the window. The impact shattered the glass into gleaming shards.

The office door swung open as Elle ran for the broken window. She vaulted out, knowing if she missed the balcony below she would fall. Landing off-balance on the balcony, she tucked and rolled, scattering a small patio table and two chairs. She also picked up an assortment of bruises that made themselves felt almost immediately.

"Down there!" someone above her called.

Elle pushed herself to her feet and ran for the railing. Silenced shots struck the wooden deck and tore splinters free. Grabbing the railing, she vaulted over, throwing her hands up over her head so they wouldn't entangle. If her feet cleared, her upper body would, too.

She hit the ground and buckled into a parachutist's roll, coming up immediately. The party was to her right. People were running back away from the broken glass.

A shadow moved to her left and she brought her fists up under her chin in a martial arts ready stance.

The man stayed back, though, and pointed his pistol in a two-handed grip. "No," he said quietly, and grinned.

Elle got her balance, standing for a moment, knowing she had to move quickly. Even then she might not be fast enough.

Standing at the open bar at the side of the big house, Joachim saw a fistful of diamonds suddenly flare to light in the air. By the time he realized the diamonds were actually broken glass, a figure bolted free of the window and dropped to the balcony on the floor below.

A shadow jumped from the window and plummeted a heartbeat ahead of a man with a pistol. The man pointed the pistol down and fired rapidly. Even though the weapon was silenced, there was no mistaking the muzzle-flashes that lashed out into the night. The screams from the surprises guests started right after that.

Joachim had a brief impression of a well-filled turquoise bikini and platinum blond hair that was at once hauntingly familiar just before the woman stood and flipped off the balcony to the ground. Before he knew it, he was in motion, going toward the action while the bulk of the partygoers were going away.

Staying with the tree line along the garden, well within the shadows even after the house's security lights flared to life and struggled for dominance against the fireworks exploding against the black sky, Joachim circled the area where the woman had dropped to the ground.

Mind flying, thinking that somehow Elle Petrenko had followed Beck, Joachim moved in. Despite the fact that his family was at risk from Günter, Joachim couldn't stand idly by and watch Elle get shot down.

She was already up, ready to pounce, when Joachim roped an arm around the security guard's neck. The guard tried to call for help, but Joachim choked off his air. The man struggled to bring his pistol to bear, but Joachim plucked it from his grasp. Then Joachim increased pressure on the man's throat, carefully not damaging the larynx but shutting down the carotid arteries.

The guard passed out unconscious.

Releasing his hold on the man, Joachim let him slump to the ground. He frisked him quickly, turning up two magazines for the pistol.

"You," Elle said.

"Me," Joachim agreed. He noticed that they both spoke German. "What are you doing here?" He glanced at the pillowcase slung over her head and shoulder.

"I don't really have time for twenty questions." Elle looked at the pistol in his hand.

"No," Joachim said. "You don't." He lowered the pistol. "Can you get off the island?"

"Yes."

"Let's go."

Elle took the lead and he followed. Together, they vaulted the low wall into the garden area, crashing through trees and brush.

Joachim cursed as branches slapped his face. One of them hit his left eye and blurred his vision for a moment.

"They're in the garden!" someone yelled.

A multitude of screams came from the partygoers.

Dodging behind a thick-boled Japanese maple tree, Joachim brought his borrowed pistol up in a two-handed grip. Closing his watering eye, he aimed at the center of the nearest guard climbing over the garden wall. He squeezed the trigger twice, riding out the recoil.

The guard went down immediately without a sound.

"What are you doing?" Elle demanded, whirling on him.

"Buying time." Joachim shoved her forward. "Go."

"You can't just kill them. They could be innocent."

Joachim didn't believe that for a moment. Vasilios Quinn wouldn't have anyone innocent around him. "I didn't. The guy I knocked out was wearing a bulletproof vest. Looked like standard equipment."

Elle ran on, fleet as a deer in the darkness. Joachim struggled to keep up, holding one arm up to protect his face.

They arrived at a patch of beach. A couple lying on a blanket glanced up at them. They guy smiled blearily.

"You're back," he said.

"I am." Elle scooped up swim fins and a scuba mask from beside a tree. She fisted the dive suit as well but didn't try to pull it on.

"Going to try to find your keys again?"

"I feel lucky," Elle assured him.

Joachim had no idea what they were talking about. He couldn't believe how calmly Elle stepped into her swim fins.

She looked up at him with those ice-blue eyes. "I've got a boat waiting." The offer was implicit.

Joachim thought about it, but realized there was no telling how the story of his disappearance from Quinn's island home would be relayed. He was certain Günter had a spy or two in the mix.

He shook his head. "No."

Her eyes turned flat and hard. "I guess the new job agrees with you."

New job? Joachim didn't know what she was talking about.

Then the sounds of pursuit crashed through the garden behind them. Flashlights whirled dizzyingly through the darkness, coming closer.

"The other guys brought flashlights, huh?" The guy showed them a thumbs-up and nodded. "Good thinking."

"Go," Joachim said roughly. But even as he said it, he gave in to impulse and leaned over to kiss her. At first, Elle didn't respond. Then, as if electrified, she pressed suddenly into him, meeting him more than halfway. Their mouths devoured each others, their hands caressing, touching every possible surface.

Joachim broke away. "No time," he gasped.

She turned and went without a word. Long strides carried her into the foaming waves of the sea crashing against the beach. She pulled on the mask and dove.

"Dude," the guy said. "You just gonna let her go?"

Joachim was asking himself the same question. She never came up again. Even with the mask, though, he didn't know if Elle was going to get away.

Turning, he stripped the silencer from his captured pistol and fired three shots into the trees over the heads of the pursuers. The flashlights extinguished as they dropped to the ground.

"Hey," the guy said. "I think they know where you are. You don't have to signal them."

A split second later, bullets tore through the air and slapped the beach only a few feet from Joachim. *They know where I am.*

Recognizing the shots for what they were, the guy

covered up his girl and huddled close to the tree trunk for shelter. He shouted, "Don't shoot! Don't shoot!"

Joachim ran, sprinting for all he was worth, heading out along the treeline away from the main house. Minutes later, he stood in hiding while the house security guards rousted the couple on the beach and started asking questions.

He wiped the pistol and the magazines down, then threw them out into the ocean. Carefully, he made his way back to the main house without encountering security guards.

Everything was still in confusion when he arrived. Several of the partygoers had headed to the marina, believing the party was being raided or attacked by armed robbers. Quinn's security staff was kept busy trying to keep the guests from stampeding like cattle. The confusion was even more complete.

Sapphira stood at the bar with a martini glass in her hand and a sour look on her face. She brightened up considerably when she spotted Joachim.

"I thought I'd lost you," she said.

"No. Almost got ran over when everyone panicked."

She studied him. An alcoholic haze reddened her eyes. "You don't look panicked."

"I'm not." Joachim smiled disarmingly. "It's an open bar." He asked for a shot and a beer, finishing the first off in a gulp and sipping the beer. He nodded toward the knot of security guards coming up from the beach. "So what happened?"

Sapphira frowned. "I don't know. Probably something to do with my father's business. He's been antsy ever since he started working on that deal in Berzhaan."

"I've never been to the Middle East."

"I have." Sapphira shrugged. "Bo-ring. It's got a lot of hot guys with attitude, but I don't like the way they treat women there."

The security team marched the nude couple into the main house. Quinn and Beck stood in the doorway.

"Who's the guy with your father?" Joachim asked.

"His name's Ross Andros." Sapphira smiled. "You and he have a lot in common, actually."

"Really?"

"Yeah. He's got a collection of knife scars and bullet wounds that he doesn't talk about, either."

One of the security guards sprinted from Quinn to the band. After a whispered exchange, the band started playing again and the lead singer called people back to the dance area.

"I want to dance," Sapphira declared, taking Joachim's beer from his hand.

"All right." Joachim took her hand and surprised her by leading her out onto the dance floor. But his thoughts were on Elle, wondering if she'd made it back through the sea to her boat.

Elle surfaced beside the boat and found her father standing watch with a Kalashnikov rifle in his hands. Finding the rifle hadn't been too difficult. The previous owner had claimed to use it as a shark gun.

"You had a bit of excitement," her father said. His words were calm, but she heard the tension in them.

"A bit." Elle caught hold of the ladder, slipped her swim fins off, and pulled herself up. She held up the sodden pillowcase. "A bit of luck, too, I hope."

"I saw that you found Joachim Reiter." Her father started the boat. The powerful engines shuddered to life.

"I did," Elle admitted. "Those infrared binoculars you were using are very good."

"The best that the Swiss make," he agreed. "What is Reiter doing there?"

"I don't know."

"He's wanted in Germany for killing a BND agent. Perhaps he's seeking new employment."

Elle shook her head. "I don't know what happened there, but he's smarter than that."

The memory of his heated kiss still elevated her pulse. *Damn* him! What had he been thinking? And why couldn't she think of anything else?

"He did aid in your escape when it might have been best if he had captured you."

"I know." Elle shivered in the cold. Thinking about Joachim Reiter left her feeling confused. On several levels. She had no clue why he had turned up here. Or how.

"There is a blanket below," her father said. "You should try to stay warm."

Elle started below.

"There is also a Thermos of coffee," her father said. "In case you happen to think of your father."

Despite the aftermath of the adrenaline surge, the confusion over Joachim Reiter and trying to figure out what her next move would be, Elle grinned. "I'll bring it out."

"I always said you were a good daughter."

Chapter 21

Mykonos Town, Mykonos
The Cyclades Islands, Greece

For two days, Elle kept close watch over Vasilios Island. The digital cameras and planners she'd stolen from Quinn's home hadn't netted any information. Whatever Quinn was up to remained a mystery.

During that time, Vasilios Quinn kept his operations buttoned down tight. He didn't go anywhere and entertained no one. No doubt her break-in had made him extra cautious.

Sapphira Quinn came and went often, brought by a small group of security men who flanked her throughout her visits to the islands and the mainland. She shopped and partied and saw a few friends.

Twice Joachim Reiter had gone with her. Both times Elle had experienced a twinge of unease and anger that she

hadn't wanted to feel. Despite her father's attempts to find
out information about the man through SVR intelligence,
no explanation could be found for Joachim Reiter's
presence in the Greek Islands.

She was hitting the bar scene, floating along through the
tavernas hoping to find Joachim's trail, or Sapphira's or
Beck's. During the last two days, she'd discovered that
Ross Andros made the party scenes in a big way as well.

Seated at one of the open-air tables at almost nine
o'clock, Elle sipped a glass of wine and watched the docks.
The tourist crowd was in full swing, and roving groups
plowed from one end of the island's bar scene and back
again, growing steadily more raucous.

Her father, dressed now in slacks and a nice shirt she'd
helped him pick out, approached her and sat at her table.
He smiled. "Hello."

"You have a reason for risking our cover?"

"Our cover is intact," her father insisted. "By now
everyone knows you're my daughter, whom I check up on
regularly."

It was true. Her father was better at getting inside a
local environment than she was. He spent his mornings
gossiping with the old fishermen who had eyes on everything and listened for news constantly. Lunches he spent
with some of the lonely women who owned their own
businesses, either *tavernas* or tourist gift shops. And
evenings he spent chasing after women much too young
for him, but getting to know the local Lotharios.

"Did you just come to chat?" Elle asked.

"You act as though you're not glad to see me."

A pang of guilt sliced through Elle. "Sorry. I've got a
lot on my mind."

"Your sister?"

That's one of the things, Elle thought. She knew they weren't going to talk about the other. "I'd feel better if I can talk to her."

"She would want to know why you disappeared and why you haven't been in touch."

"I know."

"If the CIA learn of Lenin's Lullaby, they will come into this area quickly. Too quickly. We are here and we are effective. What is that American saying? Too many cooks spoil the broth?"

"Something like that," Elle agreed. "But I think it may be an English saying."

Her father waved it away. "Whatever. The point is, we don't need outside interference at this juncture."

"I know. I just wish we were doing more."

"I had a fabulous idea today," her father stated. He smiled smugly.

"Do I have to wait to be amazed?"

"You're young," he said. "You still have plenty of time for fabulous ideas. It's good to be your father and still occasionally one step ahead of you." He waved down a harried server and asked for coffee.

"I'm getting older," Elle said.

"Do you remember the two things you can always trace men by? And most women?"

"Sex and money," Elle answered automatically. That had been one of his first lessons and it remained true today.

"Yes. Today I was talking to Nestor. Do you remember Nestor?"

"The old fisherman who repairs nets." Elle found that keeping up with the people her father met was harder than managing those she encountered. However, her father's assets were more colorful and individual than hers.

"Exactly. Well, I was talking to Nestor this morning and he was complaining to me that if he'd been smarter about things when he was younger, he'd have put away savings and been retired by now. Or at the very least owned a much nicer boat. He commented that there were any number of young people who managed investments here in the islands. So I started wondering—"

Elle knew exactly what her father had been wondering. "Who manages our target's accounts."

Her father smiled. "I did train you very well." The server arrived with his coffee. He paid her and sent her on her way.

"*We* didn't think of it two days ago," Elle said.

"*We* should have."

"A legitimate accountant won't know about our target's extracurricular activities."

"No, but we should be able to negotiate something." Her father laced his fingers across his flat stomach. "I think, if we can forge such a relationship with the man who handles our target's affairs, that we might be able to parlay it into greater leverage."

"Do we know who that is?"

"Unfortunately, not yet. But I have gotten in touch with Ashimov in Moscow and had him put his considerable talents to the quest."

Elle nodded. If anyone could turn up something on a deep search involving money, Ashimov could. "So we're waiting."

"For the moment, yes. But it is one more card we have in play." He sipped his coffee and looked uncomfortable.

Elle waited. When her father was uncomfortable with an idea, there was no getting it out of him till he was ready. She sipped her wine, feeling a little too relaxed and thinking that maybe she'd let her drinking get ahead of her. But it was nothing a good walk couldn't cure.

"I found Joachim Reiter's apartment here on the island," her father told her.

Elle's breath stilled in her lungs. Her brain suddenly raced, turning over the implications of that soft statement. If her father had viewed Joachim as a threat, which he sometimes did, then he might have moved directly to eliminate that threat.

"I have an address for him."

So he's still alive. Elle let her breath out.

Her father reached into his jacket and produced a card. "Do you remember Layna?"

"The woman who runs the coffee shop."

"There are several coffee shops, actually, but she does run the best of them."

Watching her father, Elle decided he might actually be smitten with the woman. That amazed her. However, there was something magical on the islands that brought out feelings better left buried. At least, that was what she'd been telling herself the last two nights she'd tossed and turned in her own bed while thinking of Joachim Reiter.

"As it turns out, Layna has a good friend who manages property rentals," her father went on. "I told her that my daughter had been attracted to a young man she met at a party—"

"You *did* not," Elle interrupted.

"Layna was more than happy to help act as matchmaker." He slid the card across the table. "He registered as Joachim Kleinner."

Elle took the card. "It might not be him." She tried to hide her excitement.

"It is him. I saw him there earlier."

"You didn't talk to him?"

He shook his head. "Actually, I thought you might be

the more persuasive of us." He shrugged. "I also believe you'll be better able to judge if we can trust him."

"And if we can't?"

Opening his hands, her father shrugged. "Then he needs to be removed from the game board. The closer we get—the closer *you* get to our target—the more dangerous Joachim Reiter's knowledge about you becomes." He hesitated. "There *is* a lot at stake in our mission. Not just our lives."

So she would have to kill him.

Elle took a deep breath. "Let me think about it."

Elle looked at the small house built into the hillside. According to her father's briefing, the house had six rooms to let. Joachim Reiter had taken one on the second floor.

Lights from the nearby Cavo Tagoo Hotel spilled neon into the street. Pedestrian traffic trickled through the front door as tourists returned to their rooms.

"It doesn't look as though he's in," Elle commented. She couldn't help wondering if Joachim was with Sapphira Quinn. She shut down that line of thinking.

"If he isn't, he will be." Her father took a breath. "Do you want me to go with you?"

Elle tried to appear to think about that. "No. A woman going up to the room alone won't draw as much attention. But if one of the other renters sees us together and realizes we don't live there, it could trigger a call to the police."

"Agreed. Reluctantly. This man, by all accounts, he is a dangerous man. If he feels threatened, he might not hesitate to kill you."

"I won't allow that," Elle replied. At her back, she felt the weight of the SIG-Sauer P-226 9mm her father had gotten from one of the black marketeers on the island.

"See that you don't." He nodded toward a small *taverna*

only a block away. "I will be there." He held up the walkie-talkie he carried in his jacket pocket. "If you need me—"

"I won't," Elle said. "But if I do, I'll call."

"Be careful."

"And you."

Without another word, he turned and walked down the street.

Silently, Elle took a breath and turned her attention to the rental property. She walked as if she belonged there, going up the stairs at the back and finding number six easily.

The lock was an easy one. She was through it in the time it would have taken to use a key.

Inside the rooms, she didn't use a light. If someone had been watching her from outside that would have appeared strange. But she hadn't felt anyone's eyes on her. She and her father had already checked the neighborhood to make certain Quinn hadn't assigned anyone to watch over Joachim.

The flat was simple. A bedroom/living quarters with two windows, one that looked out over the street separating the building from the Cavo Tagoo and another that looked out over the alley, occupied most of the space. A small bathroom took up the rest.

Elle stood in the center of the room and drew in a deep breath. Even over the closed-in smell of the room, she could detect Joachim's musk. A tingle raced up her spine.

Don't, she told herself. She walled off the reaction before it could get started. Forcing herself to remember that BND Agent Schultz had a family who would never see him again, she slipped the SIG-Sauer from her waistband and sat at the small desk against the wall by the window. She positioned herself so the muted light from the window never touched her.

And she began to wait.

* * *

One hour and thirty-seven minutes later, a key rattled in the lock.

Elle picked the pistol up from the desk. She'd been fighting sleep, thinking perhaps she should have brought a coffee with her but knowing that the smell of it would have given away her presence. Now, however, she was wide-awake.

She remained seated in the chair. In the darkness, a person's peripheral vision could still pick up movement. The safety was already off the pistol and a live round was chambered.

Aiming deliberately, she centered the pistol on the shadow that stepped through the doorway. The rectangle of light from outside stopped inches short of her.

Joachim automatically reached for the light and switched it on. He saw her immediately.

That was the moment, Elle knew, feeling it stretch tight and thin between them, that he lived or died. Or escaped. Though she couldn't truly imagine that because she was a good shot.

He wouldn't make it back through the door without being dead or wounded.

Instead of moving, he froze. His face was calm. "What's the occasion?"

"We need to talk."

"I gathered that from the way you didn't shoot me as soon as you saw me."

"Come in," she said. "Close the door behind you. And pull the curtains over the window."

"I didn't see the old man anywhere." Joachim closed the door behind him and pulled the curtains. He placed his hands on his head.

"Down on your knees," she told him.

Without a word, he dropped to his knees. He wore a swimsuit and an open shirt that exposed his washboard abs and tanned chest. Being near the sea agreed with him.

"Are you armed?" she asked.

"No."

Elle eased to her feet and kept the pistol tucked in close to her body so it couldn't be knocked away easily." She slipped a pair of handcuffs from her pocket. They weren't the disposable plastic kind she preferred. Rather, they were the old-fashioned steel ones that required a key. As it turned out, there were a few shops, if a person knew where to look for them, that provided for more...*exotic* tastes. Elle didn't ask her father how he'd come to learn about those places. "Give me your left wrist."

"This isn't necessary," he growled. "I'm not going to hurt you."

"I feel that it *is* necessary," Elle countered.

Cursing, he pushed his left hand behind his back.

Elle expertly hooked his wrist. "Now the other one."

Joachim slid his right wrist behind his back. As she opened the other cuff, he reared back into her, knocking her back. She went with the impact, wanting to be as far away from him as she could. Tripping, she plopped to her bottom on the floor with her back against the wall. He rushed her like an animal on his hands and knees, throwing himself at her.

He lay on top of her as she shoved the pistol against his forehead. He didn't try to take the weapon from her grip, just stared at her with those predatory gray-green eyes.

"Shoot me," he said in a hoarse voice, "and you'll be killing my family, too."

Family? That jarred Elle. No one had mentioned a family.

Was he married? Did he have children? She froze but knew if he made a move to harm her she'd pull the trigger.

"You'll also have to shoot your way past the two men that Quinn and Beck have following me around," he said.

"What family?" Elle asked.

"My mother," he answered. "My sister and her husband. My niece."

Elle looked up at him, hoping that she didn't have to kill him. "I don't understand."

"I work for a man," Joachim said. "A very dangerous man. Günter Stahlmann. He's a criminal underworld leader in Leipzig."

"Yes." Stahlmann was mentioned in Joachim's file.

"I've worked with Günter for years," Joachim said desperately. "Since I was a kid. I had to support my family after my father…died. During that time, he's always trusted me. At least, as much as Günter trusts anyone. After Amsterdam, Günter decided he didn't trust me so much."

Elle listened, feeling the weight of him against her. Her eyes searched his, but she felt that he was telling the truth.

"I'd been talking to the BND," Joachim said. "Negotiating a deal with an agent named Schultz. I was turning information about Günter's operations in exchange for my own amnesty. Günter put me in a box. I didn't have a choice about betraying him. I couldn't shake loose. Günter framed me for Schultz's death, putting me back in *his* box this time. He sent me here, to find out what Beck was doing, and he's holding my family hostage."

"He has your family?" Elle knew that was a lie.

"No. But if I don't do what Günter wants, he'll have them killed. I can't get them out of Germany." Joachim drew a breath. "Now you're going to have to make a decision to trust me." He paused. "Or shoot me. Because I can't function with one more damned restriction put on me."

Elle waited, searching his face, smelling him and feeling him pressed against her body. She was suddenly aware of how little material actually separated their flesh. Struggling against it, she felt excitement rising within her body. There was something intensely erotic lying beneath a man that could snap her neck and kill her in an instant, or that she could pull the trigger and kill in an eye blink.

Erotic, but not satisfying. She cursed the aching emptiness within her that she was suddenly aware of.

"All right," she said, and her voice was thicker than she wanted it to be. She pulled the pistol from his head.

"I apologize," he said. "I didn't mean to come at you like that. But there seemed to be no other way."

"Probably not," Elle agreed.

"Who are you?"

Elle hesitated only a moment. "Russian intelligence."

He looked surprised. "A spy?"

She nodded.

"What are you doing here?"

"Vasilios Quinn is not who he says he is."

"Who is he?"

Reluctantly, she shook her head. "If you don't know, I can't tell you."

"Why?"

"What does Günter want you to do?"

Joachim was silent for a moment. "I'm supposed to find out what Beck is doing."

"He's working for Quinn." Elle looked into his eyes. "If I tell you why Beck is working for Quinn, you'll tell Günter. That will interfere with my mission."

He didn't bother to deny it. "What do you want from me?"

"You've seen me. Beck hasn't."

"He may have known who you were before that night in Amsterdam."

"I have to take the chance that he didn't."

"How does this tie in to what happened in Amsterdam?" he asked.

Slowly, she shook her head. After an hour and a half of thinking of the questions she had to ask him, she was surprised that they had nothing to say. "I can't tell you," she whispered.

"Why did you come here?"

"To tell you to stay out of my way."

"And if I don't?" he asked, lowering his head and kissing her.

"I'll kill you," she said, pressing her lips against his, no longer able to hold back the impulses that pushed her into motion. She released the pistol, giving in to the savage need that filled her like napalm, and cupped his face in her hands.

He didn't try to reach for the pistol. If he had, she thought she could still hold her own. Instead, he opened his mouth and kissed her deeply, pushing her senses over the edge as his breathing turned hoarse. She felt his erection along the inside of her thigh as he shifted in an effort to find some degree of comfort.

His hands grabbed the bottom of her T-shirt and inched it up, baring her stomach inch by inch as if daring her to stop him. She couldn't. If anything, she wanted his hands on her more quickly. Sliding her hands inside his shirt, she stroked his chest, relishing the feel of the hard muscles working beneath her fingertips.

"We shouldn't—" he started.

"If you stop," she warned, "I'm going to break something on you that will take a *long* time to heal."

He pushed her shirt on up, found the front clasp of her bra and unfastened it with one hand in a touch that was all too knowledgeable. At the same time she thought that, his mouth closed on Elle's left breast and her head seemed to explode.

She wrapped her arms around him, pulling him close, letting him feed on her flesh. His breath was hot and ragged against her skin. His teeth grazed her nipple and nearly drove her insane. He pulled his head back and she tried to hold onto him. But his attentions were only gone for a moment as he shifted to her other breast.

Moaning, unable to help herself, Elle threw her head back and thrust her hips up against him. He was hard and insistent, and she rocked until she had him in the cradle of her legs, had the pressure exactly where she wanted it.

He cried out then, a short pant that sounded frenzied and rushed. He thrust against her, cupping her bottom in his big hands to pull her more tightly against him. He used the friction of the material of the shorts she wore to completely push her past whatever control might have been left to her. Moving his mouth from her breast, he kissed her again, maintaining the friction against her shorts and the tender flesh beneath.

Without warning, the orgasm swept her away, detonating all through her body, till it seemed that she expanded ten times her size, then coalesced back into a shuddering heap under him.

"Are you all right?" he asked. Worry showed in those gray-green eyes.

"I'm fine," she replied. She still felt him hard and demanding against her.

He started rocking against her again, and—incredibly— she felt the desire already welling up inside her. There was no doubt that she'd be able to hit her peak again.

"No," she said.

He froze.

With a quick, lithe motion, she wrapped her right leg behind his left and flipped him over. Working quickly, she slid out of her shorts and undressed him, too. She held his erection in her hand, savoring the hard flesh in her fingers. Before he knew what was going to happen, she took him into her mouth, nipping and biting and pleasing just enough to shove him close to the edge and way past the point of control. It was torture, she knew.

When she stopped, just short of where he wanted to go, his hands gripped her arms.

"Don't leave," he whispered. "We're not done here yet." He held up a condom, straightforward, no embarrassment.

"No," she told him with a smile. "We're not." She took the protection from him and fitted it to him. Sliding up, she straddled him and guided his erection inside her. It took her a moment to get used to the size. Thankfully, he allowed her the time it took to make the adjustment. Then she began the slow rise and fall that carried them toward the point of oblivion.

Her second orgasm hit her before she'd truly recovered from the first. Somehow they fit together just right, so the friction never seemed to leave where she needed it most.

Before she could move, he flipped her over, gliding on top of her and driving deeply. His hand slid between them and he caressed the core of her as he sought his own release.

Clinging desperately to her senses, Elle waited till he bucked into her a final time and exploded, then she followed him over once more.

Chapter 22

Mykonos Town, Mykonos
The Cyclades Islands, Greece

Sometime later, Elle was never sure when, Joachim had somehow found a reserve of strength that she was convinced could not have existed and carried her to bed. She had gone boneless, unable to stop him or help with her own transport.

Tenderly, he placed her in the bed and joined her a moment later. His heat radiated into her. Gently, he pulled her close and rested his stubbled chin on her shoulder, draping his large body over hers. She wanted to do nothing more than go to sleep in his arms and pretend everything was all right. But she couldn't. Her mind wouldn't stop summoning up all the complications that now lay ahead of them.

"This," Joachim said, "doesn't make things any easier."

"No," she agreed. She kissed his chest.

"If things were different—"

"If things were different we might not have ended up in bed together. We'd probably never have met."

"Possibly."

Elle leaned her head back and looked up into those jungle cat eyes. She tried to see something in them, but she wasn't sure if she couldn't find it or just wasn't sure what she was looking for. *How can I ask for answers when I don't even know the questions I'm supposed to be asking?*

"At the end of the day," she said, "I'm still a spy and you're still a criminal."

"I'm trying to change."

"That doesn't make the past go away."

A dark veil fell over his gaze. Even though he hadn't moved, he suddenly felt miles away. "You're right." His voice was cold and flat. He took his arm from her and sat up.

"That's not what I meant." Elle wished she knew what to say. She'd never been good at relationships. She'd never found anyone she especially cared to stay with. Every man in her life had been a diversion, nothing more. Some of those diversions had only lasted a night. None of them ever lasted more than a few months, and that had only been when the relationship was spread out over that time.

"Then what did you mean?"

Sitting up, Elle placed her back against the wall, brought her knees up to her chin under the sheet and wrapped her arms around her legs. She tried to think of an answer.

"We just picked a hell of a time to bump into each other," Joachim said. "Even if things were perfect—" he paused "—they wouldn't be perfect." He gathered his clothes in one hand. "I really don't need this kind of distraction."

Angry then at the thinly veiled accusation, Elle said, "This wasn't what I had in mind when I came here."

"What did you have in mind?"

I don't know, Elle thought. But she couldn't even bring herself to say that.

"My family is on the line," Joachim said. "What are you risking?"

She had no answer.

Joachim picked up her clothes and tossed them to her. He turned and headed for the shower, closing the door.

Angrily, Elle stared after him. *Distraction? Is that what I am?* She shoved up from the bed, then entered the bathroom.

Steam crawled in lazy wisps from the shower. He was a dim blur on the other side of the glass. He'd left the light off.

"I'm not a distraction," she told him. "I've got a job to do." *That's just making everything sound even worse.*

Without a word, Joachim opened the sliding glass door and reached for her. She took his hand and let him pull her into the narrow confines of the shower.

They kissed again, long and hard and just as hungrily as before, and their hands played knowingly with each others' bodies as the hot spray needled them. When her senses were reeling again, Joachim gently turned her and placed her hands on the shower tiles. She felt him move in behind her, felt the hard length of him graze her flesh, then he was deep inside her, even more distracting than before.

Afterward, Joachim wrapped a towel around his hips and stood in the bathroom doorway to watch her dress in the moonlight. *You've got yourself in a hell of a lot of trouble,* he told himself. *Things were complicated enough before this.*

But he knew he couldn't take it back. Neither could she. Even now, after everything they'd shared and how exhausted he felt, he wanted her again. The towel did little to disguise that fact. The sad thing was they were going to hurt each other and neither of them might be able to accomplish what they needed to do.

Dressed now, everything back in place, she pinned her wet hair up behind her head. He loved watching her back muscles work and the way the slope of her breast looked with her partially turned away from him. Then she picked the pistol up from the floor and tucked it into her waistband under the light shirt.

Joachim thought of all the women he'd had in Leipzig and a few other places he'd gone with Günter. Most of them had been beautiful, exotic and sensual. But none of them had been Elle. Over the years, he'd been captivated by a handful of them, but his interest had quickly waned or Krista had asked him what he thought he was doing, or he thought of having the women around Krista and knew that his sister would never approve.

He didn't know if that would happen with Elle, and he wondered—if the situation were somehow different—what Krista would think of her. But it didn't matter. There was no way he was going to have the chance to find out.

He didn't have the heart to go to the door to show her out. He didn't want her to leave. If he stood anywhere near that door, it was going to be even harder to watch her walk away.

She looked at him, her chin defiant and her blue eyes fierce. "This hasn't changed anything."

"I know."

"Don't get in my way."

Angry and frustrated, he wanted to demand what she'd do if he did. But all he said was, "I won't."

Without a backward glance, she let herself out the door and walked away. Letting her do that was one of the hardest things Joachim Reiter had done in years.

* * *

"What did you find out?"

Looking at her father seated at an outside table at the *taverna* the next morning, Elle suddenly felt guilty. She took a deep breath. "He says he's here trying to save his family. There's a man named Günter Stahlmann in Leipzig who has threatened Joachim's family. Günter sent Joachim to find out what Beck is doing here. Whom he's doing it with. If Joachim doesn't, Günter's going to kill his family."

The server arrived with coffees.

For a long time, they sat in silence.

"You are…attracted to this man?" her father finally asked.

"Yes."

"What are his intentions toward you?"

"Two days ago, he helped me get away from Quinn's people."

Her father nodded. "I remember." He sipped his coffee. "Having feelings for an adversary is not unusual."

"It is for me."

Surprise lifted his eyebrows. "You have never before…" He paused. "Negotiated a truce with a competitor?"

It was more like a surrender, Elle thought, remembering. But both of them had surrendered, then just as quickly went back to their defenses.

"No," she answered.

"I have. You need to remember that Joachim Reiter isn't a competitor. He's part of the opposition."

"True. But he is trying to save his family."

"What are you going to do?"

"My job," Elle said. *And I'm going to get revenge for my parents.*

Her father was silent for a moment. "I feel I must warn you, Elle."

In trepidation, she waited, knowing what her father was going to say. It was what he *had* to say.

"If this man gets in your way—in *our* way—make no mistake. If necessary, I will kill him."

"I know," Elle said.

Ermoupoli, Syros Island
The Cyclades Islands, Greece

Harsh morning sunlight slanted across the port city as Elle closed in on her quarry.

As the largest city in the Cyclades Islands, Ermoupoli was also the center of business in the area. Paved in marble, Lower Town spread out from the sea on the island's east side. The grand square was the city's main meeting place and commercial area. Farther north, in Upper Town, shipbuilders had erected neo-Classical mansions that were more works of art than living quarters. The blue and gold dome of Agios Nikolaos stood out among them.

Somewhere in the Vaporia district, Elle's quarry had a house. She knew the house would be well secured and protected. Fortunately, her target had a habit of coming to Lower Town for breakfast and business.

It stood to reason that Vasilios Quinn would want someone nearby to handle his international business affairs. It also stood to reason that Quinn would want someone as criminal minded as he was.

Markos Chatzidakis, the man Quinn had chosen to do business with, was such a man. Searching more deeply into Klaus Stryker's rebirth as Vasilios Quinn, Ashimov had ferreted out the fact that Chatzidakis had managed the various account manipulations that had put Stryker's money into what eventually found its way into Quinn's accounts.

Following the money exchange was, in Ashimov's biased opinion, truly the work of an artist. He'd stated that Chatzidakis was a very devious man and that only a man more cunning could follow all the permutations of his elaborate schemes. Then Ashimov had asked for a bonus.

Chatzidakis was also in SVR files and her father had accessed them. When the Communists had surrendered Russia to capitalism, several banking institutions had gone into the country and were used for criminal purposes such as washing money and deferring taxation. They'd been called "straw" banks. Chatzidakis had helped set up several of them, which had drawn the attention of the SVR.

He sat now at a table in a palm-shaded café, tapping his feet in time to a soft rock song from one of the nearby shops. Clean hands with carefully manicured nails flew across the keyboard of his notebook computer. Dressed in khaki shorts and a white crew shirt, he looked like a retiree catching up on e-mail from relatives or friends. He was overweight and soft looking, with white hair and a thin fringe of the same along his jawline, and he wore amber-tinted sunglasses and a Panama hat.

From the information in the SVR file, Elle knew Chatzidakis rarely left the island and kept three bodyguards with him at all times. They sat around the area, all of them wearing loose shirts to cover the pistols they carried. All of them looked capable and efficient.

All of them looked straight at Elle as she walked into the square. The tourist season was in full swing and Lower Town was bursting with business. Wearing a thin cotton dress that flaunted her figure and wraparound sunglasses, with her hair pulled back and a camera case under her right arm, she looked like one of those tourists.

Abruptly, she stopped and looked around as if confused.

Knowing she had the attention of Chatzidakis, his body-guards and most of the men in the area, she turned and approached his table.

The three bodyguards started closing in.

She smiled at Chatzidakis. The man held up a hand and waved the bodyguards back into their respective positions.

"Pardon me," Elle said in an American accent that could have come from the Old South, "I do believe I'm lost. Do you speak English?"

"Of course," Chatzidakis replied.

"Then perhaps you could help me." Elle reached into the camera bag and took out a guide to the islands.

"There's nothing that I enjoy more than aiding a beautiful woman," Chatzidakis said, smiling broadly.

"You are so kind," Elle said.

"Have you had breakfast? The café here is very good." Chatzidakis waved her to a seat.

Elle hesitated for a moment, putting on a show for the bodyguards, then sat across from Chatzidakis.

"Now what are you trying to find?" He took the guide she offered.

Dropping her hand inside the camera case in her lap, Elle spoke without the affected accent, "Markos Chatzidakis, do I have your attention?"

Startled, he looked up at her. Fear tightened his brown eyes.

"Good," Elle said. "First of all, I want you to know that I have a pistol in this camera case."

"I have three bodyguards."

"I know that, but here's how this is going to play." Elle slipped the sunglasses from her eyes and smiled as if they were having a friendly discussion. "If you call to them, I'm going to shoot you. My accomplice, who is on top of one of the shops—"

Chatzidakis lifted his gaze and started searching. Clearly he'd never been so close to death before. Good. His lack of experience was a great advantage.

Elle waited, knowing the man would spot her father on the tourist shop just behind her. "Do you see him?"

"Yes."

"If you do anything—anything—other than work with me, he's going to shoot you," Elle said. "He's a very good shot at this distance. Then we'll sort out your bodyguards." She paused and smiled again. "I very much doubt that you'll be in any shape to care how it all ends up."

"What do you want?" Sweat beaded on Chatzidakis's forehead.

A server came over but Elle waved him away. "I want Vasilios Quinn's personal accounts. *All* of them."

Chatzidakis protested. "Quinn will kill me."

"Quinn," Elle pointed out, "isn't sitting across from you in this chair this morning. And we're going to give you amnesty if you cooperate. A free pass. We'll get you out of the country."

Chatzidakis hesitated only a moment. "What do you want me to do?"

"Go to this Web site." Elle gave him the site address. "Then enter the information about Quinn's accounts."

"You won't get away with this."

Elle fixed him with her gaze and smiled comfortably. "Want to live long enough to find out if I do?"

Without a word, looking pained, Chatzidakis started typing.

Taking a cell phone from the side of the camera case, Elle punched speed dial.

"Yes?" Ashimov answered on the other end.

"We're at go."

There was a brief pause, then the Russian computer expert said, "I have him. Tell him to give me the information on the Swiss accounts first. I'll be better able to find out if he tries holding out on us with those."

"All right." Shifting from Russian to English, Elle spoke to Chatzidakis. "The Swiss accounts first."

The man glowered at her.

"All of them," Ashimov said. "Two are missing."

"The other two as well," Elle said, relaying the information. "List the passwords for each. Then the accounts in Barbados, followed by the accounts in the Cayman Islands."

Chatzidakis hesitated.

"Quickly," Elle snapped. "I don't have all day. Sooner or later your bodyguards will become suspicious. I can't be responsible for what happens then."

Chatzidakis complied. With Ashimov quietly directing her over the phone, Elle watched the accountant and his men. When properly motivated, Chatzidakis could type exceedingly fast. In less than twenty minutes, Ashimov assured her they had it all.

"Now," Elle said, smiling more broadly and putting her sunglasses back in place, "you get to live if you do exactly what I say."

"You already promised," Chatzidakis said. He looked ready to cry.

"I did, and I mean it." When Quinn discovered his money was missing—and he would—Elle knew that Chatzidakis's disappearance would further confuse the man. "I'm going to walk away now. Don't call out to your friends. Don't call Quinn and warn him because it's already too late. My friend is draining those accounts even as we talk. Just sit here until I'm gone."

"All right."

Elle stood and made a display of thanking Chatzidakis for his time. Then she turned and walked back toward the marina and the boat she and her father had rented.

Her father joined her as she was stepping down into the boat. "That went well," he said.

"I thought so," Elle agreed. She cast off the mooring rope as her father took the wheel and powered them up. She held her cell phone up to her ear again and called Ashimov. "Did you get it?"

"I did," Ashimov replied. A grin sounded in his voice. "You know, Elle, I've only been this rich four times in my life."

"Don't get used to it," Elle warned. "You can't keep the money."

"But he's a bad man," Ashimov protested.

"Some would say you are a bad man."

Ashimov laughed. "You know that's not true. I have worked very hard for you."

"Which is why you're getting a percentage of everything you lifted from Quinn's accounts," Elle agreed.

Her father turned the boat without incident and powered east across the open sea toward Mykonos.

"How long before Quinn finds out he's broke?" Elle asked.

"Not long," Ashimov said. "Not long at all if he's watching his accounts. Judging from the dire straits of his current finances, I would assume he keeps a close eye on things."

But not close enough, Elle thought with cruel satisfaction. Over the last day and a half, since the night she'd spent time in Joachim Reiter's arms and bed, she'd learned to detest Vasilios Quinn even more. She blamed Quinn for the confusion she felt every time she thought of Joachim.

If things had ended in Amsterdam, with the two of them sharing a few near misses and an unresolved attraction, she would have been fine. However, now she knew that her actions—necessary though they were—had placed Joachim in the line of fire. If something happened to him, she knew she was going to feel responsible. She couldn't let that get in the way of the mission.

"Are you all right?" her father asked.

"I will be," she told him, but she kept her gaze out to sea. She'd never been able to look him in the eye and successfully lie to him.

Chapter 23

Vasilios Island
The Cyclades Islands, Greece

Cold rage expanded inside Vasilios Quinn as he gripped the phone. Screaming a curse, he threw the device across the room and stared once more at the damning computer monitor on his desk.

All of his accounts in Switzerland, Barbados, the Caymans and the United States were pale, anemic shadows of what they had been.

"I take it Chatzidakis was not at home." Arnaud Beck lounged quietly in one of the expensive leather chairs in Quinn's office.

"No, he's not." Quinn went to the window that had been replaced only days ago and stared out over the pool. His daughter, Sapphira, lounged poolside with two young men.

"Joachim Reiter was not involved in the Chatzidakis matter," Beck said. "My men have had him under observation since the...disturbance at your daughter's party. He's made no attempt to hide what he's doing."

"What is he doing?"

"Judging by his actions, he's trying to find me." Beck grinned at the thought of that.

"Why?"

"His boss, Günter Stahlmann, knows me. Just as he used to know you."

"It would have been better if you'd have disappeared as I did."

"Looking back on things now, from our present perspective, I'm inclined to agree. But I would have had to find someone to murder me."

"Who has my money then?"

"My guess is the woman."

"The CIA agent? St. John?"

"Yes."

"Why?"

"To make you tell her what you know about Marion Gracelyn's death."

Angrily, scarcely able to contain himself, Quinn paced the floor. "That's ridiculous. I don't know anything about that woman's murder."

"But you shared a blackmailer," Beck pointed out. "Perhaps St. John is after her."

"She would go to these lengths?"

Beck lifted his shoulders and dropped them. "It remains to be seen. There is the possibility that you were simply robbed by an outside party."

Quinn didn't want to accept that. He couldn't. If

whomever took his money was an anonymous person, he might not be able to get his money back.

"You still have the deal with the Berzhaan terrorists," Beck pointed out. "That alone can make you wealthy."

"I don't want to give up this life I've made here," Quinn said. "I've grown...*comfortable* with it. It suits me."

"You lost your edge here, Klaus."

Hearing his old name shocked Quinn. No one called him that anymore. Klaus Stryker had died twenty years ago, just footsteps ahead of a Russian retaliation and CIA strike team.

"You need to get back to the man you used to be before you took all this soft living for granted," Beck said. He smiled but there was no mirth. "You can get back there. We grew up together. Think. Twenty years ago you would have already had a plan in place."

"If it is St. John," Quinn said, shuffling the bits and pieces that he knew, "we know she has a relationship with Joachim Reiter."

"He helped her escape the security guards here."

"We don't know that for certain."

"Certainties are for the law," Beck said. "You and I, we operate by a different set of rules. Even if we kill the wrong person, the situation becomes clearer."

When the theft had occurred, Quinn had let Joachim Reiter's probable involvement slide. That was when Beck had put him under constant surveillance. For the last few days, the German leg-breaker had maintained an interest in watching things, but stayed apart. Only Sapphira had anything to do with him, and then just to anger her father.

"They spent the night together," Beck reminded.

Beck's spies had told him that, but they hadn't identified her until the next day. At the time they had believed St. John to simply be a woman Joachim had picked up in a *taverna*, or a prostitute. Since that night, she'd been a ghost, never anywhere on his radar screen.

"For the moment, she is in command of her game," Quinn said. "We have to wait to be contacted. If she was behind this."

"I believe she was."

"But that won't stop us from adding our own dimension to the game," Quinn went on. "Bring Joachim Reiter in. We'll up the ante." He took a deep breath as Beck pulled a cell phone from his pocket and made the call. It felt good to be back in control of something.

Mykonos Town, Mykonos Island

Günter Stahlmann was growing impatient. Joachim heard that in the man's voice even though Günter tried to act sublimely confident.

Seated in one of the *tavernas* facing the harbor, Joachim tried to remain calm. That was becoming increasingly hard. At first he'd been concerned for his family, who remained in good health as of this morning. But now he was preoccupied with thinking about Elle. He hadn't seen her since the night they were together.

Images of her on top of him, under him, in his arms and in his shower wouldn't leave his mind. He could close his eyes and smell the heat of her again, feel the smoothness of her skin gliding against his, hear the sounds of their bodies straining together and taste her lips on his.

The following morning he'd woke drenched in sweat from a nightmare that had borrowed from events that night. In the dream, Beck had held Elle naked and bound on her knees, one hand knotted in her hair and the other holding a pistol at the back of her head. Beck had grinned at her and shot her. The bullet had ripped through Elle, exploding her beautiful face all over Joachim.

"How much longer am I supposed to wait?" Günter asked.

"Give me a few more days."

"And what if you have nothing to report then?"

Joachim didn't know. "Approaching Quinn isn't like going after someone who owes you money. I don't have the necessary leverage." Surely Günter understood that.

"Two more days," Günter said harshly. "Two more days, Joachim. Then we start talking about consequences. In the meantime, think about whom in your family you least want to lose. Your mother? Your sister? That still leaves your brother-in-law and your niece. Which of those should I start with? Think about it. I will."

Günter hung up the phone before Joachim could make a reply.

Joachim finished his flavored water and paid his tab. He had to get out and move. All around him, tourists and residents went on with their vacations and everyday lives. It wasn't fair. Some of the anger and helplessness he felt was almost ready to spill over onto them.

Outside, distracted by his own worries, Joachim didn't notice the men closing in on him till it was too late. He turned and started to run.

Then he saw her—Elle Petrenko—seated at a bar with a good-looking man who looked like an American. She was dressed casually, like a tourist, and she looked at him as if she was shocked to see him.

For a second too long, Joachim hesitated, wondering what she was doing there and who the man was she was with. Something sharp pierced his left thigh. When he looked down, he saw the feathered tranquilizer dart standing out from his flesh. *Not again.*

He tried to move then, but unforgiving blackness sucked his conscious mind into it. Trapped there, he witnessed the nightmare again, watching Elle's beautiful face turn to gory crimson ruin in an explosive rush.

At the table in the *taverna*, Samantha St. John tensed as she watched the man stumble. She lost sight of him as a throng of passing tourists crossed between them. When she saw the man again, he was limping between two men.

"What's wrong?" Riley asked. He sat across the table from her, looking fatigued.

"That man." Sam gestured and half stood to try to see more of him.

Riley turned and looked in the direction she indicated. "Which one?"

"I think it was Joachim," Sam said, craning her neck to get a better look at the man and his companions. Unfortunately, foot traffic prevented anything other than a few glimpses. By that time, the men were already down to the docks.

"Let's take a look," Riley said, dropping money on the table to pay for their drinks.

"Yes." Sam took the lead, moving through the crowd of pedestrians, down the incline and around the groups of fishermen repairing their nets.

The late afternoon sun slammed into her with unaccustomed intensity. For the last week they had been trying to get a lead on Elle, but whatever hole her sister had fled into seemed to have closed after her.

In frustration, Sam and Riley had gone to Leipzig, trying to pick up Joachim Reiter's trail or the one that had ended in the murder of her parents twenty years ago. She and Riley had spent three days chasing themselves. There had been no sign of Elle or Joachim.

Then, that morning, a CIA agent who had been tailing a man named Markos Chatzidakis as the result of another operation had called in complaining that "Special Agent Samantha St. John" had rousted his target. Chatzidakis had quit Syros and it looked like he wasn't returning.

Since Sam had been in Leipzig, and since the CIA agent in Syros that had identified her was a man she'd worked with before, she'd known the woman couldn't have been anyone but Elle. Though what her sister was doing in Greece escaped Sam. Nothing in the files she'd been privy to indicated any interest in Greece.

The boat "Sam" had used to leave Syros had turned up in Mykonos. Maybe Elle wasn't still on the island, but she had been there. Sam and Riley had chartered a plane and flown to Mykonos island immediately, hoping to pick up her sister's trail.

The men loaded onto a boat and cast off before Sam and Riley could get there.

Spotting a man using a pair of binoculars to ogle some of the young women draped across the prows of several nearby boats, Sam went over to him. "Could I borrow those?"

Startled, the man looked guilty and nodded. "Just admiring the boats."

Sam didn't say anything. She fitted the binoculars to her eyes and focused on the departing boat now getting under full power.

The two men had dropped their incapacitated companion in a fishing seat and belted him in. His head jerked back and forth in a loose roll, mimicking the pitch and yaw of the boat.

This time Sam had no problem identifying him. She passed the binoculars back to the tourist, who immediately elected to go elsewhere to "admire" boats.

"That," Sam said, "was Joachim Reiter."

"Let's see if we can run down the boat's registry," Riley suggested.

Sam fell into step beside Riley. "Elle isn't here with Joachim Reiter."

"What makes you say that?"

"Because those men just took Joachim," Sam said. "If Elle had been here with him, she wouldn't have allowed that to happen."

"Then what," Riley asked, "drew them both here?"

"We missed something," Sam said. "Something important."

Elle made the call from Mykonos Town just after dark. She held the cell phone in her hand and surveyed the tourists walking up from the harbor. Disguised with a dark wig, and wearing jeans and a pullover, she didn't stand out among the evening crowd flooding into the *tavernas*.

Vasilios Quinn answered on the second ring.

"Do you want to know where your money is?" Elle taunted.

"What do you want?" Quinn demanded.

"I want you, Klaus Stryker," Elle said.

Despite the use of his old name, Quinn remained calm. "Since I am out of the question, I know you're after something else."

Elle hated the smug tone in the man's voice. Ashimov had stripped his remaining millions from him. Quinn probably had some money put back, hidden away in other places kept separate from the Quinn name, but it wouldn't be much. Not enough to keep him happy as greedy as he was.

"I want Lenin's Lullaby," Elle said. *But I want you just as badly.*

"How do you know about that?" Quinn demanded.

"Does it matter?"

"What are you willing to give me for it?"

A bullet between the eyes, Elle thought. But she said, "You can have your money back."

"I don't believe you."

"Then die broke," Elle snapped. "Keep looking over your shoulder, because one day I'll be there."

"I don't think so." Quinn sounded more confident. "I, too, have something to trade. I have Joachim."

Fear punched Elle in the stomach. Her hand trembled on the phone. Breathing out, she pushed all the confusion and the emotions away. She was a spy. The SVR had prepared her for stress and pressure.

They just didn't prepare you for this, she thought bitterly. It wasn't just losing Joachim that preyed on her mind. If he died, there was no reason for Günter Stahlmann to keep Joachim's family alive.

"How do I know you have him?" she asked.

There was a pause, then Joachim yelled in pain. The sound cut through Elle, making her shudder.

"Proof enough?" Quinn asked. "Or do I have to send you a body part?"

"You've got my attention," Elle conceded.

"If you want him back," Quinn said, "in one piece, we're going to have to negotiate."

"I don't trust you."

Quinn laughed then. "See? We're already negotiating. I don't trust you, either."

"Then what do we do?"

"We swap. You get Joachim and I get my money."

"What about Lenin's Lullaby?"

"Oh, I keep that. I've already got interested buyers that I really don't want to disappoint. All those years ago I could sell it right away. I've kept it as a nest egg—waiting for a rainy day. It's pouring now."

Elle took a deep breath. "Where and when?"

Quinn gave her a longitude and latitude, then told her to be there at 6:45 a.m. "I expect everything to be put back in place before we make the exchange," he said. "Otherwise I'm going to tie an anchor around Joachim's neck and send him to the bottom. Hopefully you'll be there to watch."

"I'll be there," Elle said. Then she broke the connection before he could. She turned on her heel and started walking, thinking furiously.

Only a short distance farther on, her father stepped out of an alley where he'd been keeping watch and fell into step with her. "Something has happened."

Without preamble, Elle gave it to him.

Her father was silent for a short time. "You can still deal for Lenin's Lullaby. You can force Quinn's hand."

"Not without him killing Joachim first," Elle said.

"When you weigh the lives in the balance—"

Elle turned on him. "The lives are already in the balance. Whether the world knows about Lenin's Lullaby or not, the military departments of several countries have more than enough biological agents to wipe out the population of this planet several times over. If they don't, they will have. It doesn't matter if everyone knows that Russia made this one. Everyone's hands are dirty when it comes to this kind of warfare."

Her father looked at her silently. "I can't get a team in place in time for the meeting tomorrow. By the time I explain to the generals what we need, it will be too late."

"I know." Elle thought furiously. "But maybe I can." She took out her cell phone again and dialed Sam's home number, trusting that her sister would have her calls forwarded in case Elle called.

Sam answered on the second ring. "Hello."

"It's me," Elle said.

"I didn't expect to hear from you."

Elle tried to figure out how much anger was in her sister's words and was surprised to find that relief seemed to outweigh everything else.

"There's a situation," Elle said. She took a deep breath and let it out, realizing that honesty was the best policy. "Sam, I need help."

"Tell me where to meet you," Sam said. "Riley and I are on Mykonos."

Shock ran through Elle. "How did you get here?"

"Someone thought you were me," Sam explained. "This isn't the first time. I'll tell you later. Where can we find you?"

They met at the rooms Sam and Riley had taken at Cavo Tagoo. After brief introductions, and some tense moments, they settled down to business, spreading maps of the area over a table in the center of the room.

Despite the different political affiliations and some emotion on Fyodor Petrenko's part at seeing his adopted daughter's twin in the flesh, all of them were versed enough in their craft to concentrate on the task at hand.

"The open water is a bad place for a confrontation," her father said.

"Agreed," Riley replied, surveying the open expanse of blue on the map that spread out from the X he'd marked. "However, it's going to work against Quinn as much as it does us. Plus, I've got a few surprises I can pull as far as men and munitions. The CIA has a military staging team off the coast of Turkey that we can borrow. Mitchell Stone, our director, has already made the arrangements. The team is already en route. They'll be in place before morning."

"If Quinn thinks he's being tricked, he'll kill Joachim," Elle said. The fear inside her had died down to a constant pulse, like ashes that had been banked to make it through the night.

Although Riley wasn't completely convinced of Joachim's story about the BND agent, he'd seemed willing to listen and put aside his own judgment in the matter.

"We're not going to let that happen," Riley said. He looked at Elle. "Sam says you're good with a sniper rifle."

"I am," Elle said.

"She is one of the best I've ever seen," her father said. There was no pride in his voice, only a statement of fact.

"The men I've got coming are going to be in the water," Riley said. "But we need a sniper to make this work. I can spare one of the men, but then we lose one of them in the water."

"I can do it," Elle said.

Riley fixed her with his gaze. "I hope so, because Sam's life is going to be in your hands."

Two hours before dawn, Elle stood in front of the hotel and waited for the others. Her eyes were drawn up to the six-unit boarding house across the street, to the room where she had made love to Joachim Reiter the first time.

The first time? She shook her head, wondering where that thought had come from. *The* only *time. If we live through today, we won't see each other again.* But part of her wanted to see him again. To see him *and* to make love to him.

"Penny for your thoughts," Sam said.

Turning, Elle was surprised to find her sister there. She shook her head and tried a smile that didn't fit properly. "You wouldn't like them. They're too dark, too Russian."

Sam searched her with her knowing gaze. "He got to you, didn't he?" Sam asked.

Elle didn't say anything.

"I could tell by the way you were attracted to him back in Amsterdam," Sam said. "From the very first time you met him at the train station."

"That was hormones."

"Is it now?"

Riley and her father came from the hotel lobby, but they gave them space, standing to one side and conferring quietly.

"Now," Elle said, breathing out, "I don't know what it is. He's a criminal, Sam. Not someone pretending to be a criminal."

"If that's all he was," Sam said quietly, "if that's all he could be, you wouldn't feel the same way."

"I don't know how I feel," Elle admitted. "I think I'm more confused than anything." She took a deep breath and let it out. "Except for scared. I'm scared." It wasn't like her to admit that, or to feel that emotion this intensely. She'd always let it hang loose in the field, always felt like she could handle anything that was thrown her way.

Sam threw her arm around her sister, and it was like none of the tension that had happened in Amsterdam or at the Athena Academy had ever come between them. *This is how we're supposed to be,* Elle thought. *This is the way it would have been if Klaus Stryker hadn't come between us.*

"Come on," Sam said. "This will be cake."

"When the shooting starts," Elle said, "stay low. I'm going to be shooting from a fishing boat."

Chapter 24

At 5:37 a.m., Elle slung the thirty-pound, second-generation Barrett sniper rifle over her shoulder and climbed up into the rigging of the fishing boat Riley McLane had hired. She lay along the top yardarm, dressed in canvas-colored clothing that helped her blend in with the furled sail.

Taking her position in the narrow safety net she and Riley had manufactured as a sniper's nest, Elle ran her hands over the big rifle and tried not to think about missing her shot.

The Barrett was a .50-caliber weapon with confirmed kills out past a mile. She hoped she was shooting at half that distance.

The rifle was semiautomatic, kicking out each spent shell and seating the next on blowback. The magazine held eleven rounds. An ammo pouch held a dozen more magazines. If she needed them.

As second-generation, the Barrett had been redesigned to move the magazine receiver from the center of the rifle to the stock in a bullpup configuration, providing less recoil for a faster second shot. The .50-caliber round could punch through foot-thick walls and take out targets. Even a hit in a leg or an arm often guaranteed a kill from shock alone. Elle was extremely proficient with the weapon and had used them on other assignments with considerable success.

At 6:02 a.m., when the first creeping light of dawn showed pink in the east behind Elle, the boat Sam and her father had rented sailed into the meet site. Sam walked out onto the deck and held up a paper bull's-eye mounted on cardboard. She held it steady in the gentle wind.

Moment of truth, Elle told herself as she laid her cheek against the Barrett's stock. She kept both eyes open as she peered through the telescopic sight. Trying not to think that if she didn't hit the target the heavy bullet would take off her sister's hand or arm, she put the crosshairs over the target.

"Ready?" Elle asked over the radio headset she wore.

"Yes," Sam said.

"Steady."

"Do it." Sam never flinched.

Always restless, the blue-green swells of the Aegean rose and fell beneath both vessels. Elle timed them. At least as high up in the rigging as she was, she didn't lose sight of Sam's boat.

She took up trigger slack, squeezed and felt the Barrett slam against her shoulder.

Sam examined the target. "Two inches low and to the left. Do it again."

Elle made the adjustments to the scope. Riley had

promised that the weapon was already sighted in, but Elle knew that each shooter read a scope just a little differently. At a half mile, even a fraction of a difference measured in inches. She floated, timed the swells and entered the zero at the center of a sniper's radar, when time no longer tilted the world.

She fired again.

Upon inspection, Sam declared, "Perfect ten."

"Good," Elle said.

"All right," Riley said. "From this moment on, we maintain radio silence."

Trying to relax, trying not to think of everything that could go wrong, Elle lay quietly in the sniper's nest and waited.

"They're there."

Standing in pilot's area of his yacht, Quinn looked south southeast and spotted two boats. "There are two vessels."

"One of them is a fishing trawler," Beck replied over the radio headset. "It's a half-mile distant from the rendezvous point. You don't have anything to worry about from a fishing boat."

Quinn knew that was true. But so many things had gone wrong this past week. "Keep watch."

"I will."

The sleek executive Bell helicopter carrying Beck shot by overhead. He saluted Quinn through the thick Plexiglas.

Lifting the handset for the radio, Quinn called for Samantha St. John over the prearranged channel. "St. John, this is Quinn."

"I read you." Her voice was calm, steady.

Is she that confident? Quinn wondered. *Or does she truly believe I'm going to let her out of here?* He didn't know. Either possibility amused him.

"Get out on deck. Let me see you," Quinn ordered. He pulled binoculars to his eyes and watched the other ship as the pretty young blonde stepped into full view.

She wore a halter and walking shorts, leaving little to the imagination and even less to hide a weapon.

Are you truly that confident? Quinn wondered. He shifted his gaze to the boat's pilot. Quinn didn't know the man, but there was something vaguely familiar about him.

Beck and the helicopter circled overhead, close enough to raise additional chop on the sea. Belted into the craft, Beck and two of his men opened the doors and readied assault rifles equipped with M-203 grenade launchers.

"You didn't mention bringing a helicopter," the woman told him.

Quinn grinned. "Sue me. I like surprises."

"Surprises won't get your money back."

Cursing, Quinn waved to the two men holding Joachim Reiter between them. The German was handcuffed. Tape gagged him and he was still under the effects of a narcotic.

The two men guided Joachim to the prow and flanked him. They held him down on his knees while one of them put a pistol against their captive's head.

"No," Quinn agreed. "But he will."

"All right," the woman said. "How do you want to do this?"

"Stay there," Quinn directed. "We'll come alongside." He signaled his steersman to take them in. "Leave your boat powered down."

As they drew near, Quinn remained in the pilot area, not out in the open at all. "Move out," he said over his headset.

Immediately, the dozen armed men he had hidden aboard the yacht poured out from belowdecks and took up positions along the railing. They pointed their weapons at the woman and the man.

"Now," Quinn said, stepping out into view, "I believe you have something of mine."

Bastard! Riley McLane thought furiously. Clad in scuba gear and a black dive suit, he sat quietly in the upside-down Zodiac fast-attack boat that had been air-dropped into the sea ten miles away then steered into position.

Capable of traveling above or below the surface, the Zodiac was designed to deliver Navy SEALs and equipment to target sites. Upside-down in the water now, the rigid hull construction was at present buoyantly balanced to hang three feet below the surface, just deep enough that it couldn't be seen underwater in the early morning light. Riley felt the tide alternately lift and drop him the way it had for the past hour. The boat also carried on-board oxygen for the SEALs.

Riley peered through the miniature periscope setup SEAL team Captain James Tarlton had outfitted him with. Through it, he could see the armed men suddenly facing Sam.

Cursing himself, Riley knew they should have expected something like this. And they had, which was why Elle was set up as sniper in the fishing boat, but they hadn't thought about a helicopter.

Tarlton and his men occupied two Omega boats on either side of Sam's boat. All of the men were specialists at small-arms fire and close-quarters fighting.

Riley knew the SEAL team captain was seeing the same thing he was seeing. The SEALs also used shorthand code, tapped out on wrists, to keep each other informed.

Trying to keep his breathing regular through the regulator, Riley waited. The next move was up to Sam and Elle.

* * *

Watching the action taking shape on the two boats through the sniper scope, Elle forced herself to remain calm. She kept both eyes open but couldn't see any of the individuals on the other vessels with her left eye. Through the scope she could count hairs if she wanted to. She waited, sweeping the scope across Quinn, then settling on the man with the pistol pointed at Joachim's head.

A moment later, Sam handed over the notebook computer that she claimed had the software on it Quinn would need to reclaim his fortune. He had a satellite link on board the yacht, so he could examine the hookup immediately.

Elle kept the rifle centered over the chest of the man holding the pistol on Joachim. She saw the puff of red smoke swirl up from the notebook computer in the yacht's stern. Mixed with tear gas, the smoke grenade concealed within the computer guaranteed a moment of confusion.

Elle squeezed the Barrett's trigger, riding out the recoil and switching over to the other man next to Joachim as the empty brass cartridge spun in the gentle wind. With the difference between the bullet's velocity and the speed of sound, she knew she could have three shots in the air before the sound of the first one reached the men aboard the ship.

On the yacht, the man holding the pistol on Joachim suddenly flew backward as if he'd been hit in the chest by a sledgehammer. The second man's head came apart and Elle knew she'd almost missed the target

"Go!" she yelled over the headset as she moved on to her next target, shifting the rifle in an attempt to pick up Quinn.

"Move out!"

Gripping the Zodiac's side, Riley heard the SEAL team commander give his order over the underwater radio and felt the special forces craft shiver to life as the electric engines kicked over and powered it up. The men shifted around Riley as the Zodiac hurtled toward the yacht.

"Get us up!" Tarlton shouted.

Incredibly, the Zodiac flipped and surfaced, losing a large amount of the water through the vented sides as it skimmed along on top of the sea.

Spitting out the regulator and stripping off the face mask, Riley unlimbered the H&K MP3 submachine gun he'd been assigned for the assault. Several of the SEALs were already raking Quinn's yacht with controlled fire. Pieces of the boat's coaming blew away into the air. Armed men aboard the yacht went down at once.

In seconds, the tide of battle had shifted. But it wasn't over yet. And he didn't know if Sam was alive or dead.

Quinn flattened himself against the pilot's cabin and drew a pistol from his shoulder holster. Fear thundered through him, rattling his spine and clenching his teeth. He didn't know where the hell the armed men had come from. The sea had just seemed to vomit them up.

Dead men littered the yacht's deck.

"Beck," Quinn yelled over the headset. He searched the sky for the helicopter.

The aircraft came in like a bullet. Beck and the men hanging onto the helicopter's sides unleashed a torrent of fire that strafed the powerboat that Sam St. John had arrived in.

When fire was returned from the two military-style boats closing in rapidly on top of the water, the helicopter pilot pulled up abruptly, breaking off the attack.

Cursing Beck's cowardice, Quinn leaped to the yacht's controls and threw the throttles forward. The yacht settled down into the sea for a moment, then lunged, uncoiling explosively.

A few of the men in the strange boats made an attempt to shoot Quinn. Their bullets whined upward, missing him by inches while he stayed hunkered down.

When he looked back, he saw that he was leaving them behind him. They bobbed on the wake he left and tried to turn their craft in pursuit.

Quinn smiled, certain that he was home free. Then he noticed the small, delicate hand clutching the stern railing.

No! he thought. *It can't be!*

But it was. In the confusion, Samantha St. John had somehow grabbed the stern of his boat. He raised his weapon and took aim.

Struggling to hold onto the stern of Quinn's yacht, Sam pulled herself up. Her feet and lower legs hammered the water. Another foot or two and she would have been caught by the water propulsion jets and torn free.

Vaulting aboard this boat is definitely not one of the better ideas I've had, she told herself. But she'd intended to land astern, not barely make the grab on the railing. Taking a fresh hold, she pulled herself up, then saw Quinn taking aim with his pistol.

She ducked back down just as a bullet slammed through the space where her head had been.

Dizzy from the narcotic playing havoc with his central nervous system, Joachim forced himself to stay awake. Maneuvering on the yacht's bouncing deck would have been hard enough without the disorientation created by the drug.

He looked at the dead men beside him. One of them

was nearly headless, his face smashed by a high-velocity, heavy-caliber round. Blood ran scarlet across the yacht's deck.

Pushing himself to his knees, swaying drunkenly, Joachim stripped a pistol from the headless man's hip holster. Working the slide, Joachim made certain there was a live round under the hammer.

He leaned against the pilot cabin and went forward, catching movement from the periphery of his vision. Taking a fresh grip on the weapon, he waited, seeing Quinn alive back there with a pistol in his hands.

Then he heard someone moving in front of him. He turned, lifting the pistol in both hands as one of Quinn's men took aim with an assault rifle.

Lying in her sniper's nest, Elle watched as Quinn's yacht roared south toward the open sea. Compared to the heavy diesels aboard the yacht, the Zodiac boats would only be fast also-rans.

She took aim at the pilot's area, catching brief glimpses of Quinn and Sam. Then she saw Joachim stagger up from the deck with a pistol clasped between his cuffed hands.

Alive! The thought sang within her.

Then bullets danced through the rigging and ricocheted off the mast. By the time she realized the helicopter had circled around her position and men were now firing at her, the sound of the first shots crashed into her hearing, sharper than the reports coming in across the waves.

The helicopter hovered a hundred feet away, looking like a huge dragonfly. Elle brought the Barrett around, cursing the weapon's length and weight. Five feet long, it was hard to maneuver quickly. If not for the bullpup design that allowed her to shift the weight over her shoulder, she wouldn't have managed it at all.

Peering through the open sights, no longer having or needing the telescope at this distance, Elle took aim at the pilot's side of the helicopter. She was just tightening her finger on the trigger when Beck worked the action on the M203 grenade launcher mounted beneath his assault rifle.

Senses keyed nearly to overload, Elle saw the fat grenade leap from the launcher and scream toward her. An instant later, the explosive round detonated against the mast ten feet below her.

A concussive wave picked her up like a giant hand and shook her, hammering her back against the yardarm. Thankfully, the grenade was an HE round. High-explosive beat the hell out of an antipersonnel round. She was left deaf and beaten nearly to death, but she was alive.

Desperately, she tried to pull the Barrett back into play. Then the mast swung drunkenly and she fell.

The yacht caught a trough wrong as it sped across the sea. Leaping wildly into the air for a moment, the craft came down hard.

Sam lost her weapon when she nearly lost her grip as she struggled to hang on with both weapons. She slammed against the yacht's stern with enough force to knock the wind from her.

Evidently Quinn had seen or guessed what happened. The man rushed across the stern deck with a two-handed grip on his pistol. He shoved the pistol into her face.

Knowing she had no choice, Sam swung her body, vaulting over the railing just as Quinn fired. Her feet struck him in the chest and drove him backward just as gunfire sounded from the yacht's prow.

* * *

Joachim aimed at the center of the man's chest as the first rounds of the assault rifle chopped into the expensive teak deck. He backed away two quick steps, firing consistently as quickly as he could.

He knew his rounds were striking the man. The guard shuddered with each impact and his aim even shifted. But the rapid-fire chopping across the deck continued.

Joachim hit the wall behind him before he knew it. He was out of room to run. Even as he realized that, he shifted his aim for his opponent's face and squeezed the trigger.

Something red-hot struck his left leg, knocking it from under him. As he fell, Joachim rolled to take the impact on his shoulder and tried to keep the pistol pointed at the man, certain the next few rounds were going to shred him.

Instead, the man dropped his weapon, fell to his knees, then flopped over face-first as the yacht hit another wave badly and floundered to keep from capsizing.

Joachim caught the railing just before he went over and hung on, knowing the boat was badly out of control. He forced himself up and saw blood streaming down his leg from the bullet hole inside his left thigh. If the round had nicked the femoral artery, he knew he'd bleed out in minutes.

He lurched for the pilot area.

Sam rolled and came up before Quinn. She held her hands up in front of her in the ready position, then snap-kicked him in the face, driving him backward.

Quinn came up at once and knotted his hands into fists. He wasn't a fighter trained in martial arts, but he had years of experience in the street and knew how to make use of close quarters. He also towered over her and outweighed her by at least a hundred pounds.

Relying on instincts and training, Sam blocked his punches and gave ground. She had no choice. Footing was made even more difficult by the bouncing deck as the yacht careened across the sea.

Seeing an opening, Sam twisted and lifted a roundhouse kick into Quinn's face, popping his head back. She tried to press her advantage but he flailed out with a big hand and delivered a glancing blow to the side of her head.

Dazed, her vision suddenly double, Sam stepped back again. He punched at her but she slapped the blow away, then stepped inside his arms. She slammed the Y of her hand into his throat, paralyzing his larynx. He grabbed his throat with both hands and *hurked*, trying desperately to catch his breath.

Still on the move, Sam swept his feet from under him and face-planted him against the deck. He shivered and went still.

Breathing hard, Sam glanced up and spotted Joachim struggling with the yacht's wheel. His left leg was drenched in blood.

She picked up a pistol that skidded across the deck and shoved it into her waistband, then crossed to the wheel.

Joachim looked at her, then shook his head. "You're not Elle."

"No," Sam agreed. She spotted the first-aid kit clipped under the seat and retrieved it. Using a razor blade from the kit, she slit his pants leg. Two wounds showed on his leg, one in front where the bullet had entered and a larger one where it had exited. Both bled profusely.

"Where's Elle?" Joachim asked over the roar of the engines.

Sam pulled at Joachim's leg. "Be still. You're going to bleed out."

"Where's Elle?" he repeated.

She wrapped a pressure bandage around his leg and pulled tight, shutting down the blood flow. There was enough that she was seriously considering a tourniquet, but she hoped the bandage would hold long enough for real medical attention.

"She's on the fishing boat with her father," Sam replied in answer to his question.

Joachim looked around, then said, "You mean the one under attack by the helicopter?"

Looking up, Sam watched as the helicopter continued the attack on the fishing boat. Before she could answer Joachim's question, he steered the yacht in that direction as the mast where Elle had been sniping from exploded.

Thrown free of the sniper's nest, Elle plummeted for the deck thirty feet below. She barely had time to realize that the fall might not be survivable, then a second grenade struck the fishing boat's deck and exploded, leaving a mass of whirling fire in its wake.

Elle missed the deck by inches and tumbled through the fireball for one incredible scorching instant, and plunged into the sea. Dazed, her senses overloaded, she barely registered the fact that she was in the water. She had to stop herself from taking a breath.

Desperately she looked around for her father. He was nowhere in sight. *Don't panic. Focus.*

At the end of her arm, the Barrett dragged her down like an anchor for a moment, then she started swimming, kicking her feet and using her free arm to stroke for the surface. She didn't want to surrender the rifle. If the helicopter was still up there, it was the only weapon she had that could retaliate over the distance.

Looking up through the water, she saw the flames chewing into the fishing boat's deck and spreading across the rigging, feeding hungrily on the canvas sails. The anchor chain held the burning fishing boat idle in the water.

Elle swam for the anchor chain, took hold with her feet and started pulling herself up one-handed. She dragged the sniper rifle after her.

The helicopter swiveled around to face Quinn's yacht. Weapons blazed as Beck and his men fired.

Breaking the surface, Elle sucked in air greedily and held onto the anchor chain. The flames crackled and popped above her, gutting the fishing boat quickly.

In the yacht's stern, Sam held an assault rifle and fired steady three-round bursts. Joachim was steering. In the background, Riley and the SEAL team powered over the sea in the Zodiacs, but they were going to arrive too late.

Beck and his men readied their weapons, breaking open the breaches of the grenade launchers and feeding thick rounds in.

Grabbing a fresh hold on the anchor chain, Elle drained the water from the Barrett's barrel, then settled the weapon into the crook of her arm as the helicopter slid sideways in the sky.

Sam wasn't going to be able to do enough damage with the assault rifle to bring the helicopter down, but Beck and his team with grenade launchers would make short work of the yacht, Sam and Joachim.

Concentrating, Elle brought the rifle to her shoulder and opened both eyes wide. Mentally, she switched from her left eye to her right, choosing the field of vision she wanted dominate. She pulled the trigger time after time, steadily banging through the five rounds remaining in the clip.

Crimson colored the Plexiglas nose of the helicopter and

the pilot slumped over the yoke. Beck made a frantic grab for the controls, but he couldn't get back inside fast enough.

Out of control, the helicopter swooped toward the fishing boat and collided. Just before the impact, Elle dropped the Barrett and held onto the weapon as it pulled her beneath the sea.

The explosion vibrated through the water, disorienting her. She felt her senses fading, drifting in and out. Flames and smoke suddenly spread over the sea surface.

Releasing the Barrett to continue its descent to the ocean floor without her, Elle kicked out and swam for the surface. The headset was useless, ruined by the salt water on contact.

She came up near the yacht, which was listing badly and taking on water. But Sam and Joachim were peering over the side, preparing to dive in.

"Here," Elle called, throwing up an arm and waving.

Sam steered the boat as Joachim shoved his hand out and caught Elle's. Almost effortlessly, it seemed, he pulled her from the water and draped her against him.

Elle wrapped her arms around him, holding him tight and kissing him till they were both breathless.

"You're alive," she whispered, as if afraid to say it too loudly because just acknowledging the fact might somehow change things.

"So are you," he said. "I thought I'd lost you when the fishing boat blew up."

"Lost me?" she echoed, smiling hugely. "You haven't got me yet."

He held her head between his big hands. "I will," he said. "I can be a very determined guy."

"I," Elle told him, "happen to like determined guys. Maybe we can work something out." Holding onto him again, she saw Riley and the SEALs approaching in the

Zodiac boats. Her father was behind them in the power-boat. "Hold that thought."

She crossed the deck to where Quinn was just stirring, returning to wakefulness. Grabbing him by the hair of the head, having to restrain herself from putting a bullet through his head because he had killed her parents and cost her so much time from her sister, she lifted him so she could stare into his bloody face.

"Where is Lenin's Lullaby?" she demanded in Russian.

Quinn laughed at her.

Elle drew the pistol from her hip holster, thumbed the hammer back and shoved it into his face. "If you don't tell me, I'm going to kill you."

"I don't believe you," he said, and smiled. "You can't just do something like that in cold blood."

Elle shoved her face closer to his, till they were only an inch apart. "I," she declared in a cold, still voice, "am the daughter of Boris and Anya Leonov. Believe me when I tell you that I will kill you."

Quinn's eyes widened in recognition then.

"You killed my parents," Elle said. "The *only* thing keeping you alive is the fact that you know where that bio-weapon is. If you tell me, I won't kill you."

"It's in a safe-deposit box," Quinn whispered in a shaking voice. "In a bank in Berlin." He gave her the box number and told her where to find the key in his home.

She released him as Riley and the SEALs scrambled on board. They put plastic handcuffs on him and took him into custody.

"Elle?" Sam spoke in Russian.

Turning to her sister, Elle waited.

"What you said," Sam said. "About our parents…"

"It's true," Elle said.

Sam stepped forward and took Elle into her arms. Elle felt her sister's heart beating against hers. They weren't in tune. Maybe they wouldn't have been even if they'd grown up together, maybe other things would have pulled them in different directions.

But for now, they beat close enough.

Epilogue

The bank was small but elegant, well off the beaten path in the heart of the city.

Elle waited while her father opened the door of the Mercedes, then she got out. Dressed in a business suit with matching skirt, she accompanied him into the bank.

A pleasant bank vice president met them at the door because they'd phoned to let him know they were coming over. All the necessary paperwork from Vasilios Quinn was exchanged, and they were guided back to the safe-deposit room.

Inside the sterile viewing room they were shown to, the safe-deposit box was brought out. As though totally unconcerned, her father exchanged a few stories for a moment, then they were given privacy.

Elle waited while her father fit the key she'd gotten from Quinn's house into the box. It was possible, of course, that Quinn had been lying and that, instead of Lenin's Lullaby, the box held a final booby trap that would leave them plastered in pieces on the wall.

As she held her breath, her thoughts turned to her sister. Sam and her friends at Athena were busy tracking down leads from a computer folder that Quinn had also given them. Quinn was now in CIA custody. He didn't know much about the woman who had been blackmailing him over his past identity, but he did tell them that she was known in several circles as Arachne, the goddess of weaving and webs. The name, Sam had declared, fit the mysterious person. Whoever she proved to be.

Joachim, during his debriefing, had revealed that a woman had negotiated the deal with Günter Stahlmann that had first sent him to Amsterdam after Tuenis Meijer. At first, they had believed the woman was Arachne, but that hadn't made sense. The woman had sent Joachim in search of things Arachne would have already known.

It was a mystery that would have to be resolved at a later date. The Athena Academy women—Athena Force, Sam called them—were currently still deep into their investigation.

Elle was busy tying up loose ends as well. She exhaled and watched as her father inspected the box, then finally removed the top.

Inside was a small, insulated box as big as both her fists put together. When her father opened it, six vials containing bilious dust and liquid sat on a cut out foam bed.

There were also a number of computer discs and journals. Quietly, without a word, her father transferred everything to the metal briefcase he'd brought for that purpose. Crossing the border with the bioweapon would have been nearly impossible, so they'd made arrangements to destroy it at a lab outside Berlin that wouldn't ask questions.

Once more out in the sun, Elle felt relief wash over her. She let her father hand her into the car and unlocked his door for him.

Effortlessly, he slid behind the wheel. "I was thinking we might have lunch," he said.

"All right," she said.

"I know a place." He pulled out into traffic, sliding in with controlled grace. "Have you talked to Joachim?"

Elle shook her head. The question initiated the anxiety she'd been feeling since their separation almost twenty-four hours ago. Once debriefed in Greece, Joachim had turned himself in to the BND to plead his case. In the end, he'd pointed out that the only way he could be with her and make his family safe was to square things with his past as much as he could.

Neither of them knew when they would see each other again.

"He did the right thing," her father said.

"I know," Elle replied unhappily. "But there's no guarantee that they'll believe him. Or any idea of when they will release him."

Her father looked at her. "Do you love this man?"

Elle returned his gaze and shook her head. "I don't know. All I know for certain is that I want the chance to find out."

"He was a bad man."

Elle laughed at her father. "I can just imagine how Mom sat around daydreaming about the day she could marry a spy."

"Maybe I was not such a prize, then."

She squeezed his arm. "You were. You are. The two of you made it work. That's all that counts."

"It is," he agreed. Her father grinned, and somehow seeing him happy lightened her mood. "You have to work at it, though."

"I know. I'm still working at a relationship with Sam. *We're* still working at it. It's never going to be easy, but we'll manage."

His cell phone rang. He said yes twice, then hung up and slid the instrument back into his pocket.

Elle looked at him.

"Confirming reservations," he said. "The place I'm taking you to is very specialized."

A few minutes later, they pulled into a small parking lot beside a restaurant that looked pre-World War II. Ginger-bread surrounded the windows and the eaves, making it look like they had somehow stepped back in time.

Her father let her out of the car.

"Elle," a familiar voice called from behind her.

Heart leaping, Elle turned around and saw Joachim standing there.

He wasn't in shackles as she'd last seen him. He wore slacks, a jacket and a turtleneck, looking much different than at any other time Elle had seen him. His face still held a few bruises, but he was freshly shaved.

She walked toward him and he met her. She kissed him and felt his lips burn against hers. His arms wrapped around her and she felt the strength of him, solid and reassuring.

"Ahem," her father called. "They are very strict about their reservations here." He tapped his watch.

Breaking the embrace, Elle looked up at Joachim. "The BND released you?"

"After I agreed to give evidence against Günter." He held her hands as if afraid to let her go. He couldn't stop smiling. "They have him in custody already, and my family is being protected." He glanced at her father. "It appears your father still has favors from the old days that he can call in."

Her father shrugged. "It is a gift. What can I say? But I tell you, reservations for this restaurant were far harder to come by." He shooed them toward the door.

Leaving Joachim for a moment, Elle joined her father, embracing him and kissing him on the cheek even though she knew it would embarrass him. "Did I ever tell you," she whispered, "how lucky I have always felt that you are my father?"

"Often." He held her and kissed her forehead. "It is a very hard thing to live up to, you know. All these expectations."

"Thank you," she said.

"You're welcome." He glanced at his watch. "I'm going to have the server open a bottle of champagne to let it breathe." He looked meaningfully at Joachim and held up a handful of fingers. "You have five minutes to bring her to the table. And if things turn scandalous out here, I'd rather eat my lunch alone." He turned and went into the restaurant.

"Come here," Joachim said, taking her in his arms again and holding her tight. He kissed her long and hard. Then looked at her. "What is your father's definition of scandalous?"

"I don't know," Elle told him. "But we have five minutes to explore the possibilities."

* * * * *

The women of ATHENA FORCE *will soon face more danger, action and romance!*

Turn the page for a sneak peek at the next thrilling adventure,
Exclusive
by Katherine Garbera

Available in December 2006 at your favourite bookstore.
Only from Silhouette Bombshell!

Chapter 1

As soon as she realized that Andrea Jancey had been taken hostage, Tory Patton wasted no time. She went into action. Tory had convinced Andrea to come to UBC, the United Broadcasting Company. She felt personally responsible for the younger woman whom she'd been mentoring in the television news business. She phoned her boss and made an appointment to see him.

Next, the field producer, who was still in Suwan, Berzhaan. Tory spent ten minutes on the phone ascertaining the situation and getting whatever information she could from him. She jotted notes on the paper in front of her. A quick list of facts that she knew and that ABS News had reported.

Next she put in a call to Jay Matthews, her favorite cameraman. "Matthews."

"It's Tory."

"What can I do for UBC's top reporter?" he asked.

There was an edge to his voice that hadn't been there before their time in Puerto Isla. Before he'd pushed her for a personal relationship and she'd had to turn him down.

He'd asked for a transfer overseas and had been covering the ongoing military action in the Middle East. But she wanted him by her side if she could convince Tyson to send her to Berzhaan. "Did you hear about Andrea and Cobie?"

"Yes, how'd you hear?"

"Shannon Conner was just on ABS with a breaking story. I'm going to see Tyson in a few minutes."

"If you get him to send you, I'll work with you on this. I'll dig around and see what I can find for you. Even if they send someone else. Damn, I can't believe ABS broke the story on our missing reporter before we did."

"Pisses me off, too. Thanks, Jay."

"No problem, Patton."

She disconnected the call, turning to her computer. She sent an e-mail to Cathy Jackson in UBC research.

Cathy—
Please pull together whatever you can on Andrea Jancey and Cobie McIntire and their last known coordinates. Find out any information on who their contacts were and what story they were following.
Thanks, Tory

She also placed a called to Yasmine Constanine to see if she would be amenable to anchoring the show while Tory was in the field. She e-mailed her producer, Shawna Townsend, and ran the proposed idea past her. Shawna gave her the green light and suggested Perry for the field producer position. Now all she had to do was get Tyson to go for it.

She camped outside her boss's office for twenty minutes

making small talk with Anita, Tyson Bedders's secretary, while they both waited for him to return from a meeting. As soon as he saw her, he groaned.

"Not now, Patton."

"Yes, now, Tyson. I need to go to Berzhaan and find out what happened to Andrea."

"We're on it. You have a show now and anchors don't go into the field."

It was the same argument he'd used to keep her from covering hurricanes last fall and to keep her from heading to London after a terrorist attack. To be honest, she was sick of being an anchor. Sure it had been her dream, but she had to admit that dream had been based on reaching a goal that seemed unattainable more than on understanding what it entailed. "Then take me out of the anchor spot."

He rubbed the back of his neck. Tyson was a tall African-American man who was one of the sharpest minds in the business. He was the kind of boss that most people dreamed of having, and Tory didn't like to put so much pressure on him. "Let's go into my office where we can talk."

She followed him into his corner office. "Okay, so what's the scoop? Why did ABS get the story before us? This is one of our people."

"Shannon Conner is already in Berzhaan and the terrorists sent the video to her."

"Well, it's an interesting move on their part, to take one of our reporters."

"Did you hear their demands?" he asked. Being the head of news was on Tory's goal list but seeing the strain and the stress in Tyson as he spoke about one of their people taken hostage made her realize that much like the anchor job, there were some major cons to being the boss. She filed it away in the back of her mind so she'd have that information when she was ready to make her next career move.

"Not yet. As soon as I heard the news I started working on how to get down there and find Andrea and Cobie."

"I haven't approved that yet, Patton."

"I'm the only one you can send. I know Andrea, I trained her. I know the way she thinks. I'll find her."

"Tory, you asked for this promotion, your own news-magazine, and yet you're always in my office wanting me to send you back into the field."

She knew what he was saying. Understood that she wasn't fulfilling the commitment she'd made to Ty and the network when she'd said she'd take the anchor position. But anchoring wasn't exciting and, to be honest, with her personal life in constant flux, she craved the adrenaline rush that being in the field gave her. She missed the excitement and camaraderie of waiting at the assignment desk and seeing what kind of story she'd be given. She missed the unpredictability of always doing something new.

"What did they demand in exchange for the hostages? Who are 'they,' by the way?"

"'They' didn't tell us, just claimed to be a terrorist group. They want a total U.S. pull-out from the region in three weeks time."

"That's not even realistic. There's no way the government will go for that."

"We know."

"Come on, Ty. Let me go down there and see what I can find. I'm the best investigative reporter you have."

He rolled his eyes. "Every one of you thinks that. There's no ego like the investigative reporter ego."

Tory bit her lip. She knew her boss well enough to know

that he'd give her a shot if she didn't push him into a position where he couldn't look like it was his decision.

"This has to be the last time you leave the anchor desk. Do you remember your last contract negotiation, when you lobbied for this job? A show of your own where you could bring cutting-edge stories to the viewers at home?"

"I didn't realize that I'd be bringing home stories that *other* people researched, Tyson. That's not me. You know it's not."

"I know, Patton. That's why I usually cut you some slack, but this has to end."

She jumped up from her chair. "When I get back from Berzhaan, I'll stay put."

"I'm going to hold you to that."

She nodded, knowing she was going to have to make a few changes to make that happen. To be happy with the choices she'd made.

"I've already started working out the details for my trip. I hope to get out of town tonight."

"You need to make sure your shots are up to date. And don't tell me they are. I had Anita pull your file before I went to my meeting. You haven't even had your required yearly physical."

"Ty, that's a waste of time. I'm healthy as a horse."

"Whatever. No exam—no Berzhaan."

Tory added the exam to the growing list in her head of what needed to be done. She hated the time it would take. She needed to contact AA.gov, her alma mater Athena Academy's alumni network, to see if Andrea had been doing anything extra for them while she was in Berzhaan. Instead Tory had to focus on a stupid physical. Well, if that's what it took….

"Thanks, Ty."

He nodded. "Bring Andrea back and get the story. We can't have our competition making us look like idiots."

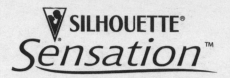

SILHOUETTE®
Sensation™

FEELS LIKE HOME
by Maggie Shayne

When Chicago cop Jimmy Corona returned to his small hometown, all he wanted was to find a mother to care for his son while he did his job. Shy, kind-hearted, Kara Brand was the obvious choice. But danger soon followed Jimmy, and only Kara stood between his son and certain death…

THE SHERIFF OF HEARTBREAK COUNTY
by Kathleen Creighton

A congressman's son is murdered and everything points to Mary Owen, the newcomer to Hartsville… but Sheriff Roan Harley can't quite make the pieces fit. At first his interest in Mary is purely because of the investigation. But where will his loyalties lie when he realises he's in love?

WARRIOR WITHOUT RULES
by Nancy Gideon

Bodyguard Zach Russell was charged with protecting risk-taking heiress Antonia Catillo, but his weakness for the beauty was getting in the way. Threats on Antonia's life were growing serious as their long-suppressed attraction rose to the surface. Could Zach crack the case before it was too late?

On sale from 17th November 2006

Available at WHSmith, Tesco, ASDA, Borders, Eason,
Sainsbury's and most bookshops

www.silhouette.co.uk

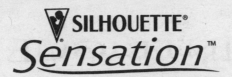

SILHOUETTE®
Sensation™

1106/18b

EXCLUSIVE by Katherine Garbera

Bombshell – Athena Force

Investigative reporting was Tory Patton's calling, and when her fellow Athena Academy graduate was taken hostage, nothing would stop her from taking the assignment to save her friend. But the kidnappers weren't who they seemed... and suddenly this crisis came much closer to the academy than anyone could ever guess.

THE BEAST WITHIN by Suzanne McMinn

PAX

The thing Keiran Holt feared most lived inside him—and possibly could cause harm to the woman he'd married. But Paige wasn't the only one who had spent two years looking for her missing husband. Would he be captured before they could save their once passionate marriage...and tame the beast within?

MODEL SPY by Natalie Dunbar

Bombshell –The IT Girls

A former supermodel from a wealthy family, Vanessa Dawson was perfect for the Gotham Roses' latest mission: Two top models were dead and it seemed a drug-ring was operating from the highest level of the fashion industry. Vanessa went undercover to get to the truth, but soon shoot-outs replaced fashion shoots as the order of the day...

On sale from 17th November 2006

*Available at WHSmith, Tesco, ASDA, Borders, Eason,
Sainsbury's and most bookshops*

www.silhouette.co.uk

▼ SILHOUETTE®
INTRIGUE™

THE LAST LANDRY by Kelsey Roberts
The Landry Brothers

Shane Landry's simple life—running the ranch and avoiding the temptation of his gorgeous housekeeper—is rocked to its foundations by a stunning revelation. Now the Landry brothers must band together to solve the murder of their parents before the secret behind Shane's heritage tears the family apart.

EPIPHANY by Rita Herron, Debra Webb & Mallory Kane *(3-in-1)*

With crime running rampant through the city of Atlanta, Georgia, quickly destroying the holiday spirit, only three hard-edged and jaded cops can save Christmas and protect the citizens from danger. And this holiday brings each detective face-to-face with his own epiphany, and his worst fears—falling in love...

THE SANTA ASSIGNMENT by Delores Fossen

She was hiding from a stalker—and from Brayden O'Malley, the man who blamed her for his wife's death. But when Brayden made an incredible request, Ashley Palmer couldn't refuse. He wanted her to give him a child, to save his son's life. But granting his wish meant coming out of hiding...and within the reach of a killer.

THE EDGE OF ETERNITY by Amanda Stevens
Eclipse & The Mists of Fernhaven

The accident that had taken her son had left Elizabeth Blackstone overwhelmed by grief—and the unshakeable feeling that she was being watched. Increasingly distant from her devastated husband, Paul, a trip to the luxury hotel in Fernhaven would prove just how deep their love went—and how far he would go to save her...

On sale from 17th November 2006

Available at WHSmith, Tesco, ASDA, Borders, Eason, Sainsbury's and most bookshops

www.silhouette.co.uk

FREE

4 BOOKS AND A SURPRISE GIFT!

We would like to take this opportunity to thank you for reading this Silhouette® book by offering you the chance to take FOUR more specially selected titles from the Sensation™ series absolutely FREE! We're also making this offer to introduce you to the benefits of the Mills & Boon® Reader Service™—

- ★ **FREE home delivery**
- ★ **FREE gifts and competitions**
- ★ **FREE monthly Newsletter**
- ★ **Books available before they're in the shops**
- ★ **Exclusive Reader Service offers**

Accepting these FREE books and gift places you under no obligation to buy; you may cancel at any time, even after receiving your free shipment. Simply complete your details below and return the entire page to the address below. You don't even need a stamp!

YES! Please send me 4 free Sensation books and a surprise gift. I understand that unless you hear from me, I will receive 6 superb new titles every month for just £3.10 each, postage and packing free. I am under no obligation to purchase any books and may cancel my subscription at any time. The free books and gift will be mine to keep in any case.

S6ZEE

Ms/Mrs/Miss/Mr...Initials ....
BLOCK CAPITALS PLEASE

Surname ....

Address ....

....

....Postcode ....

Send this whole page to:
The Reader Service, FREEPOST CN81, Croydon, CR9 3WZ